'Pray accept my d
unkind behaviou

Penelope extended h
had seen the Queen

Their hands touched, and each looked at the
other – for the touch had been oddly compelling.

Oliver was surprised, for he had been thinking of
her as still little more than a child. When
Penelope was animated one might almost call her
pretty. No, not pretty, she was something more
than that. She was totally unlike the lovely
creatures he had pleasured on his travels – or
indeed, any other women he had known.

This time when he took her hand it was to kiss
the back of it, as he had seen the French and
Italian gallants do, and again the effect it had on
them both was strong and remarkable. Oliver
because it told him that Penelope Jermaine had
begun to attract him in the deepest and most
profound manner, and Penelope because she had
never before experienced such an immediate and
shivering response.

What would happen if he kissed her? Best,
perhaps, not to find out – yet.

Author Note

When Anne Herries and I were asked to write four novels set during the reign of Elizabeth I – that exciting time when England first became a European power to be reckoned with – I was happy to agree and to open it with an account of how she came to the throne in the springtime of her youth. The story of my two young lovers, Penelope and Oliver, takes place inside the new Queen's court as she travelled slowly towards her coronation.

Pageantry and pomp surrounded her, but Elizabethan England was a dangerous place in which to live and the court was the most dangerous of all. Intrigues abounded where men and women risked everything. Those successful in them won not only the Queen's favour, but also power and wealth. Failure, however, often meant dishonour and death by execution on Tower Hill. Life was cheap and ceremony was all. To be a Maid of Honour, as Penelope is, was a great thing, but there was a price for that too. Their reputations had to remain spotless, and even a suspicion of misbehaviour could be enough to ruin an innocent girl.

Consequently, Penelope and Oliver often find themselves in difficult situations but, as the old saying has it, 'Love conquers all'. They survive – as did the Queen. But Elizabeth found that to marry the man she loved, Robert Dudley, was beyond even her power.

These are the novels which make up **The Elizabethan Season:**

Spring	-	MAID OF HONOUR
Summer	-	LADY IN WAITING
Autumn	-	THE ADVENTURER'S WIFE
Winter	-	THE BLACK SHEEP'S BRIDE

I found writing about this period fascinating, and hope that you will be captivated by it too.

Paula Marshall

The Elizabethan Season

MAID OF HONOUR

Paula Marshall

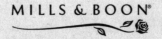

MILLS & BOON®

*First published in Great Britain 2004 by
Harlequin Mills & Boon Limited,
Eton House, 18-24 Paradise Road,
Richmond, Surrey TW9 1SR*

© Harlequin Books S.A. 2004

Special thanks and acknowledgement are given to Paula Marshall
for her contribution to The Elizabethan Season series.

ISBN 0 263 84085 9

148-0304

*Printed and bound in Spain
by Litografía Rosés S.A., Barcelona*

Paula Marshall, married with three children, has had a varied life. She began her career in a large library and ended it as a senior academic in charge of history in a Polytechnic. She has travelled widely, has been a swimming coach, and has appeared on *University Challenge* and *Mastermind*. She has always wanted to write, and likes her novels to be full of adventure and humour.

Other novels by
Paula Marshall

AN UNCONVENTIONAL HEIRESS
JACK COMPTON'S LUCK
RINALDI'S REVENGE

Prologue

10th November 1558

'Yߩou promised to marry him when he came home, you know that you did. You told me so at the time.'

It was nigh on noon at Shelford House on the Strand in London on a fine cold morning, and Penelope Jermaine was hotly reproaching her elder sister, Mary, for being faithless. She had just learned that her parents, with Mary's full approval, had arranged her betrothal to William Vassall, Earl of Castleford.

Mary, who was as blonde and beautiful as Penelope was brown and ordinary—as she never failed to remind her—smiled scornfully and patronisingly at her sister.

'Pray do not be so childish,' she drawled. 'We were but children, Oliver Woodville and I, when we played together before he left for Europe, and as children we

delighted in talking such nonsense. We meant nothing
by it.'

'You were not children,' exclaimed Penelope angrily, 'you were both fully grown and you even exchanged rings with him on the night before he left.'

'Rings?' Mary's beautifully arched eyebrows rose
in derision to match her voice. 'They were but trumpery things. No one would expect me to be bound by
such an exchange of worthless trifles.'

'It is you who are a trumpery thing,' Penelope told
her angrily, 'not the rings, since it seems that your
solemn promises mean nothing to you.'

Mary Jermaine's laugh was an ugly one. 'Come,
come, sister, you seem to be living in a dream. When
Oliver and I were friends you and I were but poor,
dowerless gentlewomen, the daughters of a nobody,
and he was a good match for me then. Once our father
had inherited a fortune and the great house in which
we now live, and we became his heiresses, everything
changed. It was immediately possible for us to make
grand matches, go to court, and live a life free of the
restrictions to which we had previously been condemned. As a consequence I am well pleased that I
am to marry a great man and not a nobody like Oliver
Woodville.'

She paused, before adding spitefully, 'You would
do well to think of yourself, sister. Since no one will
be minded to marry you for your looks, a quiet decorum added to your dowry would be a better mode

of behaviour than running around busily trying to tell your elders and betters how to do their duty.'

Penelope flushed hotly. She had always known that Mary despised her for being more interested in book-learning than in the give and take between the young men and women who lived on the edge of the Tudor court. 'But what,' she asked, 'will Oliver think—and how will he feel—when he comes home to find you married to another—and to a man old enough to be your father?'

Mary had a ready answer to that: she seemed to have an answer for everything. 'What he will think is no business of yours—or of his. Since he has probably spent his time enjoying himself with various ladies in France and Italy, he will probably not be surprised to learn that I have changed my mind. He will have to be content to marry a person of his own fortune and settle down in the country with her. You know, sister dear, since you are so troubled by my decision to show a little common sense by changing my mind about Oliver, why don't *you* marry him? Life in a quiet village would suit you both down to the ground—or to the earth, rather.'

Despite herself, Penelope's eyes filled with tears. She was wise enough not to believe that Mary cared for her deeply, but to learn that, to her sister, she was such an object of scorn and mockery was almost more than she could bear. It was useless to try to appeal to her sense of honour since it was plain that Mary had none. But Penelope remembered only too well that last day, three years ago, which Oliver had spent with them before he left for a tour of Europe in Harry Grantly's retinue.

She was sure, by everything which he had said and done, that he expected Mary to wait for him. She remembered something else, though, something of which she had thought little at the time, since she had only been fourteen to Mary's eighteen. He had wanted to speak to her father, to ask him that they should be formally betrothed before he left, but Mary had demurred.

'Time enough for that when you return,' she had told him.

Had she already learned that her father's cousin was gravely ill, and that when he died they would no longer be poor and unconsidered? To accept Oliver Woodville's suit when they were nobodies and he had a reasonable, if not large, inheritance was one thing, but to remain true to him when Fate had given her the opportunity to marry into a great family was quite another.

Nothing which she could say would change Mary's mind, so best, perhaps, to say nothing more. Poor Oliver! What an unpleasant surprise would be waiting for him when he returned home. Best not to think of that, either. To hide her distress Penelope paced slowly about the room, a room in which she could take no pleasure for all its beauty. Unlike Mary, she wished that she was back in the pretty, if small, manor-house which had been their home until two years ago their father's inheritance had changed their life.

Mary's mind, though, was already running on other, more important, things.

'Father wishes to speak to us about Queen Elizabeth's Coronation, which will take place soon after her sister Mary's death which should not now be long delayed. We are sure to be invited to the service at Westminster Abbey since I am to marry Lord Castleford. It is most important that we both look our best. Mother is already ordering our clothes and arranging a trip to the jewellers.'

She looked Penelope critically up and down. 'She will have a deal of trouble making you appear other than one of the crowd, which is too bad, but will have to be endured…'

What more she would have said to Penelope to remind her of her lack of looks and presence was cut short by a knock on the door and the entry of the Jermaines' Steward, John Brewster, carrying his new white wand of office.

'Ladies,' he announced oracularly, 'your father awaits you in the Great Hall. He has news for you. So pray be ready to leave with me immediately.'

Penelope could barely stifle a disrespectful giggle. One of the few things which amused her in her new life was the way in which Brewster had transformed himself from a rather bumbling flunkey into a grand official, suitable in manner and bearing for the coming new Queen's court.

They followed him down the stairs and through the double doors which led to where their father and mother were waiting for them, in yet another splendidly furnished room. John Jermaine, like Brewster, had changed himself completely. He had been a soberly dressed hard-working country gentleman but he was now accoutred like a grandee, fit to rival the Spanish courtiers who had accompanied the dying Queen Mary's husband, Philip of Spain, to England's less spectacular court.

His wife, however, still clung to her former mode of plain dressing. Agnes Jermaine was a modest woman who sadly remembered her quiet life in the country, preferring it to the new honours which she was now trying to enjoy. She refused to wear the stiff and over-decorated apparel which was the current fashion.

All that was to change, it seemed, since one of the pieces of news which John Jermaine wished to share with them was that the Queen had decreed that no expense would be spared at her Coronation.

'She wishes the whole world to know,' he told them gravely, 'that whatever they can do in splendour at their own courts we shall be only too happy to rival here—so Castleford says—and he is still in high favour with the new Queen. Our apparel must match her wishes—and that goes for you, too, my dear,' he said, turning to his wife.

'The other piece of news which I have to tell you is that the new Queen will appoint Mistress Mary

Jermaine and Mistress Penelope Jermaine to be two of her new Ladies in Waiting.'

Penelope stared at him. No, this could not be true. It must not be true. She had not the slightest desire to be a Lady in Waiting to the Queen. She could think of no post around the court which was less attractive, unless it were that of the kitchen-maid! On second thoughts she might even have preferred to be one.

Mary said jealously, 'Whatever made her ask for Penelope as well?'

Their father smiled. 'I doubt me that she did. One of her ladies left her for some reason, marriage perhaps, and Castleford suggested Penelope's name to her, now that she has become in some measure one of his family. You are quiet, Penelope! Have you no words to express your pleasure at being the recipient of such a signal honour—no gratitude for what your soon to be good brother has done for you? How fortunate for us that she is minded to overlook the sad fact that he still tends towards the Catholic religion.'

'No, yes,' stammered Penelope, aware of Mary's jealous eyes boring into her, and the disappointed expression on her mother's face at her lack of pleasure at this unlooked-for promotion. So now even her mother had deserted her. There would be no more secret conversations about how much they missed their old life with its pleasant round of rural duties.

'Now I have some unhappy information to give you,' John Jermaine announced solemnly, his manner more like his Steward's than ever. 'Sadly, I have heard from my good friend, Nicholas Grantly, that his son's party arrived at Dover several days ago and that, from thence, he has received a letter telling him that his son, Harry, died in Italy of the Roman fever, but that his two companions, Masters Oliver Woodville and Bevis Frampton, are in good health.'

Penelope could not prevent herself from saying, 'Oliver will be most disappointed when he learns that Mary is to marry Lord Castleford. After all, they did exchange rings before he left.'

Mary gave a great sigh and her father said, repressively, 'Child's play, my dear, child's play—as I am sure Master Woodville will understand. I hope that you will not be foolish enough to raise the matter when you see him—although I believe that you will be unlikely to meet him now that you will be part of Queen Elizabeth's court.'

Of course her father would approve of Mary's proposed marriage, for had he not arranged it? Mary was right, she was being childish in believing that, in the new world in which they were now living, such things as honour, duty and keeping one's word were of paramount importance.

Nevertheless, whatever the cost, she, Penelope Jermaine, would try to live up to the precepts which the Bible, and the priest in his sermon on Sundays, had laid down for her.

Oliver Woodville sighed heavily. He was standing on the quay in the port of Dover watching his and

Bevis Frampton's baggage being unloaded from the vessel which had brought them on the last stage of their journey from Europe.

Their early travels in France and then in the north of Italy had been extremely happy; once they had arrived in Rome, however, everything seemed to have gone wrong. After a glorious fortnight during which they had all enjoyed inspecting the remains of the Roman Empire, Harry and Bevis had suddenly engaged in a fearsome quarrel which had ended with Bevis storming away and Harry retiring to his room to sulk—something quite uncharacteristic of his usual behaviour. What the quarrel had been about Oliver never found out, since by the end of the week Harry was in the throes of the fever which had killed him.

So now Oliver had the unpleasant duty of telling Harry's family the bad news. Bevis, having taken over Harry's sulks, had barely spoken a civil word to Oliver on the way home—which was a sad ending to a journey which had been so successful until the moment they had left beautiful Florence for historic Rome.

It was useless to repine. Oliver had written from Paris to tell his father that he and Bevis were on their way home by the first boat which would take them across the Channel to Dover. On his arrival there, one of the port's officers had informed him that there was a packet of mail waiting for him.

It was to be hoped that the news in them was not so bad as that which he was bringing home. He had already learned, shortly after landing, that Bloody Mary, as his Protestant family always called her, was at the point of death and that her half-sister, Elizabeth, would shortly be Queen. Bevis, who, so far as Oliver could make out, was neither Catholic nor Protestant, had grunted at the news and said something under his breath which sounded like 'as well one as another'.

Oliver thrust the mail packet into his pocket, since he dared not find time to read his letters until he had checked that his belongings were safely ashore and loaded on to a waiting cart. After that one of the customs officers would wish to inspect them, and only when he had completed his search would he be able to retire to the inn not far from the quay, eat a good meal and read his post. There was sure to be a letter for him from Mary, and after Harry's unexpected death the thought of reading it and seeing her again was the only thing guaranteed to raise his spirits.

Bevis came up to him, saying in his crawling and semi-wheedling way, 'I am off for home. We do not need each other's company now that we are safe in England.'

Oliver nodded agreement. Three years of living with Bevis had destroyed any small rapport which had once lain between them. Bevis had been Harry's friend, although he was most unlike him in every way. Harry had been tall and golden-haired, every Continental nobleman's idea of an Englishman. Bevis was nondescript. Neither tall nor short, his hair was a dirty blond and his body was as thin and powerless as Harry's had been athletic. He had an unpleasant habit of cringing away from anyone to whom he was speaking.

Oliver was quite unlike either of them. He was tall, but not remarkably so. He was of a dark complexion, with thick and curling black locks, grey-green eyes, and possessed the nose and profile of a haughty eagle—as Mary had once told him. Although he was strong he was, again unlike Harry, not remarkably so. For all that, he was a better swordsman than Harry had been and could always beat him at real tennis, since he had the acute sight of an eagle, with an eagle's reflexes. Bevis had been content to watch the pair of them playing their many games, rather than take part in them himself, since he did not excel at any form of sport.

Once he was seated at table in the crowded inn, Oliver eagerly began to examine his mail. To his great disappointment there was no letter for him in Mary's familiar and careless hand. She had once told him that she left the art of penmanship to Penelope since, unlike her younger sister, she was more interested in the art of enjoying life than in book learning.

Never mind that; he would be seeing her soon, which would be better than mere words on paper, and he looked fondly at the ring on his right hand. What matter that it was a cheap thing, merely a simple circle: it stood for the deep love which lay between them, and that was better than any gaudy piece of jewellery with no affection behind it.

What did cheer him up, even if it surprised him, was what his father had to tell him in his letter. It seemed that once Elizabeth became Queen, his old friend Lord Robert Dudley would be one of her leading courtiers. The consequences of that, his father wrote, were fortunate for their family, since the Woodvilles and the Dudleys were distantly related and now that Robert had favours to dispense, some of them would be going the Woodvilles' way.

'I mind me,' Lord Robert had written to his father, 'that your son is a great equestrian and since the Queen is talking of appointing me to be her Master of the Horse, he would make me a useful Gentleman in Waiting when he returns from his tour of the Continent. I shall be at Greenwich and would wish to see him as soon as he is able to visit me.'

Oliver put down the letter. It was plain that his father wanted him to accept Lord Robert's offer. It would mean that he would attend the new Queen's court and that there would be plenty of opportunities for advancement. Before he had travelled to France and Italy Oliver might have refused such an offer, but while he had been abroad he had discovered in himself an ambition which he had not known he possessed. He had seen the great ones of the courts of France and Italy and had thought that many of them had less sense and understanding of the world than he, an inexperienced young country gentleman, did.

Why should he not try to take his place in the arena where the mighty ruled and carve for himself honours and a fortune as Lord Robert's father had done? He, too, had been a nobody until chance had put him in the way of power and he had been created the Duke of Northumberland. That Robert's father had ended his life on the scaffold was the consequence of his flying too high, which was something which he would try to avoid.

Oliver laughed at himself a little. Here he sat, contemplating an offer of a relatively humble post, and he was already dreaming of ennobling himself and ending up as the chief adviser to the monarch—for that was what Lord Robert Dudley's father had ultimately become before he over-reached himself and met his untimely end.

He picked up the letter again and began to read on. There was other news, about the family and also about old friends. 'You will be interested to learn,' his father wrote, 'that in your absence John Jermaine has inherited the fortune and great estates of his cousin, Reginald. He has taken up residence at Shelford House in London and is often to be seen about court. You would scarcely know him.'

And that was all. There was no mention of Mary. Oliver put down the letter with a disappointed sigh and opened another. This one was from William Cecil, who had held high offices in the reign of the two previous monarchs. What could such a man be doing writing to him? He had been one of his father's friends in youth—but what of that? To his surprise

Cecil was also offering him a post—this time to serve with him.

'Even if you decide against this,' he wrote, 'I would still wish to see you on your return. The Queen's reign will shortly begin and consequently there will be many opportunities for a man whom Nicholas Grantly held in such high regard that he asked for him to accompany his son to the courts of Europe.'

No, he would not accept Cecil's offer, since the position appeared to be merely a clerkly one, but one thing was plain. The new reign was creating new opportunities and he was arriving back in England in time to be able to seize them. He would, with luck, give his dear Mary a better and richer life than the one which he had originally planned for them both.

All that now remained was for him to write to Lord Robert accepting his offer of an interview and, better than that, to meet his beloved as soon as possible and tell her the good news.

Chapter One

Penelope was seated in what her father now called his library. It was a smallish room, with an oak press on one wall containing a variety of printed books and manuscripts. In his absence she was working at his desk translating Livy's *History of Rome* from its original Latin. As a very young girl she had spent two summers at the then Princess Elizabeth's country home and had joined enthusiastically in the daily lessons which the Princess was taking with various tutors.

It had been one of the happiest times in her life and ever afterwards she had done her best to improve on what she had learned during those few months. One good thing about becoming one of the Queen's Ladies in Waiting would be the possibility that she might meet again some of the scholars whose instruction she had enjoyed.

The rest of the family had gone out visiting. She

had asked not to accompany them, saying she had letters to write to her old friends whom she had left behind when they moved to London. This was not a lie, for she had not opened her Livy until the letters were ready to be posted.

She was disturbed by a resounding double-knock on the door, which undoubtedly heralded Brewster's arrival—he had adopted it to distinguish himself from the other servants, who were only allowed one. Penelope could not imagine what he might have to tell her.

'Enter,' she called, putting down her pen.

In he strode, his wand of office prominent before him, like an actor in a play proclaiming his office.

'Mistress, you have a visitor. It is Master Oliver Woodville. He has come, he says, to pay his courtesies to your father and mother and to speak to Mistress Mary. I told him that she, together with your father and mother, have gone on a visit to some of their new friends in Westminster.'

He paused significantly, and gave a slight cough before continuing. 'I thought it best not to tell him aught else about Mistress Mary. I mentioned that you were present today and he asked if he might speak with you. I said that I would ask you if it were convenient.'

Convenient! Of course it wasn't convenient. If she agreed to meet Oliver in her sister's absence she would have the unhappy task of telling him that Mary had abandoned the vows which she had made to him and was soon to marry middle-aged Lord Castleford. Could she refuse to meet him by saying it was not convenient for her to see him, leaving Mary to tell him the truth at a later date?

No, she could not. For here she was, as free as air, with no reason to turn him away after she had lain down the strict rule for herself that truth was to guide her life and her conduct. But which would be the worst course—for him to learn from Mary of her treachery—or from Mary's unconsidered sister?

Since their argument the other day Mary had not uttered another word about her one-time love. Oliver and his affairs had disappeared from the world in which she lived. She was so busy preparing not one, but two, trousseaus—the first being for the Coronation and the second for her marriage to Lord Castleford early in the New Year—that she had had no time to worry about how much she was going to hurt Oliver when he discovered that she had broken her word to him.

'You may send Master Woodville in,' she said at last. Perhaps God would tell her what to say and do for the best when she met him.

Brewster bowed and disappeared, to return a few moments later to announce portentously, 'Master Woodville at your service, Mistress Penelope,' and disappear again, leaving them alone together.

Their first thought on meeting again was a similar one—how much the other had changed. Oliver had always been good-looking, and now he was proudly handsome with the remains of the tan of Italy on his aquiline features. He was dressed in what Penelope took to be the Italian mode, too, and oh, how it suited him. His clothing was all black and gold and cut in beautiful long lines which showed off his powerful arms and legs.

Merely to look at him made Penelope feel weak. How could Mary reject such a fine figure of a man and accept instead the middle-aged, nondescript, fat fellow which Castleford was? Quite easily, of course, for Castleford was a peer, a man of power, one of those who, like William Cecil, had managed to survive the very different reigns of Henry VIII, Edward VI and Mary without losing his head—which no doubt said something for him, but quite what, she wasn't sure.

Penelope often found herself silently asking such searching questions and getting no reasonable answers. For the twentieth time she made up her mind to try to stop doing it. She hoped that she didn't look as distracted as she felt.

For his part Oliver remembered her as a little, thin child who turned big golden eyes on him whenever he came to visit Mary. For some reason he had remembered her eyes when everything else about her had faded. She had been quiet, so quiet that there had been something almost disturbing about her, as though, even at that early age, she was busy summing up everyone whom she met—including him. She was, however, always willing to talk to him.

Now she was quite tall, not so tall as her sister perhaps, and by the way she was studying him she had not lost her assessing look. Her hair, what could be seen of it beneath her cap, was a deep brown with golden lights in it, and if she were no conventional beauty she had an appearance of what he thought of as quiet strength. No longer thin, her face and figure reminded him a little of the many classical statues of women which he had seen on his travels.

She waved him to a large chair, one with arms which was her father's favourite, and sat down behind her desk again, after he had bowed low in her direction.

'You have grown, Mistress Penelope,' was all that he could think of to say to her. He remembered that even as a child she had always wanted him to tell her nothing but the simple truth.

She smiled, and in some sort the smile transformed her serious face. 'Not surprising, Master Woodville, since it is some years since we last met and I had not then attained my final height.'

'True,' he said, and then to his surprise, for he was no popinjay who wondered what women—or men, for that matter—thought of his looks, he asked a question concerning them. 'And I, Mistress Penelope, have I changed?'

She considered him for a moment. 'Indeed, you left as a boy and have come back as a man.'

It was the best answer she could think of which did not betray how much he affected her. As a child she had offered him silent worship, and if the years since she had last seen him had taught her anything, it was that few men or women deserved such unthinking homage—she was reluctant to call it love.

Nevertheless there was now something formidable about him, whereas before he had left England he had been but a gallant youth, full of promise. To tell the truth—which Penelope always tried to do—he reminded her of the heroes of the legends of Arthur, or of the tales of courtly love which she had read in the intervals of improving her more serious learning.

Oliver laughed. 'You were always an honest child so I take that remark as a compliment.'

Penelope smiled sweetly at him. 'If you like,' she said, offering him another small smile.

'I do like,' he said, although what he would have liked even more was to be exchanging banter with the older, not the younger, sister.

'What I would also like,' he added, 'is for you to tell Mary of my visit and to assure her that I shall, if it is convenient, call here on the morrow and renew our vows so that we may shortly marry.'

When he spoke of Mary he looked so eager and so much like the ardent boy who had left England three years ago that Penelope's heart bled for him. Whatever the cost she must tell him the truth. It would be cruel to allow him to live in a fool's paradise where simply to be re-united with Mary would mean that they might start making plans to be wedded as soon as the ceremony could be arranged.

Her face must have changed when she thought this, for he looked anxiously at her, saying, 'Are you well, Penelope? I thought that for a moment there you seemed faint.'

She shook her head. 'Quite well, but, oh, Oliver, there is something which I ought to tell you, and which will grieve the pair of us in the telling.'

'Mary!' he exclaimed. 'Do not tell me that she is ill—or has been ill?'

'No, not that. I scarce know what to say, or how to say it…' She paused. 'Let me ring for Brewster to bring you a glass of hippocras before I do.'

Oliver stared at her. He had left his lodgings that morning full of hope that he might be seeing Mary before noon. Instead he had found her younger sister, who was looking at him as though there had been a death in the family.

'No,' he exclaimed, roughly for him. 'I thank you, but no hippocras for me—simply tell me your news.'

'Very well, it is this. Mary is contracted in marriage to William Vassall, Earl of Castleford. The preliminary public, and binding, pledging *de futuro* which signifies the betrothal has already taken place. The final contract of *verbis de praesente*, followed by marriage, will take place early in the New Year after the Queen's crowning.'

Penelope knew at once that she had dealt Oliver a body blow. His face had turned as white as hers had done a few moments ago.

'No, I don't believe you,' he said at last. 'And if

your news be true then her father must have forced her into this union against her will. He surely knew that we exchanged vows before I left.'

The truth: she had vowed always to tell the truth and so she must not deceive Oliver however much telling it might cost her.

'All has been done with her full co-operation. I cannot say more than that. It is for her to explain her reasons to you when you meet.'

He turned away from her and walked to the window to look out on a lawn with a herb garden on its far side, a sundial in its middle. He had left behind a young woman of modest fortune who had seemed to be happy to marry him but had returned to find that her family had gone up in the world, that she was co-heiress to a large fortune and was contracted to marry a powerful nobleman.

His face ravaged with pain, he swung back to face Penelope, exclaiming, 'Are you telling me the truth? I cannot believe it of Mary: that she would throw me over for another.'

Penelope's answer was a simple one, simply given. 'I would not lie to you,' she said.

'Forgive me,' he begged her. 'I was wrong to accuse you of such a thing. I must speak to her myself, though, to hear what has passed from her own lips when I call on the morrow.'

It was plain that he was having difficulty in believing that Mary had abandoned him. Despite his stoic expression his pain was evident to Penelope, and in knowing that, she knew of another thing: that she had always loved him, but that, as her sister's suitor, he had been denied to her.

Now he was doubly denied, for in telling him the truth about Mary she would always, in the future, be a symbol of his pain.

'Indeed,' she replied. 'I am sure that she will wish to see you.'

His smile was bitter. 'Will she? I trust that you will forgive me if I ask to leave immediately.'

'No forgiveness is needed,' she replied, but even as she spoke, there was a commotion outside and the sound of voices, most probably those of her parents and her sister returning early from their excursion. His meeting with Mary would be now, not on the morrow.

Oliver said, 'Does that noise mean what I think it does? That your parents and sister have arrived?'

He was well aware that it was a stupid question, because he knew the answer, but for some reason he seemed to be unable to think clearly. The news of Mary's desertion of him had been so unexpected that it had shaken the foundations of his life. Perhaps Penelope was mistaken, or even lying—but no, that was a piece of folly, for why should she lie to him? Or was it possible that she could have been misled?

In any case, when he met Mary he would shortly discover the truth of the matter for himself. In Rome he had lost Harry, his best friend, and now, in London, it seemed that he was about to lose the woman whom he loved.

Penelope had risen, and was saying, 'You will want me to inform my father and mother—and Mary—of your arrival. You might wish to remain here until I do so.'

What could he do but agree with her? To be left alone would give him time to gather his errant thoughts, time to collect himself, time to be calm when he saw Mary again.

'Yes,' he said, 'that might be best,' and said no more.

He looked out of the window so that he might not see her leave the room, for, as Penelope had suspected, the sight of her was painful to him. He had returned to find the wrong woman still free—and the right one promised to another. Once he was alone he walked over to stare at the book she had been studying when he had disturbed her—to find that it was no light poem or courtly romance, but Livy's *History,* and that she had evidently been reading the Latin easily, for she had made some notes in that language on a piece of paper—for future reference, perhaps.

Oliver clenched his fists. Penelope, at least, had remained constant to something, even if it were only her desire for learning, a desire which had caused her elder sister to tease her constantly. For some reason her steadfastness, so different from Mary's, enraged him. As a consequence when the door opened and Mary and her father and mother walked in, immediately after the officious Brewster, his desire to be temperate in manner proved difficult to sustain.

'Well met, Master Woodville,' said John Jermaine, all affability. 'I learned but this morning that you had returned, and am greatly pleased that you chose to visit us haste, post haste. First, I must commiserate with you on the loss of your friend, Harry Grantly: it must have been a sad end to your journey.'

Oliver noticed that, most uncharacteristically, Mary was hanging back. Her mother was smiling at him.

'Thank you for your sympathy,' he said shortly, for it would be barbaric of him not to offer a response in proper form to John Jermaine's courtesy. 'I am pleased to discover that you are all well, however, and have had some great good luck during my absence. I felicitate you on that. I also understand that Mistress Mary has been contracted to marry Lord Castleford—something which surprises me greatly.'

All three looked at him, expressions of great astonishment on their faces. Even Mary had the gall to look amazed by what he had just said.

Her father, puzzled, addressed Oliver, stiffly. 'Pray, Master Woodville, why should you be surprised by my good news? My daughter is surely free to marry anyone, even someone so high in favour as Lord Castleford presently is.'

Oliver, who knew that at the moment he was, unfortunately, not in favour with anyone, including the woman whom he thought that he had come home to marry, replied coldly, reining in his temper with difficulty, 'I believe that Mistress Mary was already bound to another by the most solemn vows before she so much as met Lord Castleford, and will therefore be unable to marry him.'

This robust declaration had his three hearers look even more stunned than they had after his first remark about her.

'I,' said John Jermaine portentously, 'had expected to receive your congratulations about her coming great honour, not a denial of her right to receive that honour. What, sir, do you mean by implying that she was already promised to another?'

'That, as Mistress Mary well knows, we exchanged rings before I left on my tour of Europe, as troth that we should marry on my return.'

He held up his left hand, saying, 'Here, Master Jermaine, is the one which she gave me.'

Agnes Jermaine uttered a faint cry, whether of distress or otherwise, could not be told. Mary would have spoken, except that her father forestalled her.

'This, sir, is nonsense which you speak, most palpable nonsense. Neither you nor Mary told me of this. Such an agreement, without witnesses and without parental permission, cannot stand. Mary, my child, does this man speak true? I find it difficult to believe that *you* would deceive me—even if *he* dares to.'

'Tell your father the truth, Mary, I beg of you,' Oliver said, trying desperately to control himself in the face of Mary's cool indifference.

'Yes,' agreed her father, 'the truth, please.'

Mary smiled. 'Dear sir—and Oliver—what can I say? What happened before you left us was but children playing, exchanging rings without a word to our fathers—or so I thought. We had played such games all our lives, had we not, Oliver? And meant nothing by them.'

She held up her hand. 'See, I wear no ring. I put it in my little jewel box, long ago. I am sorry if you are disappointed, Oliver, but think, you were off to Europe and we had no notion of when we might meet again. That alone should tell you, dear father, that we were but playing.'

'I was not playing,' said Oliver quietly.

In the face of the untruths she was offering her father, all his anger had leached out of him and left him with a deep sadness. He would never trust a woman again, never. He could tell her father that he had wished to ask him for Mary's hand in marriage before he left, but that she had persuaded him to wait until after he had returned. But what good would that do? It would be his word against hers. All the love which he had felt for her, and which had sustained him during his time out of England, had dropped dead before him in the face of her duplicity.

He pulled the ring from his finger: the ring which he had looked at so fondly so many times, the mere sight of it being enough to bring his beloved's face and figure before him, and said, 'It may not mean anything to you now, but I would wish you to have it.'

Mary ignored his extended hand, on which the ring

lay, and shook her head, saying coldly, 'Nay, I wish it not. Keep it in memory of our happy childhood.'

Oliver's face was suddenly stone.

'By my troth, I want it not, either. Those days deceived me.' He walked across to the desk at which Penelope had earlier sat, happily reading her Livy, and laid the ring upon it.

'Sir, and ladies, I bid you good day, and Mistress Mary, I trust that in the times to come you will receive all those favours which God cares to bestow on you as a reward for your behaviour.'

He bowed to them, and began to leave.

John Jermaine said, 'Let us not part in anger, Master Woodville. After all, it was but a child's mistake.'

'No,' said Oliver before he reached the door. 'I leave you in indifference, not anger, and Mary was not a child when we pledged our troth.'

Once the door had closed behind him Agnes Jermaine, who had remained silent during the whole sad interview, turned to Mary, saying gently, 'Tell me, daughter, did you say true—that it was but child's play? Or was it more than that that he should come here, haste post haste?'

Her husband said, 'Now, now, wife, do not trouble our daughter…'

He was interrupted by Mary, who had never looked less troubled in all her life.

'Of course I was speaking the truth. I do not understand why he should cause such a pother over this.

Was it likely that I should pledge myself to a man who was leaving me for years, perhaps for ever? After all, Harry Grantly did die in Rome.'

'But the rings,' persisted her mother.

'Oh, the rings!' exclaimed Mary carelessly. She walked over to the desk, picked up Oliver's and waved it at her parents. 'As mine was, this is but a trumpery piece, by which you may see what an empty thing all this talk of a betrothal was. No, I go to my Lord Castleford with a clear heart and a clean conscience. As for Oliver, I wish him well, in the hope that he will not take too seriously the next lady with whom he chooses to play games.'

So saying, she tossed the ring back on the desk. She had said true when she had averred that she did not wish to have it back.

Agnes Jermaine opened her mouth—and then shut it again. She thought that there was more to this sorry business than her daughter claimed, but she could tell by her husband's expression that he wanted to hear nothing more of this supposed betrothal. Whether or not he was convinced that his daughter was telling the truth was not the heart of the matter. Above all he wished Mary to be Lord Castleford's bride, with no shadow hanging over her marriage. Everything had turned out for the best, and so he told his wife.

'I wish to hear no more of Master Oliver Woodville and his claims. It is my opinion that he has heard of our daughter's great dowry and had hoped to get hold of it by blowing up the childish passages which occur between young people before they settle down in life. Now let us eat. Mary, my dear, do not trouble yourself over this, I beg of you.'

Mary offered him a demure, smile beneath which deceit crawled like a snail, leaving its slimy track behind. 'Indeed, father, I shall not. I vow that I have quite forgot it already.'

'Good girl,' he said, 'and now let's to table.'

Penelope sat on a settle in the Great Hall. She had refused to accompany her parents and sister into the library, saying that she had already spoken her fill with Master Woodville. She had no wish to see his face when he was compelled to understand that Mary had, in truth, abandoned him.

She was not surprised to watch him walk through the library door, his face white and strained and his expression grim. Nor was she surprised that he did not acknowledge her, striding past her as though she were not there, for the very sight of her must be that which the Catholics called anathema: something cursed, which had given him news which he had no wish to hear. Brewster ran vainly after him in a doomed attempt to see him out with all proper ceremony.

A moment or two later her father and mother, followed by Mary, also appeared. Her father paused to speak to her.

'Come, child, it is time to sup. Our untimely guest has delayed our meal.'

Oh, so that was what Oliver was, was he? An untimely guest!

She rose. 'Pray excuse me, father and mother, I have no wish to eat.' The truth being that the food would choke me, would it not?

He shrugged. 'If that is what you wish.'

'I do wish, father.' She curtseyed to them, avoiding Mary's mocking eyes—to no avail, for her sister said, 'I suppose, Penelope, that you prefer to ring a funeral peal over Oliver Woodville rather than eat with us today.'

Penelope rose from her curtsey, and smiled at her. She could make no reply to her sister, for what she wanted to say was unsayable.

Instead, she walked away from the three of them, the only one in the family to mourn for a friend whom they had known since he was five years old, but who was now, quite plainly, a friend no longer.

Livy would be preferable to food. She returned to the library where a part of her life had come to an end and sat down in front of the beautiful book—to discover that lying there was Oliver's ring, which Mary had carelessly thrown down on it.

Penelope's eyes filled with tears before she picked it up, to kiss it before slipping it into the little pocket which depended from her waist. Mary might not want the ring, but she would keep the so-called trumpery thing not only as a symbol of a lost past, but also as a talisman against the dark into which the past had dissolved.

While she lived his name and memory would not be entirely lost to the Jermaine family. And there was one other thing to remember: the original Penelope, from whom she derived her name, was Homer's heroine who had waited patiently over many long years for her husband—and lover—Odysseus to come home from the Trojan wars, to claim her at the last.

Chapter Two

'I thought, Master, that our wanderings were over when we left that plaguey France behind,' grumbled Gib, Oliver's body servant, who, having laid out his master's clothing for the day, was now packing a small trunk preparatory to their visit to Hatfield where Lord Robert Dudley was currently staying as part of the new Queen's household. She had succeeded to the throne on the 17th of November.

'Well, *I* have a great mind to leave plaguey London behind, so keep a quiet tongue in your head unless you wish to stay here as a kitchen lackey on a kitchen lackey's pay,' snapped Oliver, whose temper had been uncertain since Mary's desertion of him.

What flea's biting him these days? was Gib's internal comment on that. He had always counted himself lucky to serve such a mild-mannered fellow as Master Woodville. Master Grantly had been a trifle haughty and as for Master Bevis Frampton! Well, best *not* to think of him. But ever since they had come to London, Master Oliver had been most unlike his usual self.

Oliver, who didn't like himself at all, because he found he was so short-tempered these days, had decided to accept Lord Robert's offer of service with him. The further away he was from Mary Jermaine the better. He regretted snarling at Gib, who was a good fellow who had helped him to weather the worst days after poor Henry's sudden death, but there it was. With luck a complete change of surroundings might find him cheerful again.

The only thing which he regretted about his parting with the Jermaines was that he had swept past poor Penelope without a word. It was not her fault that her sister was a faithless hussy, and as a gentleman who prided himself on his proper conduct towards others, he should at least have bidden her farewell, if only briefly.

Never mind that; what was done, was done, and now he would try to carve a career for himself with one of the new Queen's nearest and dearest friends.

He was still pondering on this on the following day at Hatfield while he waited to be led into Lord Robert's presence. An elderly Steward was keeping him waiting in an ante-room where there was not even a bench or a settle on which to sit.

'I believe he is with the Queen's Grace at the moment, but he may be inclined to see you immediately if it so pleases him,' the man had said, after Oliver had shown him Lord Robert's letter to his father. Pray God, Lord Robert's offer had been a serious one and that he was not wasting his time.

Shortly afterwards the Steward appeared again. 'Lord Robert will see you, Master Woodville,' he said. 'Pray follow me.'

He was led into what was plainly, by its size and magnificence, the Great Hall, where the Queen's Grace sat in an ornate chair-cum-throne before a large window at its far end. A tall, dark man was bent over her. He was apparently whispering something in her ear, for she suddenly began to laugh, tapping the back of his hand with an ornate fan while she did so.

Around them were an array of finely dressed men and women. One of the women stood a little way forward from the rest. Her expression, Oliver saw, when he drew near to her, was severe in the extreme.

The figure of the Queen on her throne, though, drew his attention the most. He had not quite known what to expect, but what he saw of her as he walked towards her was entrancing. She was slender and delicate-looking, with silky red-gold hair and a face which resembled the finest porcelain, so purely white was her complexion. She was no conventional beauty, that was sure, but she had something more than that— grace, character and an unusual presence. Her clothes were exquisite, a dream of gold and crimson patterned brocade. They were carefully cut to reveal her tiny waist, and the simple elegance of her figure.

She ceased to pay attention to the man who was

talking to her and turned it on Oliver himself, speaking before the Steward could announce him.

'Fie, Robin,' she said, laughing. 'Cease your gossiping and take note of the young fellow whom you asked to see. What is your name, sir? And for what purpose have you asked to pay court to Lord Robert?'

Her manner when she asked this was friendly in the extreme, since Oliver Woodville was a comely, tall and athletic man, exactly the kind of fellow of whom the Queen most approved. God grant that he had a good intellect as well as a fine body—if so, he would be a useful addition to her court.

Oliver thought rapidly. Lord Robert, she had said! So this was the Queen's friend to whom he was distantly connected. He was, as Oliver had already noted, uncommonly tall, with a dark, handsome face and with an air so haughty that it approached arrogance. He was even more finely dressed than all the other men in the vast room.

Oliver bowed low to both great personages before replying.

'I am called Oliver Woodville, Your Grace, and I have a letter from Lord Robert to my father asking me to present myself to him if I wished to serve him as a Gentleman in Waiting. I am, I believe, his distant cousin.'

'This is true, Robin?' she asked of her companion.

'Quite true, madam. Master Woodville has been journeying in France and Italy. I have had good reports of him from Sir Nicholas Grantly as both an honest and educated gentleman and a horseman of some repute. He would make an excellent addition to my family—if he cares to join it. I believe he speaks truly when he claims to be my cousin.'

The Queen turned her amazing blue eyes on him.

'How say you, Master Woodville? Will you serve with my Lord Robert?'

Oliver bowed again. 'With pleasure, Your Grace.'

She smiled at him so sweetly that Lord Robert looked sharply at her. 'As for his being your cousin,' she said, 'I believe that I am the cousin of half the gentry and nobility in Wales—to say nothing of those in England. Why, I might even be yours. My Lord Robert, you will wish to interview your new gentleman in private, I believe, at a later time—but for the present, he may remain in our company and sup with us. I give you leave, Master Woodville, to join my other companions,' and she waved a hand at the men and women who surrounded her.

It was his congé. Oliver bowed and moved back to melt into the crowd, some of whom were regarding him jealously for having occupied more of Her Grace's attention than they had ever done. For his part, he welcomed his anonymity, temporary though it might be. So much had happened to him since he had returned to England, it was as though he were living in a new world where some things proved to be surprisingly bad and some surprisingly good.

He was not to remain unconsidered for long. A middle-aged man, almost as finely dressed as

Lord Robert, approached him, saying languidly, 'Woodville, did I hear? If your father is also Oliver, then I believe he held some minor office at court during the young King's reign, did he not?'

'I believe so, sir?' This was said with a slight question in his voice, so that the fellow said to the Steward, 'Introduce us, man. Do not leave Master Woodville to swim in strange waters alone.'

The agitated Steward bowed. 'Master Woodville, I have the honour to present you to m'lord the Earl of Castleford.'

So this was Castleford who was to marry Mary! This middle-aged man, running to fat, with a soft face, was the man whom she preferred to him. He tried to look suitably honoured and deferential and must have succeeded because the fellow smiled at him.

'I hear that you have recently been visiting Paris and Rome, so you may not be aware that I am to marry again—Mistress Mary Jermaine, the daughter of a family who were once your near neighbours.'

'Pray accept my great good wishes, and a happy future with your new Countess,' said Oliver, lying in his teeth.

'I have also arranged for her and her sister, Mistress Penelope Jermaine, to be appointed to be two of the Queen's Grace's Ladies in Waiting. They will be in attendance at Lord North's home, the Charter House at the Barbican, when the Queen moves there in a few days' time,' continued Castleford. 'A signal honour for the young ladies, which I am sure they much appreciate.'

'Oh, yes, indeed, my lord,' returned Oliver, lying again, since he was certain that Penelope would almost certainly prefer to live a quiet life far from the intrigue and gossip of the court. He was rapidly discovering that lying was something he would be required to do regularly now that he was a member of Lord Robert's family. Court life was not a place where the truth could ever be safely told.

As an example of this rule of conduct, he saw nearby a gentleman whom he knew and who had told him not so many days ago that he was off to his home in the North: Bevis Frampton.

Now what in Satan's name was *he* doing here? Why had he lied about returning home on the instant? And why should the sight of him be enough to conjure up Satan? Only, perhaps, the memory of Harry's breach with him in Rome where, according to Harry, Frampton had plainly been in the wrong. If Harry were telling the truth, that was, since he had never seen fit to reveal to Oliver what the quarrel had been about.

By his manner Bevis was not exactly happy to see him, either.

'What brings you to Hatfield?' he hissed at Oliver once Castleford had finished patronising him.

'I might as well ask how you come to be here,' retorted Oliver. 'You told me that you were going home immediately after we docked.'

Bevis was stiff. 'I changed my mind.'

'And I am here at Lord Robert's invitation—a sufficient reason for my presence, I believe.'

Bevis said no more. He turned on his heel and walked away, leaving Oliver to wonder why he was so annoyed at finding him to be part of the new Queen's retinue—if that was why he was truly here.

In the days that followed Oliver had little time to worry over this, or anything else, for that matter, since, as one of Lord Robert's men, he became heavily engaged in the business of moving the new Queen's court to the Charter House and preparing for her Coronation. Not only that, once Lord Robert had discovered that he wrote and spoke French and Italian with ease, he was given the task of looking after all the correspondence in those languages.

The morning after they had reached Charter House, he was busy translating a letter which had recently arrived from the Duchy of Milan, when the door opened and the Steward entered.

'Master Woodville, I have been asked by Master Cecil to require that you attend on him at three of the clock this afternoon—if you have no other appointments, that is.'

'Tell Master Cecil that I shall do as he wishes,' replied Oliver. He remembered that Cecil had written to him offering him employment, but since the Queen had made him her Privy Councillor and Secretary of State he had seen him only at a distance. What could be the meaning of this summons? Why should William Cecil wish to see him, a comparatively lowly member of Lord Robert's family, so urgently?

He was soon to find out. Master Cecil was seated at a long table covered with papers and documents when the Steward ushered Oliver into his room with a great deal of ceremonial. Elizabeth's premier minister asked Oliver to sit down in front of the fire which was roaring in an ornamental hearth.

'I remember your father,' the great man began, 'as a person possessed of profound common sense. I am hopeful that you resemble him in that. You are now a member of Lord Robert Dudley's household, I believe.'

Oliver agreed that he was. He had already discovered that Lord Robert and Master Cecil were somewhat at odds—the Secretary of State mistrusted the friendship between Lord Robert and the Queen, whom they both served.

'I am sure you understand that we may be facing difficult times in the future, once the Queen has been crowned. Lord Robert has decided to consult Dr Dee, asking him to draw up an astrological chart in order to decide on the most propitious date for her Coronation. Presumably in the hope that it will result in a long and prosperous reign for her.'

Was there sarcasm in Master Cecil's dry tones? Oliver was not sure. 'I know,' Master Cecil continued, 'that your father is a follower of the Protestant

faith and I am judging that his son is of the same
kidney. If not, pray inform me.'

'As the father, so the son,' said Oliver, who was
rapidly learning that in his new life the less he said,
the better.

'Excellent. I am therefore hoping that if the son
hears of anything untoward which might threaten our
kingdom and the person of the Queen's Grace, he will
not hesitate to inform me.'

So the spider—for thus Oliver had begun to think
of Master Cecil—was busy spinning a web of safety
around his mistress and was asking the fly which was
Master Oliver Woodville to be his spy in Lord
Robert's camp. It behoved him to be careful and not
end up crushed and ruined between two great personages.

'Indeed, sir,' he replied, as dryly as he could,
'should I learn anything which appears to menace the
safety of the realm, or of the Queen's Grace, I would
not hesitate to inform those whose duty it is to guard
it. So far, I assure you, all appears to be well.'

Master Cecil smiled at this somewhat two-edged
speech. 'Excellent,' he said. 'I see that you are becoming used to court life. You will drink wine with
me, Master Woodville, in the hope that our kingdom
might not need your services in this matter. You will,
I am sure, keep a guarded tongue in your head—for
your own safety as well as Her Grace's. The punishment for failure these days is a harsh one.'

He paused and then said something which was not

at all related to what had gone before. 'You travelled in Europe with Master Bevis Frampton, I believe.'

He believed! Cecil knew, of course he did, that Bevis had been one of his companions—even if he were not one whom Oliver would have chosen himself. So thinking, he took the goblet which Cecil handed him, trying to work out what he meant by this seemingly chance-spoken reference to Bevis Frampton, since he did not believe that the man opposite to him ever spoke idly of anything.

'Yes,' he said, before drinking the good wine he had been given. 'Master Bevis Frampton was with me on my travels, but he was Master Harry Grantly's acquaintance, not mine.' And he said no more.

Oh, the young man was learning fast, was he not! Master Cecil almost grinned at him, but contented himself after that with asking Oliver questions designed to discover how learned he was—Cecil, like the Queen, being a learned person himself.

Master Woodville passed that test, too, before Cecil dismissed him, saying at the last, 'You will not forget what I have asked of you, I trust.'

Oliver shook his head. 'No, indeed, Master Cecil, I am determined always to serve my country—be sure of that.'

He did not like being asked to spy on Lord Robert—or anyone else—but of one thing he was certain. He did not like treason, either, whoever plotted it, Catholic or Protestant, male or female, Lord or Commoner.

* * *

'Been closeted with the old fox, have you, Woodville?'

It was Bevis Frampton who was questioning him. On leaving Cecil's rooms Oliver had found him in the corridor outside—whether by chance or not he could not tell. Before Cecil had sent for him he might have thought nothing of meeting Bevis, but one thing the Secretary of State had done was to rouse his suspicions of everyone—and why had he mentioned Bevis to him? And had Bevis been following him? And why was he beginning to think that something evil lurked behind every corner?

'Briefly,' returned Oliver. 'He knew my father years ago and wished to be acquainted with the son.'

Which was something of the truth, even if only half of it.

'Aye, your father being Protestant, perhaps, or facing both ways like the fox himself.'

This came out with a sneer. Oliver shrugged, and made no reply other than, 'You will forgive me if I leave you, I have work to do.'

'For the Queen's suitor, who would be king, I suppose.'

Would Cecil wish to be told of that cavalier remark? More to the point, did he wish to tell Cecil? And why was Bevis suddenly using his evil tongue on him?

These two questions occupied Oliver's mind as he made his rapid way back to his duties—Lord Robert

wished the letter he had been working on Englished
as soon as possible.

That night Oliver's dreams were troubled ones. For
some reason the wretched Frampton fellow haunted
them. They were all in the Colosseum again, and
Bevis was a little way away from him and Harry.
Harry was admiring the power and splendour of the
building which surrounded them. Bevis, as usual, was
glowering at Harry. Somehow this provoked Oliver—
in his dream—into a violent fit of the shivers. The
sky grew dark and the shivers persisted, until suddenly all was clear again and he was in an English
field in spring and Penelope Jermaine, of all people,
was holding out her hand to him, a posy of bluebells
in it. He reached to take it; the dream vanished, he
was awake again—and then he fell at once into a deep
and dreamless sleep.

In the morning he had forgotten his dream—except
for Penelope's part in it—and he had no notion of
what it might have meant.

'I really can't imagine why Castleford should have
insisted that you became one of the Queen's Ladies
in Waiting as well as me,' fretted Mary Jermaine to
Penelope. She resented Penelope's presence, but since
Castleford had insisted that they should be installed
at Charter House so that they might both be presented
to the Queen when she arrived there on her slow procession into London, there was little she could say.

'I can't imagine why, either,' Penelope retorted. 'I

would certainly prefer a quiet life, but I expect your future husband believed that he was doing me a favour by his patronage. I like the notion as little as I imagine the Queen will like moving on to the Tower of London for six days, before she travels to Somerset House on the Strand while Whitehall Palace is prepared for her and her staff. The Tower must hold painful memories for her. If she is willing to endure that, then I can't complain about serving her.'

Mary shrugged her shoulders. 'At least you might have tried a little harder to look as though you are about to become part of her household. That dress you are wearing has seen better days. I must say that you look rather like an underdressed mole.'

Mary herself, Penelope thought rather unkindly, looked more like a painted maypole. She was arrayed in yards of garish brocade, her giant circular ruff nearly extinguished her and her hair was pulled dramatically high inside a gilt net decorated with minute rosebuds. She was obviously preparing to be Castleford's over-decorated Countess. Penelope wondered whether she knew that one of the ladies at Charter House who was also awaiting the Queen's arrival had told her that the Queen insisted that the wives of the men in her retinue would not be allowed to attend her court, but were to be sent away to their husbands' country homes.

Amy Dudley, Lord Robert's wife, who had been Amy Robsart, was living at Cumnor Place, but Lord

Robert at least had the excuse that she was gravely ill and not fit to be present at court.

Without thinking—or was she?—Penelope said, 'I wonder where Oliver Woodville is, and what he is doing?'

'Back in dreary Leicestershire, among the sheep and cows, one supposes,' returned Mary nastily. 'One can't imagine him here. Oh, listen…' and she ran to the window '…I do believe that the procession has already arrived. I thought that I heard the sound of trumpets.'

Penelope followed her to the window. Sure enough the outriders and the heralds were already streaming through the stone gateway into the courtyard, followed by the soldiers guarding the Queen and then by Elizabeth herself, Lord Robert Dudley riding a little behind her.

Lady Greville, who was in charge of the Ladies at Charter House until the Queen arrived, came bustling into the room. 'Come, young ladies, you must make haste to join the others already assembled in the Entrance Hall to greet the Queen's Grace. Remember to bow low if she stops to speak to you when you are presented to her.'

Penelope, eager to see more of the procession, hesitated at the window for a moment. Yes, there was the Queen herself, followed by Lord Robert and a host of mounted gentlemen. Was that Oliver Woodville she could see among them? Surely not. He must already be at home again, as Mary had said.

'Mistress Penelope Jermaine, this is a poor start to your duties,' called Lady Greville, reproachfully, 'to be backwards in them already. Pray hurry into the Entrance Hall to take your place there, or I shall inform Her Grace that you are scarce fit to be one of her ladies.'

Mary, who had rushed to be one of the first in line, sniggered at this reproof. Penelope took no note of her, and was happy to stand at the far end of the assembled company so that she might see how she ought to behave in the presence of Royalty.

The Queen was prettier than she had imagined her to be. Her red hair and her porcelain complexion went well together, and she held herself like a true sovereign both on and off her horse. As for Lord Robert, he was the most handsome man she had ever seen, even more handsome than Oliver, yet there was something about him that Penelope did not quite care for. He seemed so very sure of himself in a proud, careless way—but perhaps that was how men near to the throne looked and behaved.

Now it was her turn to bow and curtsey to the Queen. She did so, dropping her head so that she could see quite plainly her sovereign's beautiful shoes.

'This,' said Lady Greville, who had already presented Mary to her as one of her new Ladies and as Lord Castleford's betrothed wife, 'is Mistress Penelope Jermaine, sister to Mistress Mary Jermaine, whom you have also appointed to be one of your

Ladies in Waiting. She is well aware of the honour you do her, are you not, Mistress Jermaine?'

Something in Penelope's somewhat restrained manner must have caught the Queen's attention, for instead of moving on, she remarked in a kind voice, 'It is Mistress Jermaine who honours me in being willing to attend on her monarch. I trust that you will be as happy to serve me, as I am to serve my country.'

'Indeed, Your Grace, indeed, I'm sure that I shall be,' said Penelope, bowing low again, and almost feeling Mary's anger that the Queen should bestow such a distinction on the younger sister, not the elder.

The Queen smiled at her and moved on down the line of waiting courtiers and servants. Elizabeth, during this formal presentation, had been attended by only the senior members of her own and Lord Robert's household. The rest had ridden straight to the stables, so that Penelope was unable to discover whether or not she had imagined that she had seen Oliver among them. The day seemed full of surprises and the Queen's speaking to her so graciously had added to them, almost overwhelming her, since it was something which she had not expected.

'Well,' said Mary, when the Queen had finally processed further into the house, leaving them all standing there, 'I'd heard that she occasionally spoke to minor personages like yourself whom she chance meets in her duties, but I had never thought that you might be honoured when I was not, particularly when my future husband is part of her immediate retinue.'

Penelope almost blurted out, 'It was not my fault that she spoke to me,' but said nothing. After living for a few days at Charter House she was beginning to learn to be more discreet and less outspoken—even though, inside, she was still the forthright Penelope of old.

One thing was sure, though: she would try to discover, as soon as possible, whether it had been Oliver Woodville whom she thought that she had seen among the horsemen. If he were, what would she do then? One thing was certain, she could not approach him after he had ignored her so dreadfully on the day on which Mary had rejected him. Oh, she fully understood why he had, but because of it she must not be forward. She must remember that a slight inclination of the head would be the right thing to do if she met him when he was one of Lord Robert's attendants.

Lady Greville had spent the last week driving home the message that for the Queen's Ladies discretion was all. Others might romp and play, and joke with the men around the court, but her Ladies must be models of decorum.

'You may be sure,' she had said when ending her last sermon on the subject, 'that Mistress Kat Ashley, her chief lady, will keep a stern eye on you until she is certain that you can be trusted.'

She had hardly moved away before the young woman next to Penelope, one Janet Saville, related to the Yorkshire Savilles, who was also joining the

Queen's Ladies, muttered, 'I do hope, if all I hear is true, that Mistress Ashley is keeping as stern an eye on the Queen when she is closeted alone with Lord Robert as she is going to do on us!'

Lèse-majesty, thought Penelope. I'd better be careful what I say to Mistress Saville if she is often as loose-tongued as she was just now. It's fortunate that Lady Greville didn't hear her.

All in all, her stay at Charter House was introducing her to a whole new world where it obviously behoved her to be careful in what she said and did. So she made no answer to Janet Saville's indiscreet remark and tried to seem as innocent as she had probably appeared to the Queen.

But not so innocent that she would not look out for Master Oliver Woodville.

Master Oliver Woodville, too, was rapidly growing accustomed to court life. The worst thing about it was his loss of freedom, the best was being at the seat of power in the country. Although that also had its drawbacks. One good thing was that he had not seen Bevis Frampton lately. A discreet question to Jack Chancellor, one of his more reliable new friends, revealed that he was, temporarily at least, one of Castleford's gentlemen, but was now supposed to have been despatched on some mysterious errand for his master.

'Probably to do with one of the Earl's women— his ladybirds, he calls them,' Jack had told him merrily. 'He's supposed to be getting married to some nobody with money. The joy of that being that no-bodies with money can easily be kept from Court—it's hard to be so severe with some great family's daughter. I gather that his future wife is becoming a trifle demanding. Gossip says his secretary, Bevis Frampton, is supposed to be a great hand at persuading people to do what they don't want to.'

Well, apart from the news that Mary Jermaine's ambitions might shortly be thwarted, this was also a new piece of information about someone who had never persuaded either Harry, or himself, to change his mind. It was with an odd sense of relief that he learned of Bevis's absence. What disturbed him more at the moment was the possibility of someone's presence—although why he should worry about Penelope Jermaine was beyond his understanding.

On the late afternoon of their arrival at Charter House he thought that he had seen Penelope, as well as her sister, walking along the minstrels' gallery—so she was already a member of the Queen's entourage. The thought of her charming innocence being damaged by the duplicities of court life disturbed him—and was the source of his worry.

He would have worried even more if he had known that Elizabeth had spoken to Lady Greville about Penelope once she was settled into her Privy Chamber.

'The young girl I spoke to this afternoon. Know you aught of her? She seemed a promising lass.'

Lady Greville smiled. 'She has a mind of her own, Your Grace. The other young women say that she is too learned for their tastes.'

'Too learned?' queried the Queen, smiling. 'Tell me, is it possible to be too learned? I would have thought that that kind of distinction was reserved for those who are too ignorant. Has she any musical talents?'

'She plays the virginals, Your Grace, and I am told that she writes little songs of her own, but will not perform them in public, only for herself in private.'

Something in Lady Greville's manner told the Queen that she did not entirely approve of Mistress Penelope Jermaine—and that intrigued Her Grace more than any praise of the young woman would have done.

'Does she so? Learned, musical, writes poetry: a most interesting young woman. Has she any Latin?'

Lady Greville would have liked to reply, 'I fear so,' but remembered Her Grace's prowess in the tongue in time to prevent a tactless answer.

'Yes.' She hesitated, before adding, 'In fact I believe that when much younger she attended some of Master Ascham's classes at which you might also have been present.'

'Well, that settles that, then,' said Elizabeth, smiling again. 'She shall be promoted to be one of my Maids of Honour. I have a mind to talk to this young woman. She seems full of promise. I need intellect, as well as beauty, around me—not that she is over-backwards in the latter. I would hazard that her looks will improve with age—unlike those of the ungracious sister. You may send her to me on the morrow, after you have informed her of her elevation.'

Her hearer marvelled all over again at how quickly her mistress was able to gauge the men and women whom she met, even after only the most cursory inspection of them. She had rapidly seen that the older Jermaine girl was a light-minded piece, and was probably pleased that after marriage to Castleford she would be exiled into the country.

On the other hand Mistress Penelope Jermaine's future was assured. Lady Greville wondered what that independently minded young lady would make of it!

Chapter Three

'So there you are, Woodville? For once not closeted with our Lord and Master?'

To be successful was to rouse jealousy in others less fortunate, Oliver was rapidly finding. Even in the few days he had been in Lord Robert's service that astute nobleman had discovered that he had acquired a most useful aide.

He smiled as pleasantly as he could at Roger Temple, another of Lord Robert's men, but one who had not had the advantages of the extra polish which Oliver's travels in Europe had given him.

'No, indeed,' he replied as coolly as he could, 'but I am on an errand for him. He is unable to visit Her Grace this morning as he had promised and he has asked me to convey his regrets and deliver this letter to her. In other words I am today nothing but a superior kind of postman.'

This artful answer did not mollify his hearer, although it made his new good friend Jack Chancellor stifle a guffaw. Oliver did not stay to indulge in further badinage, but walked on until he came to the Queen's Gallery where a Steward took him in to see Her Grace.

Instead of Lord Robert hanging over her he found his second patron, William Cecil, with her. They were busily discussing a lengthy document which lay on the long table before them. But it was not the pair of them who engaged his interest but the sight of Penelope Jermaine sitting among the Queen's Maids of Honour at yet another table placed before a stained-glass window. She was playing chess with a pretty young woman who was moaning and wailing under her breath at her inability to offer Penelope a game.

The Steward coughed. Her Grace looked up, first at him, and then at Oliver who stood in his rear. Her smile for them was a dazzling one.

'I see,' she said, waving her right hand in the air, 'that Master Woodville has chosen to visit me this fine morning. Are you here on your behalf, sir, or on that of your patron? Master Cecil, you will forgive me, I trust, if I honour Master Woodville with my attention for a moment.'

'Always, madam,' murmured Cecil. So, by the fashion in which she was treating young Master Woodville, the Queen's eye for a handsome and clever man was not failing her.

'Come, then, Master Woodville,' she bade him. 'What is it you have to say to me?'

'Only this, Your Grace,' began Oliver, who was now being stared at by Penelope, as he had stared at her—it would have been difficult to decide which of them was the more surprised on seeing the other. 'I come merely as Lord Robert's postman to hand you this letter, and to ask that you pardon him for having been called away this morning on urgent business.'

'More urgent than that of his mistress, the Queen?' riposted Elizabeth, taking the letter from him. 'No, no, Master Woodville, no need to answer me. But does Lord Robert straightway require an answer?'

Oliver shook his head. 'I know not, Your Grace. Perhaps his missive will tell you.'

She laughed a little at that and opened the letter while saying, 'You may wait on me a while, Master Woodville. My Maids require amusement, particularly since my latest acquisition, Mistress Jermaine, plays a better game of chess than any of them, is a divine mistress of the virginals, and also has the temerity to sing like an angel and read Livy in the original.'

She called across to Penelope, who had risen on hearing her name, 'I give you leave to entertain Master Woodville. He is as new to Lord Robert's service as you are to mine. The virginals are before you, Mistress Jermaine, play a quiet tune on them for him—that should serve to keep the pair of you behaving yourselves as a pious lady and gentleman ought. You have my permission to attend her until you leave, Master Oliver.'

Master Oliver, indeed! William Cecil's face was grim when he heard the familiar way in which his Queen spoke to this new favourite. Oh, yes, Master Woodville was plainly destined to be one of her courtiers—and for her pleasure, not that of her Maids of Honour. She would expect him to direct all his attention to her while keeping his hands off them. In return he was to be teased and charmed by her, but she would always remind him that she was Queen and he but her latest toy.

What will Robert Dudley think, reflected Cecil, when he learns that one of his own suite is to be admitted to the circle of honour? If he has any common sense at all he may simply argue that Master Woodville is merely the newest addition to her stable of young gallants and, as many have observed before me, there is always safety in numbers.

Oliver, a little surprised by the Queen's warm reception of him, walked over to where Penelope had already seated herself at the virginals. He said, keeping his voice low, 'I gather that Her Grace does not know that we are already acquainted.'

'For sure,' said Penelope, trying not to blush with pleasure at the sight of him so near to her, and speaking kindly to her, 'and, who knows, that may be a good thing, or a bad thing. I have already been told by Mistress Ashley that were she aware that we have long been on friendly terms, she would not have thrown us together. We are expected to ignore young men, rather than encourage them—unless she tells us to, and even then only in public, of course.'

Oliver nodded—it was safer to say nothing here—and sat back to listen to her when she began to play for him, and for the other maids who had seated themselves on cushions in the window embrasures nearby. For the first time he looked at Penelope without seeing her as the mere junior appendage of her beautiful sister. There was a tranquillity about her which pleased him. Not only that, but she was no longer the skinny child she had been before he left on his travels. To top that she had, most unexpectedly, instead of being a mere Lady in Waiting, become one of the Queen's Maids of Honour, who were the Queen's intimate companions, ready at all times to entertain her, both in matters light and in matters learned.

He wondered how her sister had received her being given this singular honour; badly, he supposed. Oliver suddenly felt that he needed a friend, a true friend from his uncomplicated past—and who better than Penelope with her downright common sense—for he also remembered that about her.

'I am told that there is a Knot Garden at the back of the house,' he said, still keeping his voice low. 'After dinner—which I understand you will eat with Her Grace—I intend to visit it. I have been indoors too much. It would please me, if by chance, you would care to meet me there. I have somewhat to say to you concerning a matter which is a cause of self-reproach for me.'

Penelope, having ended her song, let her hands rest on the keys. 'You must understand that my time is not my own, but I shall try to oblige you—if only in memory of our long friendship. Fortunately, the Knot Garden is not overlooked from the house. There is a small pavilion by the path where we may talk in private. I shall be waiting there for you if my duties allow.'

Even before she had finished speaking she had begun to play again, a plaintive song, one which she had performed before company in her old home when she had been little more than a child. Since then her musical abilities had greatly improved and now that he heard her singing it again, Oliver found that it was one which he remembered. It was about a man whose lover had deserted him. It had often haunted him in the midnight hours when sleep was hard to come by—particularly since he had lost Mary.

So rapt was he that it was a moment before he realised that the Steward had come over and was urging him to attend upon Her Grace, who was about to hand him a brief letter for Lord Robert, to be delivered at once.

'After which Her Grace commands that you attend her at dinner in her suite at noon precisely—and Lord Robert, too, of course, if his duties so allow him by then.'

'It will be a great honour for me to obey Your Grace,' bowed Oliver, taking the letter from her shapely hand and wondering how, in a few short weeks, he had been transformed from a nobody of a country gentleman into a favoured member of the royal court. A thought which occupied him, on and off, until it was time for him to make for the Knot Garden and Penelope.

With luck, Lord Robert might not need his services that afternoon, since Jack Chancellor had informed him with a snigger, before dinner began, that Her Grace had ordered him to attend on her privately once the meal was over.

Which left him able to eat the excellent food in peace, since he knew neither of his neighbours, both of whom favoured him with a hard stare—and never once spoke to him—something for which he was grateful. He must never let himself forget that court life was a nest of intrigue.

Penelope waited inside the Knot Garden's small Pavilion on a stone bench, nervously wondering what it was that Oliver wished to say to her. Like everyone else she had noticed the favour with which the Queen had treated him. If only she could be as easy in his presence as most of the women were with the men around them. The trouble was that being with him made her feel breathless—but she must not let him know that.

Was he aware that Mary would be sent to Castleford's home in the North after her marriage had taken place—and been consummated—which would only happen once all the rituals connected with the Coronation were over?

Nervously she twisted her hands together, looking anxious, until she heard someone walking briskly along the gravel path and rose to greet him; but alas, it was not Oliver so she sat down again. Perhaps he would not trouble to come. Now that the Queen had taken notice of him would he find time to consort with a mere Maid of Honour?

Penelope had learned long ago that time ran slowly while you waited for something—or someone. Nevertheless, after she had been waiting for what seemed forever, she began to think that, for one reason or another, Oliver must have decided against meeting her. Despite the long and warm fur coat which Janet Saville had lent her when she had told her that she wished to walk in the garden, she was beginning to feel the cold.

She rose and gathered her skirts about her—one drawback of Court Dress being that it was so much heavier than the thin cottons and satins which she had always previously worn, even if it were warmer—left the pavilion and set off down the path, back to the house.

She had almost reached the back door when she saw Oliver emerge from it and come hurrying towards her. His clothing, like hers, was stiff and elaborate, certainly not designed for rapid walking. All the same, he had never looked more handsome, and Penelope's heart wrenched a little in her bosom.

Oh, if only once he would look at her as he had so often looked at Mary—with longing mixed with love—she would die happy. But that would be too much to ask for, so be thankful for small mercies, my girl, she told herself briskly: be thankful that he has not forgotten you after all, but has kept his given word. When they finally met she could not stop herself from smiling at him, although she had earlier decided to greet him coolly so that he should not guess how much the sight of him affected her.

'Pray forgive me, Mistress Jermaine,' he told her, panting a little, 'but when I was about to set out Lord Robert suddenly thought of yet another errand for me. I was fearful that I might not have finished it in time to meet you in the gardens as I had promised.'

'Penelope,' she said, before she stopped to think. 'I am not Mistress anything to you, Oliver. I have known you too long for that.'

'So you have, Penelope—but will the Queen excommunicate us if we are overheard being so familiar with one another?'

'Fortunately no one, at the moment, is near enough to us to be able to tattle to her,' she told him.

'True, but I feel that we might be even safer if we went into the Pavilion where we can be more private—as well as warmer. On the way here I had the strangest feeling that someone was following me—but looking back I couldn't see anyone. Nevertheless, let us be wary.'

To be alone with him, in the Pavilion, with no

Mary nearby to mock at her, would be nothing less than a taste of heaven on earth! Together they mounted its three steps and walked into a porch which was ornamented by a stone statue of Pan, playing on his pipes. From thence an archway led into a small room. Several stools were arranged in its middle and wooden benches ran round the walls.

Oliver gallantly helped Penelope to sit on a bench away from the entrance so that she might not be seen, while he pulled up one of the stools in order to be opposite to her, saying, 'You will allow me,' before he sat down, for it was customary for a gentleman to ask a lady for permission to sit in her presence.

'Yes,' returned Penelope, 'if you will continue to be Oliver to me, and not Master Woodville.'

'Then Oliver will sit,' he replied, 'and Oliver will offer you his apology in comfort.'

'An apology?'

There was a question mark in her voice. He had mentioned something about self-reproach earlier. Could it be that he regretted not having spoken to her when he had left on the day that Mary had turned him away?

For his part Oliver wondered what it was about Penelope which had changed, for there was no doubt that consciously or not she was teasing him a little, something which she had stopped doing before he had left for the Continent. When was it that she had ceased to be easy with him—and why?

Had Oliver thought hard, he might have remembered that her behaviour towards him had changed after he and Mary had become sweethearts. This had happened when Penelope had been little more than a child. The slight friendship which had existed between a youth, nearly a man, and a very young girl, who asked him questions about his reading, had disappeared. Her manner to him had become distant, she had even tried to avoid him—which had wounded him somewhat, though he had soon forgotten it in the heady delights of courting Mary.

He was not to know that Mary had reprimanded Penelope for talking to him so often—she was always asking him for advice about what she ought to be reading once she had learned that he had distinguished himself at Oxford University.

'A young man of his age does not want a child following him about and pestering him with silly questions,' Mary had said to her once, among other critical and unkind remarks, ending with the words, 'I suggest that you keep to your room when Oliver visits.'

Their similar—if separate—musings could not have taken long, because Oliver was replying almost immediately to her last remark.

'Yes, an apology, I fear. When I visited your family on my return from my tour of the Continent, I passed you by in the most discourteous manner when I left the house. That I was deeply troubled is no excuse. I should not have done so. I remember you as a very well-behaved child, always anxious to do your duty and, to my shame, I did not do mine that afternoon.'

Was there compassion in the look which she was giving him? Compassion for his loss of Mary? If so, she deserved something more from him in return. Like a knight to his lady, or one of the handsome courtiers he had seen in the various palaces he had visited in Italy, he bowed his head and went down on one knee before her, saying, 'Pray accept my deepest regrets, Penelope, for my unkind behaviour. I shall try to be more gentlemanly in future.'

Penelope extended her hand to raise him, as she had seen the Queen do. 'They are accepted, sir. I was well aware how distressed you must be—and *my* deepest regret after you had left was that I was losing an old friend, even if I did not see you very often before you went away to the Continent. And now, let us forget all that—and start again.'

Their hands touched, and each looked at the other—for the touch had been oddly compelling. Neither knew exactly what to say. Penelope, in particular, was almost disturbed by it. For a brief moment her whole body seemed affected by him and his presence in the strangest way.

Until Oliver—who was even more surprised than Penelope, for he had been thinking of her as still little more than a child—came out with, 'Willingly, most willingly, since you have been so gracious as to forgive me for my churlishness. But I do have a question for you to answer, which is, How came you to be one of the Queen's Maids of Honour?'

'By accident, solely. The Queen, for some reason which I shall never know, spoke to me when I was introduced to her as one of her new Ladies in Waiting, an honour I gained through my future brother-in-law's influence. Something which I said, quite unwittingly—I know not what—must have interested her, for she spoke to Lady Greville and immediately ordered that I was to take the place of a Maid of Honour who had just left to be married. It seems, among other things, that we shall read Livy and Cicero together—whenever she finds time to indulge herself, that is.'

When Penelope was animated one might almost call her pretty. No, not pretty, she was something more than that—something strange and different. She was totally unlike the lovely creatures he had pleasured on his travels—even Mary had been right about that—or indeed, any other women he had known, including Mary herself.

He was not to know that the Queen had seen character in her face and the promise of a mature and rare beauty, for Penelope was full young for her age— quite unlike her sister when she had been eighteen.

'You have achieved your wish to be learned, then? I remember, years ago, when you were but a midget, that you asked me questions about my studies. Oddly, I was flattered that you should consult me—and then, quite suddenly, you stopped doing so.'

He had remembered! Mary had been wrong—he *had* liked her for asking him questions, and he had not been at all annoyed! Penelope's eyes shone and she answered him eagerly, 'Yes, and I understand that Lady Greville informed her in detail of my interests— and since the Queen is very learned, beyond my poor abilities, she likes those about her to be learned.'

For no real reason, Oliver said softly, 'Mary is not learned.'

Penelope said nothing. She did not wish to speak of her sister—least of all to the man whom Mary had treated so cruelly.

For a moment or two they sat there in silence. Oliver remembered that Penelope—according to her sister—was too forthright when she spoke, which wasn't often, but, as he had discovered earlier, her tranquillity was most welcome after the hectic pace at which court life was lived. Speech was good, silence was sometimes better. He had had a hard day of it and simply to sit in the Pavilion with her was strangely soothing.

But Penelope must be beginning to feel the cold— after all, it was late November outside—and that would never do. He rose, 'I regret to say it, Mis... I mean Penelope, but we must part—and separately. It would never do for you to be the target of unkind gossip when you have been generous enough to forgive me for my sins.'

This time when he took her hand it was to kiss the back of it, as he had seen the French and Italian gallants do, and again the effect it had on them both was strong and remarkable. Oliver because it told him that Penelope Jermaine had begun to attract him in the deepest and most profound manner—which was a surprise because he had never thought to lust after someone who was so unlike, not only Mary, but those other women whom he had bedded.

Penelope was the more disturbed because she had touched many men's hands when dancing and never before had she experienced such an immediate and shivering response. Oh, it was all over in a minute, but that it had happened at all was a wonder which she did not quite understand. Was it only Oliver who could cause this? And, if so, it surely confirmed the love which she had felt for him the first time she had met him—a love which she might have otherwise dismissed as childish.

More than that, did he experience the same powerful physical response when he touched her? If so, what did it tell her about him—and his feelings for her?

And if merely to touch hands with him could provoke such an immediate and pleasurable response, what would happen if he kissed her?

Best, perhaps, not to find out—yet.

It was late in the afternoon, the candles had been lit, and most of Lord Robert's men were seated at a long table in one of the galleries. He was away in the

Queen's suite, and they had been playing cards—and drinking—to pass the time until supper.

Now they were gossiping, and as ever, the talk had turned to the ever-present question of who the new Queen might marry. Most of those round the table who had not already laid their money out on one of her many foreign suitors were joining in the fun of trying to prophesy as to who, of them all, might be the fortunate man. Oliver was the only one who, so far, had not risked any of his wages, or of his winnings at cards, on making a bet—something of which jolly Jack Chancellor was about to remind him.

'Come, Master Woodville,' he bawled down the table, 'pray give me an honest answer. Is it true that you have not yet wagered anything on guessing who might be the fellow fortunate enough to marry Her Grace? Fie upon you, not to lay out some of your winnings.'

Oliver thought that it was a good thing that Lord Robert wasn't present to hear what his followers got up to in his absence, particularly since, if he were not already married, he might have been the Queen's most favoured suitor.

'My money is on a foreigner,' continued the half-drunk Jack, 'for I cannot believe that she will marry a subject. But which foreigner? Aye, there's the rub. Erik of Denmark or the Archduke Charles? Or even brother-in-law King Philip of Spain. How say you?'

'I say,' returned Oliver, 'that it is a poor thing that while the last Queen is waiting to be taken to St James to be buried, we should be betting on who will be the new Queen's husband.'

This only served to earn him shouts and jeers of, 'Turning parson, are you, Woodville?' and other insults. Since he was one of the few people at table still sober, he decided not to take offence lest worse might follow. He could scarcely justify his prudence by pointing out that his refusal to bet partly arose because he was, unlike many present, not exactly flush with money, and the wages Lord Robert paid his followers were not high.

The noise they were making grew until the door opened and the unlikely combination of William Cecil and Lord Robert entered, followed by assorted flunkies.

This had the effect of a snuffer descending on a candle. Silence fell.

Lord Robert was looking down his nose at them all. He was dismally sure that Cecil's followers would not be misbehaving themselves like this—they would be too frightened of the consequences. On the other hand, who wanted to be surrounded by a pack of pious old women wearing men's clothing?

When at last he spoke it was in a most formal and constrained manner. 'I am here,' he said, 'to inform you that the Queen and the musicians await us in the Great Hall. She has decreed that we shall dance this evening.'

William Cecil was nodding his agreement. Oliver wondered why these important personages had been sent to make this announcement, and not one of the royal Stewards. He was not to know that they had annoyed the Queen by bickering in her presence and, as a punishment, she had ordered them to carry out this menial errand so as to remind them that she was their monarch and that her word was law. It had not helped matters that the bickering had been about the Queen's marriage—a subject of which she was growing heartily tired even before she had been crowned.

A dance! None had taken place at court since the late Queen's death. All those present leapt excitedly to their feet. Visitors to England—and many of those whom Oliver had met on the Continent—frequently remarked on the English love of dance.

What a splendid opportunity to get close to the pretty Maids of Honour and the other ladies who attended Court! Had it not been for the presence of their superiors, the assembled gentlemen would have rushed out of the room on the instant. As it was, they walked decorously towards the Great Hall, from whence the strains of music were already coming.

The Queen sat at one end of the Hall on a small throne, all her ladies around her. Since any event at court was always conducted by following a strict ritual, no one was yet dancing, because the Queen always had to be the first to take to the floor unless she ordered otherwise.

She beckoned to Lord Robert when he arrived and he walked across to where she stood, waiting for him, so that he might lead her forward to dance that lively measure in triple time, the Galliard. After that the other dancers streamed on to the floor as their partners claimed them.

Mary Jermaine, a discontented expression on her face, stood watching her future husband leading out Janet Saville and not her. Earlier that afternoon she had told him how much she was looking forward to attending court with him once they were married. He had immediately told her that on the contrary, she was to be sent into exile at his castle in the distant North after their marriage had been consummated. She had promptly begun a furious argument with him—which she had lost—after begging and pleading with him to change his mind.

Castleford, to punish her for daring to disagree with him, had ignored her and asked another lady to join him on the floor. Fortunately, after standing there alone, hurt and feeling betrayed, she saw Oliver Woodville walking towards her.

Would it not be delightful to partner him again? To look adoringly at him and make Castleford jealous, perhaps? At the back of her mind a suspicion was growing that it might have been better not to have turned Oliver Woodville away. Castleford was such a dull stick that the prospect of being tied to him for life, and exiled to the wastelands of the North, was much too big a price to pay for becoming a Countess. Were she to be allowed to attend court, she would be prepared to endure him, but otherwise…no.

So she smiled a welcome at Oliver, who replied with a distant bow before moving on.

To invite Penelope of all people to be his partner in the dance! Mary's fury knew no bounds.

Penelope, by contrast, was delighted when Oliver held out his hand to her and led her into the middle of the fun of the Galliard, which she had thought that she was going to miss. The best bit of all, she discovered, was when Oliver put his hands round her waist and tossed her into the air—nearly as high as Lord Robert was throwing the Queen. Breathless, she descended into his waiting arms, whereat he whirled her around in time to the music which was coming from the dais where the players sat.

On and on they danced, like the Italian men and women in one of the paintings on the walls which showed them to be enjoying themselves in similar fashion. All too soon the dance ended, but only after Penelope had discovered that the strange feelings which Oliver's kissing her hand had excited were as nothing to those which she had experienced when they were dancing together.

Her breathlessness was more from the result of that than from the physical exertions of the dance itself, so in some odd way she was almost relieved when it ended—and what did that mean?

Oliver, taking note of her flushed face, her glowing eyes, their pupils dilated, knew exactly what it meant. For the first time he realised that what he had shared with Mary was nothing but calf-love—the tepid feelings of an immature young man for an equally immature girl. This was something quite different.

Unaware that Mary was glaring at them, he led Penelope back to her place near to the Queen's small throne, saying, 'I am told by those in the know that the Galliard is usually followed by the Pavan—which is slow and stately—to allow us to get our breath back.'

'Isn't the Galliard a trifle immodest?' Penelope breathed back at him.

'Not if the Queen sanctions it,' smiled Oliver.

'I suppose not—but Lord Robert did throw her very high.' She did not add, *and the old Queen not yet in her grave*, but if she had she would only have been echoing what many of the spectators were thinking— and what some of them were saying.

Oliver did not remain with her—etiquette forbade—so he retired towards the corner where many of the other young gentlemen sat. But he never reached them. William Cecil, who had been one of the silently disapproving spectators—and who had been talking with the Spanish Ambassador, Feria, while the music played—said to Oliver when he walked past him, 'A word with you, Master Woodville.'

Perforce Oliver had to obey him. Cecil led him towards the far end of the Gallery and, raising his hand to point at one of the paintings there—a Holbein sketch of the late King Henry VIII—said, as though he were describing its excellence to his hearer, 'I must ask you, whether, in your duties around the Lord Robert, you have heard aught of a possible plot—inaugurated by someone unknown and mysterious—to arrange matters so that the Queen's Grace is compelled to marry a Prince of the Catholic persuasion. A someone, I am told, who has recently visited the Continent.'

Before Oliver could reply, a pair of courtiers came within earshot of them so that, Cecil, quite smoothly, said, as though continuing a long monologue inspired by the portrait, 'This fellow Holbein was, of course, a master at showing the true character of the personage whom he was painting. Note how skilfully he has conveyed the late King's power and majesty…'

And then, when the pair had passed on with cursory bows offered on all sides, he continued, just as smoothly as before, saying, 'I ask you again, have you knowledge of this?'

Oliver shook his head and replied bluntly, 'No, only that it is not I who am doing the plotting.'

Why, at this point, did he think of Bevis Frampton? Other than that he, too, had visited the Continent lately?

'No, I do not suspect you,' lied Cecil—for he suspected everyone, only a fool would not. 'I fear that they may force the Queen into this marriage by discrediting her and those around her.' So saying, he looked across the vast room to where, once again, Lord Robert was tenderly bending over his royal mistress.

His meaning was unmistakable, but Oliver did not allow Cecil's superior rank to push him into saying anything unwise, or to let him know that he understood the message which lay behind Cecil's seemingly innocent words. Instead he replied, looking as naive as he dared, 'I assure you, Master Cecil, that being a loyal subject of the Queen, I would report to you anything which I thought to be treasonable or which might affect the safety of her realm.'

Cecil looked at him and smiled wryly. 'I believe, Master Woodville, that you may yet be very successful in the dangerous world which you have chosen to inhabit. A still, or a discreet, tongue in one's head is a wise thing to possess—but I would rather that you did not palter with me, sir—though your last statement of intent is one which I commend. Now walk a little further with me and I will discourse on yet another painting for you. It is one more of the many which have come from Italy. It is essential that others think that it is simply a shared love of the arts which is the cause of our conversations. Most useful that, since we increase in knowledge after a double fashion—or so I trust.'

All the same, Lord Robert's eyes were hard on the man who was his enemy showing such favour to someone in his service. He wondered how far he could trust Master Woodville in the intrigues and the game of wits which involved all those living near the monarch. Both he, and the Queen also, watched them gesticulating while they discussed the painting's won-

ders. It showed Orpheus and Eurydice at the point
where he had lost his dear love for ever.

The room was hot, and Lord Robert, by reason of
his exertions in the Galliard, was hotter, but all the
same the sight of the painting set him shivering as
though he were standing in the cold outside—and he
briefly wondered why this should be so.

Penelope discovered that Oliver had been right.
The Galliard was succeeded by the Pavan. To her
surprise, immediately the music began, Mary's betrothed walked over to her—cutting Oliver off on the
way—and said, after offering her a most formal bow,
'We ought to become better acquainted, Mistress
Penelope, seeing that you are soon to be my sister-
in-law. To that end I ask you to dance the Pavan with
me.'

Penelope had no wish at all to dance with Lord
Castleford. Until this very moment he had completely
ignored her. Oh, he had been stiffly polite to her on
the few occasions on which they had met, but he had
never before tried to engage her in conversation or
shown any willingness to enjoy her company.

So, why this ingratiating smile? And why was he
not dancing with Mary as he ought? She could not
refuse him, however, even though she would have
preferred Oliver to be her partner.

'Most honoured,' was all that she could murmur.
At least they could enjoy the dance in silence—but
no such thing, he immediately began to ask her how

she was enjoying herself at court, and from then on questioned her about all her doings. What in the world had possessed the man that he should single her out so?

What possessed William Vassall, Lord Castleford, was the realisation that he had completely miscalculated the nature and temper of the woman to whom he had proposed marriage. At that time he had thought Mary to be gentle and biddable—as well as beautiful. He had compared her favourably with her quiet, plainer sister, who had sat silent while beautiful Mary entertained him with her lively comments on everything around them.

Once betrothed to her, however, she had changed completely. Her previously charming submission to him before their betrothal disappeared completely and she became impossibly demanding, not to say domineering. He was beginning to gain the impression that he was to marry an ill-tempered shrew and had started to believe that the plainer, quieter sister would have been a better proposition as a malleable Countess. After all, their dowries were equally large, so he would lose nothing if he could exchange them.

The dowry, of course, mattered greatly to him. His own wealth was largely imaginary. In the new world of commerce and industry his lands possessed no coal-pits and no iron ore, which elsewhere were serving to enrich other noblemen and enabling them to make a greater show at court than he could. Perhaps, somehow, he could rid himself of the bad-tempered

Mistress Jermaine and gain the gentle one instead. There were always ways and means of doing such a thing.

He must ask young Frampton for advice on this— he seemed to have a clever and a devious mind and had proved useful in their behind the scenes intriguing for the Catholic cause by furthering the prospects of those suitors on the Continent who were devoted to the old religion. He had even sent several convincing stories which were highly critical of Lord Robert on their way round the court.

In the meantime he could gently woo the younger sister. Besides, it would not do for her to become involved with one of Lord Robert's retinue, so cutting Woodville out as a prospective suitor would be no bad thing. He had no wish to have someone from a Protestant family as a future brother-in-law. He laughed to himself when he watched Mary walk over to Woodville, who was now also without a partner, and begin to talk animatedly to him.

His internal laughter grew the more when it became plain that Woodville wanted no more of her. Mary, in their earlier and happier days, had made a mock of him, saying that he had been a most presumptuous suitor. He had later discovered that she made a mock of everyone—particularly the little sister and anyone she disliked. So it would be all the sweeter if he could manoeuvre matters so that he married Penelope instead!

Penelope, meanwhile, was finding that dancing

with Castleford was quite different from partnering Oliver. To begin with he was so much less athletic than Oliver that he was unable to follow the intricacies of the dance, stumbling over his feet once or twice—and hers on at least one occasion. The frissons of pleasure which coursed through her body whenever Oliver was her partner were quite missing—instead she was repelled by Castleford's slightest touch. Unlike him she did not watch the spectators and therefore missed the sight of Oliver refusing her sister's importunities.

Had there been a playwright present who could disentangle the emotions and behaviour of most of those in the Great Hall, he would have delighted in the criss-cross of their passions, from those involving the monarch and her would-be lover down to the lesser characters present.

Mary, with mounting fury, had watched her betrothed ignore her again, in favour this time of Penelope, of all people. Fortunately that meant that Oliver was without a partner, and when he moved in her direction she decided to accost him and remind him of the happy days which they had once shared—in virtual childhood, of course.

Alas, the face he showed her when she touched him on the shoulder when he passed her was a forbidding one.

'Mistress?' he queried her with a perfunctory bow, as though he did not know her.

'Mistress?' she trilled back at him. 'You must mean Mary, Oliver. Surely you have not forgotten me?'

'No, Mistress Jermaine, no one could forget you.'

'There,' she exclaimed, tossing her head at him, 'you are as gallant as ever,' completely unaware that it was no compliment that he was paying her, merely seeking to remind her, instead, of how cruelly she had treated him. Thus misled, she turned her most dazzling smile in his direction, saying, 'Surely such gallantry will allow you to invite me to join the dance with you—seeing that we are both without partners.'

'Oh, but I am not without a partner, Mistress Jermaine. Mistress Janet Saville awaits me. Now that your future husband has asked your sister to dance the Pavan with him I intend to fulfil a promise that I made to take the floor with her tonight.'

He bowed—and left her—to move on to the wretched Saville girl so that she was compelled to stand there, alone and rejected, and watch others enjoy what she had thought to be hers by right—a loving, or a friendly, partner.

The Pavan wound its stately way to its end. Penelope tried to take her hand out of Castleford's but, alas, he merely clutched hers the more firmly, saying, 'Come with me, Mistress Penelope, I have not yet seen enough of my betrothed's pretty sister. It is most fitting that, for the passage of this evening, you become one of my family. I am sure that the Queen's Grace would surely not begrudge you that.'

What could she do without making a scene, but

allow herself to be dragged over to where Mary stood? Her sister was glaring at her as though it were she who was pulling along fat Lord Castleford and not the other way round.

'Was my poor Penelope so bereft of partners, Castleford, that you felt compelled to invite her to dance?' was Mary's unkind greeting to them.

'On the contrary, my dear, I had to cut young Woodville off before he could offer for her. I thought it only fitting that she should join us for a time. It must not seem that we are ignoring her. That would never do.'

'But what does do,' exclaimed Mary, clumsily ungrammatical in her speech as a result of what she saw as yet another affront, 'is apparently for me to go partnerless through two dances while my betrothed squires other women.'

Penelope closed her eyes and managed to extract her hand—scarlet as a result of Castleford's determination to make Mary endure the sight of her despised younger sister being favoured by him—and said, 'I do have duties to perform for Her Grace, Lord Castleford, so I trust that you will allow me to return to her.'

In the face of that blunt statement he was compelled to allow her to leave them. Mary could not prevent herself from unwisely snarling at her sister, 'Yes, do go, Penelope, we have no need of you here.'

By God, yes, he would get rid of Mary, by hook or by crook, for there was no doubt that the younger sister knew how to conduct herself properly—which was more than the elder one did.

Consequently he continued to refuse to invite Mary to dance with him, but recommended her to retire to the dormitory of the Ladies in Waiting so that she could rest in order to dispel the black humours from which she unfortunately seemed to be suffering.

This came out so authoritatively that Mary had no choice but to appear to obey him. He was beginning to frighten her, which led her to regret even more that she had agreed to marry him. If there was any way in which she could escape her unpleasant fate she would take it, although such an outcome seemed very unlikely.

In the meantime, once he had left her alone… again!…in order to ask that dowdy old woman Lady Greville to partner him, she decided that one way to counter his control of her would be to persuade another of the gentlemen present to ask her to dance.

She looked around her. Jack Chancellor appeared to be unclaimed. He was leaning against the wall, arms folded, enjoying the fun. The Branle was an even noisier dance than the Galliard. It was unlike him to be without a partner. Fanning herself, Mary walked steadily over towards him, trying to appear as though she, too, was merely happy to be an observer.

Jack saw her coming, uncrossed his arms and smiled at her. It would be a jolly piece of fun to dance with that fat fool Castleford's betrothed.

'What, no partner, Mistress Jermaine?'

She smiled back at him. 'Oh, I am alone at the moment, for my future husband has his duty to do by entertaining those unfortunates who otherwise might not be able to take part in the dance.' Which statement was true so far as Lady Greville was concerned, but certainly did not apply to her sister, nor to Janet Saville.

If Jack saw through this excuse he did not say so, merely bowed elaborately and said, 'But you would allow me to be your escort in the Branle, would you not, since I, too, am alone?'

'It would please me greatly,' replied Mary, putting as much condescension into her voice as she could, as though she were doing Jack the greatest favour.

'Well, then,' said Jack, and together they processed on to the floor, where Castleford, on seeing them laughing and giggling together, after he had told her to leave, was more determined than ever to rid himself of his unwanted encumbrance.

All in all it was a typical evening at court, where intrigue and double-dealing reigned supreme. At least, for the present, everyone felt that their head was safe upon their shoulders, but, all the same, it would be wise not to be careless nor to tempt fate and the devil lest the worst befall, since one must never forget that Queen Elizabeth was very much her father's daughter.

Who knew what the new reign might bring in? At the moment all seemed set fair—but how long would that last? Moving through the dance, laughing, talking, and joking, the assembled company, for a brief moment, were able to forget their cares.

Tonight was pleasure, but work and duty would soon follow as the preparations for the burial of the late Queen and then the Coronation gathered pace.

And once the Queen was crowned, what then?

Chapter Four

'Thank you, Mistress Penelope,' said the Queen, 'for keeping me company today. I dare say that you might have preferred to have gone riding with the others.'

'Oh, I can do that at any time,' Penelope returned truthfully, 'whereas an hour spent with you and Tacitus is a rare and happy event.' She was not flattering her royal mistress, even though the Queen might think so.

'And now we must cease. First Master Cecil is coming to trouble me, and then Lord Robert. The cares of state take precedence over everything else—which is something that those who are not monarchs do not understand, nor do they grasp how wearisome it might be.' She indicated by a wave of her hand that Penelope was to leave her.

Penelope bowed, rose and walked out of the Long Gallery and down the main staircase towards the rooms where the Maids of Honour retired when the Queen dismissed them. A group of men, led by Lord Robert Dudley, were assembled at the bottom of the stairs, among them Oliver Woodville, who was attired in clothes suitable for riding on the rainy day that this was proving to be.

Earlier Lord Robert had commanded his presence. He had begun by saying, somewhat brusquely, 'I saw you in private conference with Master Cecil yesterday. I was not aware that you and he were acquainted.'

'Through his friendship with my father at University, merely,' replied Oliver. 'I had not known him before I came to court.'

'Hmm!' Lord Robert lay back in his chair of state. 'You seemed closer than that.'

'Only because he knew that I had been to Italy and he wished to discourse with me on various matters to do with the art of painting—in which I, too, take an interest. He was kind enough to enlighten me on the subject of the canvas hanging in the Long Gallery.'

'And that was all?'

Oliver was careful to look puzzled, although he knew quite well that Lord Robert was testing him to discover whether his real loyalties lay with Cecil.

'Indeed, m'lord—the matter arose because Master Cecil had heard that I had sojourned in Europe. Was there aught else I should have discussed with him?'

Lord Robert smiled and waved a languid hand. 'No, nothing, but he is a cunning fellow, and the less said to him on matters of import which affect me and my household, the better. Do you understand me, young Woodville?'

'Truly, yes, m'lord—which is why the conversation turned only on such minor matters as interested us both.'

'Then let it remain so. Know that I am sending a party of my most trusted followers to the house of Dr John Dee, the necromancer and astrologer, this afternoon. He will be told that I am inviting him to consult the stars and decide on the most propitious day for the Queen's Coronation. When he has done so I shall have him brought to where the Queen is residing at that time in order to explain his reasoning. I wish you to be one of the party. You may go now to prepare yourself. I am summoned to the Queen else I would accompany you, but I dare not delay treating with Dee any longer, so you must all be my eyes and ears.'

Truly the court was a place where one would be well advised to tread with care! Even flighty Jack Chancellor said the same thing to him later when they were assembled in the hallway before leaving. It was he who first saw Penelope coming down the stairs. Whereupon he poked Oliver in the ribs, saying, 'Look Woodville, here comes your pretty girl. Her Grace is favouring her these days—and not the elder sister. Mistress Mary deigned to dance with me last night only when everyone else had passed her over. Now that we are to visit Dr Dee this afternoon you ought to have your own horoscope drawn up in order to discover whether Mistress Penelope is to be your fatal fair—by which I mean your wife.'

'I had it drawn up in Italy,' replied Oliver, 'and all that the necromancer could tell me was that I would marry the woman who would bring me happiness— which is as little as telling me what I already know, for I am not likely to marry anyone who I think might bring me unhappiness!'

'Ah, but Dee is better than that—or so I'm told. At least Lord Robert believes so.'

Oliver was not sure how much Lord Robert's advice on anything could be relied on—other than that to do with horses and pageantry. By this time Penelope had reached them and Jack forestalled him by detaining her.

'Stay a while, Mistress, we are waiting to take our leave, and you may relieve our boredom while we do so. Is not that so, Master Woodville?'

Oliver smiled. 'Indeed, she may.'

Penelope blushed, but while she was pleased to have two handsome men soliciting her company, she would have preferred to have only one—and that one Oliver. Nevertheless it was Jack she addressed, saying, 'Of what would you wish me to speak, Master Chancellor?'

'Oh, do not Master me,' replied Jack with a grin. 'We must surely be Jack and Oliver to you by now.'

'Then, Jack and Oliver, since you are dressed for riding, for where are you bound on this rainy afternoon?'

Before Jack could reply, one of the men nearest to Lord Robert called him to his side, which left Oliver to answer her.

'We are visiting Dr Dee on behalf of Lord Robert,' he said.

Caution kept him from saying more, but he need not have troubled, for Penelope said eagerly, 'Then it is true that the Queen's Coronation date will be decided by Dr Dee and that Lord Robert is arranging for him to be consulted?'

Jack, who had been delaying his departure, overheard this and turned back, while Oliver, jaw dropped, exclaimed, 'Now how do you come to know of this, Penelope, when we have only just been informed of it?'

'Oh,' she said, puzzled, 'I'm surprised that you didn't know. It's been common gossip among the Maids of Honour for the last few days.'

Oliver began to smile: Jack, slapping his thigh, started to laugh, saying between each gust as it overcame him, 'Here was Lord Robert keeping it a secret from us until a few moments ago and all the time, the Queen's Ladies have been in the know. If I were a Spanish spy searching for State secrets I wouldn't be haunting Lord Robert and Master Cecil's bureaux but I'd deck myself out as a servant to one of the Maids of Honour and listen to their gossip.'

His excessive mirth was causing heads to turn in their direction. Lord Robert called out, 'Master Chancellor, pray tell us what it is that is amusing you

so much.' He knew that Jack was his retinue's un-
official jester.

Jack, suddenly sobered, and greatly to Oliver's
amusement, replied, his face solemn again, 'Mistress
Penelope has been relating to me one of the Queen's
fool's latest jests.'

'Has she, so? Then, perhaps you could share it with
the rest of us while I await Her Grace's command,
and give you the order to leave.'

Jack looked wildly around. Even he couldn't imagine, on the spur of the moment, anything outrageously
amusing enough to have caused him near apoplexy,
or death by laughter. Fortunately he was saved from
answering by the sight of the Steward coming downstairs to lead Lord Robert to the Queen.

'Later,' said that nobleman on passing Jack. 'You
may tell it to me later, after you return from visiting
Dr Dee. You may all start your mission to him now.'

'Yes, m'lord,' gabbled Jack, relieved. He felt certain that he could invent something on the journey
into central London—or, on the way back—which
would amuse his patron.

'And a good reprieve for friend Jack that was,' remarked Oliver to Penelope, laughing himself. 'I hope
to see you on my return if that is convenient to you.
There is something I have to tell you—although if the
Maids of Honour are privy even to the Royal secrets,
you may probably know my news already.'

Penelope, who was only too eager to see Oliver as
soon as possible, immediately agreed to his request.

She watched him and his fellows stream out to where their horses awaited them, secretly amused to discover that what had been hidden from them all had been commonplace gossip to the Queen's Maids of Honour.

She was already learning that there were few secrets at Court—except those which were the deepest and the most dangerous. She walked on towards the Maids' rooms, only to be stopped at the door by a little man whom she had seen before, but whose name she did not know: a man who seemed grey already, although he was not yet past his first youth.

He bowed to her, detaining her by moving in front of her.

'Mistress Penelope Jermaine, I believe.'

Why did she dislike him on sight? There was so little of him to dislike. She returned as coldly as she could, 'You believe truly, sir,' while trying to pass by him.

'Stay a while, Mistress. I am one of your future brother-in-law's gentlemen. He has asked me to deliver this to you.' He handed her a letter with a very prominent seal. 'I am to wait while you read it, and give me an answer to take back to him.'

Penelope took the offered letter and opened it. The message inside was brief.

'Mistress Penelope, I beg of you to do me the honour of waiting on me in my rooms this evening. I am giving a supper at which your sister will be present. I look forward to receiving you also.

   'I remain your very humble servant,
   'Castleford.'

What to do? She had already promised Oliver that she would meet him that evening, but Castleford out-ranked him and, more than that, was to be her future brother-in-law. To refuse him was to snub him. A way out presented itself. She would ask Janet Saville to give Oliver a note in which she would explain her absence.

Reluctantly, for she did not much like Castleford, she told the little man to inform his master that she would be pleased to accept his invitation.

The little man bowed. She asked him, for she did not wish to appear to snub him, either, 'We have not met before, sir. You know who I am, I would wish you to inform me who you are.'

He bowed. 'I am Bevis Frampton, one of Lord Castleford's gentlemen and happy to do his bidding. I will give him your message. It will please him greatly.'

But it does not please me, thought Penelope sadly. I had much rather have met Oliver. But I must do my duty—as he, doubtless, is doing his.

Oliver, and the party of which he was a member, arrived at Dr Dee's London home: his clerical living was at Leadenham in Lincolnshire. The group's leader was Sir Alaric Saville, Janet's cousin, and it was he who would present Dee with Lord Robert's commission on behalf of the Queen. Two gentlemen, one of whom was Oliver, would accompany him when he interviewed Dee, the rest would remain on guard outside his house, once they had stabled their horses. Jack, who had hoped to be chosen alongside Oliver, had lost the opportunity by his frivolity before their setting out, and had been replaced by Roger Temple.

Oliver was very anxious to meet Dr Dee, as who would not be? Not only was he an astrologer and conjurer of great repute, but he was also experimenting with the Philosopher's Stone: that talisman which would enable those who possessed it to change base metals into gold—and other minor metals into the greater and more precious ones.

Dee turned out to be a tall and imposing figure, fair-haired with a thin clever face. The room in which he met them was a beautiful one, full of strange, mysterious objects, and with a carpet from Turkey on its polished wood floor. He listened carefully to Sir Alaric while he told him of Lord Robert's wish that he choose the most propitious date for the Queen's coronation: a date which would ensure her a long and prosperous reign. Some years earlier, when she had merely been the then Queen's younger and unimportant half-sister, Dee had cast her horoscope.

In that he had foretold a great and powerful future

for her—something which, Oliver thought, was not very difficult, since if her sister died, Elizabeth was almost certain to become Queen herself, however much the Catholics disliked the notion. Now, however, he was being asked to do something much more difficult in forecasting a possibly precarious and changeable future.

Oliver's scepticism was dispelled a little by his being forced to admit that the man himself was most impressive. He possessed a stern eye, a beautiful voice and his replies to Sir Alaric were measured, grave and learned.

'You do me great honour,' he said, slowly, 'and though it will demand all of my powers to carry out Lord Robert's proposal, you may rest assured I shall use them to the full.'

'That is most reassuring, sir, and when your labours have resulted on a suitable date, Lord Robert asks that you will deliver it to her in person. May I now take back to him your agreement to this commission?'

'Indeed, Sir Alaric, I am greatly honoured by it. I trust that you will confer a favour on me by drinking a toast to the success of this enterprise and in praise of the Queen's Grace herself.'

'Willingly, sir—provided that you will include the rest of my retinue in the invitation. They are at present guarding your house.'

Dr Dee laughed, but the laugh was a kind one. 'No need for that, sir, my neighbours respect my reputation—and they also know that I have put a curse on anyone who might seek to harm me and mine. You may invite them all in.'

He called a servant to him to set out the wine and the biscuits to eat with it while Sir Alaric sent Roger Temple to invite the rest of the party to join them before accepting Dee's invitation for him and Oliver to be seated. Dee handed Sir Alaric a small, but beautiful, book to examine. It was, however, surprisingly enough, Oliver to whom he paid the most attention.

'You will forgive me, Master Woodville,' he said, 'if I deduce from your manner that you are a trifle sceptical as to the extent of my powers. I wonder why that is so.'

'Oh, I am sceptical about everything,' Oliver returned, 'and you are no exception to my rule.'

'Hmm,' said Dee, eyeing him thoughtfully. 'What would you say if I told you that I sense danger all around you—and danger to those whom you love? The reason being that you have been exposed to an evil of which you are not yet aware: an evil which seeks to destroy you—something which might not be difficult now that you are employed so near to the seat of power.'

He stopped and repeated, 'What would you say?'

What could Oliver say? He had no wish to antagonise a man who was obviously trusted by his superiors who ruled England. A man who was also reputed to have strange powers and to be able to use them. He chose his words carefully.

'I would say that until there is some evidence that

what you have told me is true, I would suspend judgement of you and your predictions regarding myself.'

Dee began to laugh, and again, the laugh was kindly.

'Shrewdly said, sir, and I see that young though you are, and relatively inexperienced, you have a good mind and are not afraid to use it. You have recently travelled in Italy, have you not?'

Now this was surprising, since Dee could have had no previous knowledge of their visit nor of who would be among the visitors—and yet—and yet, he knew of Oliver's recent Continental tour. And then Oliver began to laugh himself. The explanation for Dee's successful guess—for he was sure that that was what it was—was not difficult, but he would not tell Dee that he knew that it was a guess and how he knew.

'You, Dr Dee,' he replied, 'do possess strange powers—although whether they are truly magical I do not, as I have just said, yet know.'

'You talk in a double fashion,' smiled Dee, 'and now that your fellows are arriving, let me advise you to guard most particularly the young woman whom you love—and that, sir, is all I have to say to an honest man. There are not many of those about, God knows, and so I honour you.'

Oliver did not know whether to honour Dr Dee or not. When they arrived back at the Charter House Sir Alaric took him on one side before reporting to Lord Robert.

'I could not help but overhear what Dee was saying to you and how you answered him. I will not tell you my opinion of him, but when he spoke to you of your having made a recent journey to Italy, you seemed to indicate that you did not believe that he had used magic powers to be aware of that. How so?'

'Oh, it is simple. He could see that I am wearing clothes in the Italian style—that my face is still darkish-brown in hue, although summer is long gone here—and I have a foreign-styled jewel in my ear and on my little finger. It was a good guess. I think, though, that you may hold a different view of him— and I would respect that, too.'

Sir Alaric laughed. 'You are a level-headed fellow, Woodville, and a cautious one. Hold to that and your future at court is assured—but you must beware of jealousy. Furthermore, Dee might not be wrong to suspect that you are in danger.' With that he left.

But not tonight, Oliver told himself. For tonight I shall be seeing Penelope—and where is the danger in that?

Penelope duly wrote a short note for Oliver telling him that she had been compelled to accept an invitation to supper from Castleford and would therefore be unable to meet him as she had promised. She gave it to Janet to hand to him when he came looking for her after he had returned from the visit to Dr Dee. She had not seen Mary that day, but that was not surprising. Their duties were different. The Queen had

dismissed her Maids before Lord Robert's visit—
something which caused a great deal of gossip—and
she did not send for them once he had gone.

Castleford's suite was at the top of the Grand
Staircase. There was a footman before it who had
obviously been given orders to admit her. She entered
to find Bevis Frampton seated at a table just inside
the first room. He leaped to his feet when he saw her.

'Mistress Jermaine, so punctual. My master will be
exceedingly pleased by that.'

'Courtesy demands no less,' returned Penelope
briefly, reflecting that she disliked pointless flattery.
Nevertheless she gave him a weak smile and allowed
him to conduct her through several rooms before they
reached a small one where a table was laid for supper
before a blazing fire. Castleford, splendidly dressed,
was seated in a chair of state some way from it. What
was surprising was that there was no sign of any of
the guests of whom he had spoken, including Mary.

'Ah, Mistress Penelope,' he said, rising. 'You are
truly in looks this evening. Allow me to compliment
you.'

Penelope said nothing to that, merely curtsied before looking around her and remarking, 'Where are
the other guests, m'lord? You mentioned my sister
Mary in your letter.'

'Alas, your sister has a megrim and is unable to
attend. As for the remainder for one reason or another
they have cried off—there is a deal of work to be
done at court these days with the Coronation so near.'

'In that case, m'lord, I think it best to leave. I should not be supping alone with you.'

'Not m'lord,' he said, smiling. 'Castleford will do, and as for the proprieties, I am soon to be your good brother and when have brother and sister ever been forbidden to dine alone, eh?'

'Nevertheless,' said Penelope taking two steps backwards as he took one towards her, 'you are not yet my brother-in-law and what would my sister think if she were to discover that we had been supping tête-á-tête? So I bid you good evening and take my leave.'

He was ready for her when she turned towards the door, slipping agilely to put his bulk between her and it.

'Not so fast, my sweeting. Not only do I wish to sup with you alone, but there is an important matter I must discuss with you, so you may not yet depart. Frampton, you will see that the outer door is locked— we cannot have our guest leaving by it. So, sit you down, my dear, and let us talk before we eat—always a good rule, that.'

'Sweeting' and 'my dear', what was the man thinking of that he should use such words to her? There was a look in his eye which she did not like. She was innocent enough to be unaware that it was cunning mixed with lust—but not so innocent that she was not frightened by it.

And what was it that he wished to say to her without Mary present? And why should she believe that he was not telling her the whole truth about Mary's absence?

'I am sure, m'lord,' she said, trying not to sound desperate, 'that you are honourable enough to allow a lady to leave when she does not wish to remain in a situation which is distasteful to her.'

'Oh, my intentions towards you are strictly honourable, as you will shortly discover. Come, let us eat and drink, for there is no way you may now leave, nor will you wish to when I have explained myself to you.'

Penelope had heard of the evil eye. Was it something like the looks with which both Lord Castleford and Bevis Frampton were favouring her? She truly hoped not, and wondered what it was that he wished to say to her so urgently that he had contrived this elaborate trap for her. She answered him as steadily as she could, trying not to show the fear which was growing in her the longer she was with him.

'I have no wish to eat, drink or talk to you in private, m'lord,' she told him, trying not to sound hysterical, 'so instruct your man here,' and she pointed at Bevis, 'to open the door and allow me to return to my room.'

'You were not listening to me, sweeting,' Castleford said, smiling greasily at her. 'Come,' and he held out a chair for her to sit at the supper table, 'all will soon be made plain.'

What, in the circumstances in which she found herself, could Penelope do but sit, as he bade her, holding her head so that she might not see the smirks which Bevis was casting in her direction.

'I will remain here,' she said, although she quite understood that what she was saying was mere bravado, for she was, in truth, his prisoner, 'long enough for you to tell me why you have played this scurvy trick on me—and no longer.'

'Very well,' he replied, sighing as though she were the one being most unreasonable and not he. 'I have made a grave mistake in asking your sister to marry me. She is not the woman I thought she was. She is frivolous, stupid and disobedient. You, however, are exactly the kind of woman I should most wish to marry. You are serious, learned, quiet and behave yourself at all times with propriety. I have therefore decided that I will find some means to cast your sister off and marry you in her place.'

Penelope jumped to her feet. 'You are quite mistaken, sir. You do not know me. I am opinionated, disobedient, boisterous and given to speaking my mind. You would not like me at all. Besides, I would never marry a man who gained me by betraying the vows he had made to my sister.'

'Now, now, sweeting,' he said tenderly. 'You are not to try to deceive me as to your true character. I have been watching you most carefully, and my mind is quite made up. I shall find some excuse to rid myself of her and then you may be my wife—and to be Lady Castleford is a great thing, as I am sure you understand.'

'I don't understand at all—and that being so, I would ask you again: please allow me to leave.'

His answer to that was to walk round the table, pull her to her feet and clasp her in his arms.

'Do not make me take by force what I would have you freely give me,' he murmured into her neck. 'For if I do take you by force, as I surely shall, if you continue to refuse me, then once I have made you mine you will be compelled to accept my proposal, for otherwise you would most certainly be ruined. Believe me, sweeting, for if you do not accept my splendid offer I will tell the world that you freely lay with me in order to try to take your sister's place— and that I was obliged to punish you, before refusing you.'

Penelope cried, 'No, you would not tell such dreadful lies, you would not dare…'

At which he murmured still gently, although his grip on her grew the more tight, 'Oh, I dare do anything to gain what I wish, and, one way or another I shall have you—either in honour, or dishonour—and the choice is yours.'

Choice! She had no choice, and there was Bevis grinning at them and here was she a prisoner, for there was no way in which she could prevent Castleford from carrying out his wicked will. She could struggle, but she could not escape him.

Penelope gave a great sob and called silently on her God to save her as Castleford's mouth descended on hers…

* * *

'Master Woodville, a word with you.'

Oliver was on his way to his room when he was stopped by Janet Saville, who had just discovered that the company sent to interview Dr Dee had returned. She was holding a letter which she gave to him, saying, 'Mistress Jermaine asked me to hand this to you when next I saw you.'

Oliver eagerly took it, opened it and read it. He was disappointed that he was not about to meet Penelope, something to which he had been looking forward all afternoon, and asked Janet, 'Pray, Mistress Saville, do you know what is in my letter?'

'Oh, yes, Mistress Jermaine told me of it and said how sorry she was to have to postpone meeting you, but she could not ignore a command from Lord Castleford…'

She hesitated a moment before continuing, 'There was something odd about the invitation, Master Woodville, for she told me that it was to a large supper party which her sister, Mary, his betrothed, would also attend, but I have just learned that Mistress Mary Jermaine has spent the whole day confined to her bed with a severe megrim.'

She looked so distressed that Oliver's curiosity was roused. 'You seem worried by the news that her sister will be absent, Mistress Saville,' he said. 'May I ask why?'

'Because, and perhaps I should not be saying this to you, but m'lord Castleford has a bad reputation

where the Maids of Honour and the other ladies about
the court are concerned. We all try to avoid being
alone with him, but since Penelope is his future sister-
in-law no one liked to warn her not to trust him overmuch. Unfortunately, it was only after she had left to
attend the party that I discovered that her sister was
unwell—too late to warn her. Not only that, but there
are no reports of any such large entertainment being
given by Lord Castleford. I would not like to think
that she might be alone with him.'

Oliver took her hand and kissed it. 'I thank you,
Mistress. Tell me, where exactly is Lord Castleford's
suite of rooms?'

'On the first floor, in the annexe to the right of the
Grand Staircase.'

'Thank you. I think that I will pay him a visit.'

'That would be wise.'

It might be that Janet was starting at shadows, but,
all the same, Castleford was not a man who inspired
trust in Oliver, and it would not hurt to try to find out
whether all was well with Penelope. He rapidly made
his way to Castleford's quarters, only to be denied
entrance by the footman guarding the entrance.

'M'lord wishes to be private and will admit no one
this evening.'

'You could, perhaps, inform him that Master Oliver
Woodville wishes to speak to him about some urgent
business.'

'My orders are firm, Master Woodville. Tomorrow,
perhaps.'

And perhaps not, thought Oliver, who was of the opinion that Janet Saville's worst fears might be coming true. What to do next? He walked as swiftly as he could, for there was no time to waste, to his own room, where he found Gib unpacking one of his trunks.

'Well met, master,' Gib said. 'I was looking for a clean shirt for you. The Queen is giving a dinner tomorrow for all Lord Robert's men—I would not have you disgrace me.' And then, on seeing Oliver's expression, as worried as Janet's had been, 'What is it, master?'

'What sort of reputation does Lord Castleford have so far as women are concerned?'

'Bad!' said Gib succinctly. 'Why?'

'No matter. Tell me, if I wanted to enter his rooms by other than the main doorway, is there any other entrance I could use?'

Gib laughed. 'There is a backstairs on every floor which serves a narrow passage behind each room. It is for the servants to use in cleaning and fire-setting so that they do not soil the main stairway.' He read Oliver's expression correctly. 'You did not know that, master?'

'No, for I have never seen any doors which might indicate such an entrance.'

'They're usually hidden—behind a curtain or a painting. There's one here, see.' And he pulled back a tapestry which showed the Gods feasting on

Olympus. Behind it was a plain door which, as he had said, gave on to a dark passage.

'Then take me to the backstairs which serve Castleford's rooms and quick about it,' Oliver ordered him.

'At once, master—but why?'

'I've no time to dally—get along with you, at the double.'

Gib's grimace was a work of art, indicating that he wondered what bees had invaded his master's bonnet—not that he was wearing one at the time, of course. His curiosity was the more intrigued when Oliver said while they raced up the backstairs towards Castleford's rooms, 'You are not to tell anyone of this—you understand me. I shall turn you off if you so much as breathe a word.'

'Understood, master. Now here is the passage that you want.'

'Leave me,' said Oliver, and again, 'Mum's the word—no gossip with the other servants.'

'Understood,' repeated Gib, and went ahead.

Oliver pushed open the door, to find himself first behind a tapestry and then, pushing it on one side, in a splendidly furnished chamber where his first view was of Bevis Frampton, who was laughing—at what? Something in the room which opened off this one, no doubt, from which came the sound of voices, one of them feminine and frightened.

Spurred on by this, he walked forward to find out

what was so entertaining that worm, Bevis, who, on hearing him, turned to see who the intruder was.

Shocked, he exclaimed, 'By Satan, what are you doing here, Woodville? And how did you gain entrance? You must leave at once—m'lord will be greatly angered by your uninvited presence!'

'Now why should that be?' retorted Oliver, and, knocking Bevis on one side with such force that he fell to the ground half-stunned, made for the opening into another grandly furnished room. There he saw a man pushing backwards the woman in his arms, who was trying to free herself. The man was Castleford. He was laughing and saying, 'Come, sweeting, struggle no more—'tis all to no avail.'

The woman was Penelope and she was crying out for help.

'To no avail, say you,' shouted Oliver, 'I'll soon change that tune! Let go of her at once, damn you, or I'll turn you into cat's meat!' Afterwards, he was surprised by his own savagery. He could have killed Castleford on the spot.

Castleford released Penelope the better to face the intruder and, shocked, witlessly exclaimed, 'Where in hell did you spring from, Woodville? You weren't invited! I'm merely entertaining my dear Penelope, who came here of her own free will.'

'No, no,' exclaimed Penelope, running to the refuge which Oliver presented, and hurling herself at him. God, it seemed, had answered her prayers after all. 'He deceived me, Oliver, I thought that I was coming to a supper party.'

Castleford roared at Oliver who, after putting Penelope gently to one side, was now advancing on him with the force of a leaping leopard. 'She lies, damn her, she lies. She was my willing partner in this…'

His last words were cut short when Oliver caught him by the throat. Only the sudden arrival of Bevis Frampton saved him from strangling Castleford on the spot.

Bevis, having recovered from his fall, ran into the room and, catching him around his middle, began to pull Oliver away from his master. Oliver, compelled to release Castleford, who staggered dizzily away from him, now had to deal with Bevis. Not that Bevis took much dealing with. The two men wrestled together for a moment before Oliver, the bigger and more athletic of the two, finished him off by hurling him across the room, where he crashed into the elaborate sideboard, the impact knocking him unconscious.

Castleford, meanwhile, was making for Penelope, for what purpose neither he nor his intended victim could have said. Before he could reach her Oliver was on him again, this time with no Bevis to prevent him from finishing off his prey.

It was Penelope who saved him—and Castleford— by pulling at his right arm before he could injure him too severely, shouting, 'Oliver, don't kill him. Think of the scandal. He isn't worth your death on Tower Hill, and you have saved me from him.'

The blood lust left Oliver as quickly as it had claimed him. He released Castleford, who fell to the floor, moaning and clutching at his much-abused throat. Oliver stared down at him.

'Since Penelope wishes it, and for that matter, my own common sense, I will spare your miserable life— on one condition. That what has happened here remains a secret. She and I will leave and no one will be told anything of what has passed. Before we go I'll try to convince your vicious lackey to hold his tongue.'

Bevis, who was already stirring, shouted from where he lay supine on the floor, 'I'll see you in Hell for this, Woodville!'

'For what?' retorted Oliver. 'For sparing you and your master? Content yourself with thinking up some convincing lies to explain the damage you have both suffered. You, Frampton, will see Mistress Jermaine and myself out with all due form.'

Bevis snarled at him, but did as he was bid. Castleford had sunk into an armchair and was moodily contemplating the collapse of his attempt at seduction. Penelope, her face white, but her gallant spirit still strong, took Oliver's arm, and the reluctant Bevis, unwilling to suffer further injury, escorted them to the door.

Once outside, safely down the staircase, and in a long empty gallery leading towards the Maids' quarters, Penelope finally spoke. She stopped walking, took her hand from Oliver's arm, and turned towards him.

'I have been wrong in not thanking you before, Oliver, for saving me from that vile man. I thank you now for rescuing me so gallantly. You do believe me when I say that I was not aware that Lord Castleford had invited no one but me to his supper party, despite what he wrote in his letter of invitation?'

It was all that Oliver could do not to take her in his arms. Only the thought that he had prevented her from being involved in one scandal stopped him from possibly creating another.

'Of course I believe you. I know you too well to think that you would begin an affair with your sister's future husband.'

Penelope's immediate relief on hearing this gave way to quite another emotion. 'Oh, Oliver, what am I to do? I hate the thought of Mary marrying such a monster as Castleford, but I hardly dare tell her what he was intent on doing. I know that she would think me jealous—or that I was mistaken. He told me that he had changed his mind and did not wish to marry Mary—but would marry me instead. He said that he would find means to call the match off. When I told him that I would never agree to marry him he said that he would ruin me so that I would have no choice, for if I then refused him, he would say that I was his willing mistress.'

'What? He said that?'

Penelope bowed her head.

'Yes.'

It took Oliver all his strength not to turn back immediately and treat Castleford as he deserved. He said through his teeth. 'If I had known that upstairs I would have killed him and risked execution. I am of a mind to risk it now.'

Penelope clutched at his hands. 'No, Oliver. He is not worth it. God will punish him in another way, I am sure. I asked God to save me—and he did, by sending you. How did you know that I was in danger?'

'Janet Saville,' he said, and told her of the chance which had brought him to Castleford's rooms in time to prevent her from being violated.

'She is my good friend—almost my sister,' said Penelope smiling. 'And you are my true knight—even though the Queen has not yet honoured you.'

Oliver took her hand and kissed it, not on the back, but on the palm this time. Penelope had feared, after Castleford's attack on her, that she might not be able to bear a man's touch again, but Oliver's gentle kiss gave her an exciting feeling of pleasure.

'A true knight's reward consists in his being able to serve and save his lady. Are you my lady, Penelope?'

Penelope flushed. She had never thought to hear him say such a thing to her. On the other hand, the very ferocity with which he had attacked Castleford had shown how much he burned to defend her. Did he burn in other ways, too? All the poets spoke of the flames of love. Was that what had made her hand tingle so? The flame of love?

'If you wish,' she said shyly, her head drooping a little.

'Oh, I do wish. Look at me, Penelope, I have something to say to you.'

Alas, he could not say it then. The sound of men talking heralded the approach of Jack Chancellor and Roger Temple.

'Ah, there you are, Woodville,' said Jack cheerily. 'We wondered where you had hidden yourself once the report to our lord and master had been made. And a good day to you, too, Mistress Penelope, I have never seen you rosier. All Woodville's fault, I'll wager.'

It was Oliver who was mumchance, furious at Jack's tactlessness, innocent though it was. Penelope, however, stood her ground, quipping back at him, 'And if it were, what business is it of yours, Master Chancellor?'

'None, I suppose. Well, we'll leave you to it. See you at supper, Woodville, and a good even to you, Mistress Penelope.' And he winked at them.

'That fellow is a fool,' said Oliver furiously, only to find Penelope laughing. 'But a jolly one, do confess,' she gasped. 'He means nothing by it. He would never treat a woman as Castleford tried to treat me, I'll be bound.'

'No doubt, but he has a loose tongue in his head, all the same.'

The true reason for Oliver's anger was that he had been about to say something tender to Penelope, but Jack's intrusion had ruined that happy moment.

'Never mind that, Oliver, now you may take me to the Maids' quarters and we had better behave ourselves on the way there. You know how severe the Queen is about her ladies' conduct.'

'And very right, too,' Oliver proclaimed. 'If only that swine Castleford felt the same way.'

Nevertheless he managed to kiss and fondle her hand again before Penelope disappeared through the door, to be greeted by Janet Saville and to tell her that no, nothing out of the ordinary had happened, and that Oliver Woodville had met her on the way back to her quarters—for that was the story which they had concocted between them which would serve to save everyone's good name—even Castleford's.

Back in Castleford's suite m'lord was cursing Bevis Frampton.

'I thought that you were my watchdog,' he ended. 'I would have done better with one of the lackeys. How, in hell's name, did he manage to enter our rooms?'

'By the backstairs,' wailed Bevis, cringing. 'He was on me before I knew he was there. He had the advantage of surprise.'

'So you say,' snarled Castleford, 'You had better

have that advantage yourself the next time that you deal with him. I want him dead. Do you understand me? Dead after such a fashion that no one will know that I had anything to do with it. And I mean to have the woman, too. More than ever now that she has managed to escape me this time.

'Oh, and one further thing. I think that it would be advisable for you to be discreet, to hide yourself lest anyone think you my creature. Do what work I give you silently, drop discreet poison in other's ears—it is not necessary for scandal to be brayed abroad for it to be successful—until, of course, one deals the enemy a final blow. For more violent errands I shall use other tools than you.'

Bevis wanted Oliver Woodville dead, too, and not only for having been manhandled that day. The tally of hate which he kept in his rabbit warren of a mind was mounting daily—but there was no need to tell Castleford of that. The less others knew about his own ambitions, the better.

Yes, he would be discreet, so discreet that not even Castleford would know of all that he was doing—and if Castleford became too overbearing, too demanding, then… He fell into a delightful reverie in which he danced on the bodies of all his enemies—and some of his so-called friends, too.

Chapter Five

After each night at court the mindless gaiety of the dance was followed on the next day by the serious business of preparing for the removal of the Queen and her household to their next destination, the Tower of London. The bustle which this created meant that there was little time left for anyone to pursue their private interests. As usual Lord Robert's powers of organisation proved equal to the task: the Queen's procession was as splendid and inspiring as anyone could wish when she rode towards a place which held such painful memories for her: a place where for several agonising days she had waited to hear whether or not she was to be executed.

Mercifully for Elizabeth, and for most of her retinue, this, her first visit to the Tower as Queen, was to be a short one. Never mind that Sir Henry Bedingfield, the Lieutenant of the Tower, and his staff gave her an elaborate welcome—even if he had been

her former gaoler—it could not erase her own unhappy memories of the place, nor those of many of
her court. They were all relieved when the time came
to move on again.

Oliver had been kept so busy in his somewhat
cramped quarters that he rarely had time to leave
them, which meant that he had hardly had a chance
to speak to Penelope, but he consoled himself with
the thought that he would soon be seeing her more
often when they reached the splendid and spacious
surroundings of Somerset House and the Strand. Like
everyone else he was happy to leave the Tower and
try to forget the suffering which had occurred there.

By chance he saw Penelope on the evening before
they left. Lord Robert had sent him with a message
for the Queen which he had duly delivered, but on
the way back to his room he met her in one of the
darker corridors not far from the Maids' quarters.

Her face lit up at the sight of him. She had been
wondering where he was billeted and what he was
doing, but she had been unable to look for him because Kat Ashley had kept her so busy. Oliver's pleasure on seeing her was also written on his face.

'Well met,' he said. 'I had thought you banished
to the Scilly Isles and the rest of the Maids with you.'

'How strange—I thought the same of you,' was her
teasing answer. 'Yet here we are. We have had a difficult time of it lately. The Queen is working harder
than ever, so hard that Master Cecil has become quite
testy, for she constantly sends for him when she needs

advice—once in the middle of the night! Not only that, living at the Tower is making her most unhappy and when she is not working we have to try to amuse her in all the different ways we can think of, but nothing seems to answer. She puts on a brave face in public, but in private it is a different matter. Perhaps I should not have told you that.'

'I shan't pass on what you have just said. I'm not surprised that the Queen is unhappy in the place where her mother and her cousin, Lady Jane Grey, were executed and she herself imprisoned. I often think that she likes Lord Robert's company so much because he was her only friend when they were in the Tower together.'

'Well, we are not prisoners here,' Penelope said soberly, 'but I shan't be happy until we are safe in Somerset House. I hear that despite the late Queen's death we are to have some splendid Christmas revels there and at Whitehall, too, so perhaps we shall be able to forget this gloomy place while we are enjoying them.'

'Amen to that—and now we must part and await the day when we may be together again, away from the scene of so many terrible memories. My prayer is that our new Queen will be less bloodthirsty than either her father or her sister.'

'Amen to that, too,' echoed Penelope. 'I suppose that since you are Lord Robert's man you know that we are to travel by river to Somerset House. The Queen has ordered that one of the barges shall be filled with musicians and trumpeters so that all may hear, as well as see, her arrival.'

'Indeed, and Lord Robert has managed to fit that into the order of the procession—if you can call travelling by water a procession. There is also to be a tilting match when we arrive there, which he, of course, is expected to win.'

'And you, will you take part in the match?'

'Alas, no. I am a reasonable rider, but my skills are more suited to the tennis court than the tilt-yard.'

Penelope thought that he might be being overmodest, but she did not say so. Instead she smiled, saying, 'Au revoir, I hope to see you when we reach Somerset House,' and made him a saucy curtsey before she left to complete her own errand.

Oliver was still smiling at the memory of this happy meeting with her when he reached his little room again. He, too, could scarcely wait to reach Somerset House, comfort—and Penelope.

On St Nicholas's Eve the people of London turned out in great numbers to watch Elizabeth arrive by water. She smiled and waved to them, her recent unhappiness forgotten in the sight and sound of their simple joy. The trumpets and music of which Penelope had spoken accompanied her progress, and the sight of her being rowed both up and down river served to show her subjects that she did not wish to retreat behind the walls of her various palaces, but was willing to be seen by everyone—commoners as well as Lords.

On arrival at Somerset House an announcement soon followed that Queen Mary was to be buried with great ceremony and state at St James's Chapel on the 14th of December, but the manner of her burial did not please those who had been her Catholic followers. The new Queen was so studiedly careful in her references to both groups of believers when planning the service that her Protestant subjects were not satisfied with her half-sister's form of burial, either. She was not willing to commit herself, so early in her reign, to either group, even if her sympathies were markedly Protestant.

So far as Feria, the Spanish Ambassador, was concerned, however, this outcome was a happy one—and so he told Lord Castleford, a prominent Catholic sympathiser, when they met privately.

'Not only that but best for us all, too, that she marry—and soon—to a Catholic prince,' was his final judgement. 'My master, King Philip, would make a most suitable husband for her. She would be wise to accept him. After all, she surely cannot mean to wed one of her own subjects—and a Protestant at that— but she is showering so many favours on Lord Robert Dudley as may lead us to believe that that is what she most wishes…' And he shook his handsome head.

'Lord Robert cannot marry her,' replied Castleford. 'He has a wife still living.'

'But dying, they say, of some disease which cannot

be cured. Were she soon to do so…' and Feria paused significantly.

'Such a marriage would not be popular,' Castleford replied, for once speaking the truth.

He did not add that her marriage to a Catholic would be even less popular. The devil of it being, as Feria later said to William Cecil, that everyone agreed that she ought to marry someone. No woman was fit to rule alone. Such a situation was neither right nor proper.

Cecil privately agreed with him. Yes, it might be best for the Queen to marry. No, she ought not to marry Lord Robert, who was far too light a character to have the realm of England handed to him to play with. His stable of secret informers was keeping him posted as to Lord Robert's intentions and his wife's failing health.

He thought that Lord Robert's frivolity was never better in evidence than when he was chasing after that dubious character, Dee—for William Cecil did not believe in Dr Dee's magic powers. It was even proposed that when Dee finally decided on the most propitious date for her Coronation he should personally present his documents to the Queen. This was not, he considered, the fashion in which great powers should be governed.

But if not Lord Robert, then who? Better perhaps if she never married at all—or, at least, not yet. Cecil was as Protestant as Castleford was Catholic, and while he agreed in part with the Spanish Ambassador, he also believed that it would be a gross mistake for her to marry her late sister's husband, King Philip II of Spain—even if the Pope was willing to give him the dispensation which the Papacy had refused in a similar case to Henry VIII, the new Queen's father.

One of the most annoying things about the times in which he was living was that all the petty fools in the country felt that they were entitled to voice their opinion about everything. Even the Queen's Maids of Honour appeared to believe that they had the right to advise their mistress on affairs of state.

He was not far wrong about that. Penelope, Janet Saville and a new Maid, Alys Belsize, were busy discussing the Queen's marriage in the Long Gallery while they waited for her to arrive and start the day's work. Kat Ashley, who was in charge of them—and the Ladies in Waiting—had just come in looking most put out about something. They were later to discover that Her Grace had been with Lord Robert who was telling her of Dr Dee's latest report concerning her Coronation date. All the world knew that Kat despised Lord Robert and thought her mistress's favouring of him most unwise.

Janet, who came from the North, where Catholicism was rife—London and the South being the hotbeds of Protestantism—was voicing her belief that the Queen ought to marry one of the Austrian princes, 'Although,' she ended, 'my father says that Erik of Denmark might be a better choice.'

'Perhaps,' said Penelope, thinking of how she

might feel if she were Queen and surrounded by a lot
of quarrelling men offering her different advice about
which husband to choose, 'the Queen does not wish
to marry anyone, but would prefer to remain single.'

'But every woman must wish to marry,' said Alys.
'We are nothing else.'

'But the Queen is not every woman,' Penelope reminded her. 'Think, at the present moment she is sole
ruler, but if she were to marry she would, inevitably,
be the lesser partner, as her sister was with King
Philip. She might prefer to reign alone rather than
share her power. After all, she is very learned and
knows her own mind.'

'King Philip was making eyes at her when she was
but Princess and he was married to her sister,' offered
Janet.

Kat Ashley, who had come over to them in time to
hear this piece of scandal, said sharply, 'Have you
nothing to do all day, ladies, but gossip? You are
supposed to be embroidering the new kneelers for Her
Grace's private chapel at Whitehall, not sitting here
idle, indulging yourself by talking nonsense about
King Philip's supposed favouring of her.'

'It wasn't nonsense,' muttered Janet, when Kat had
swept on to reprimand another group of Maids for not
doing their duty. 'Everyone knew of it. They were
always laughing and talking together.'

'Best not to say so,' remarked Penelope, but Alys
said, her voice wistful, 'I wouldn't want to reign
alone. I'd prefer to be married.'

Her remark ended the conversation, for during it the Queen entered, followed by Lord Robert and many of his followers, including Jack and Oliver. In their rear, William Cecil and his retinue walked in.

Everyone stood up while the Queen mounted the dais to arrange herself carefully in her Chair of State. Once she was seated, the leading Royal Steward banged his white staff on the ground and announced the arrival of the French, Danish and Spanish Ambassadors, who had come to present letters and despatches to her.

From where the Maids sat in the light of a distant window, Penelope had an excellent view of the Ambassadors and their heralds, all dressed in the utmost splendour as befitted their rank, but she could hear nothing. She had already come to the conclusion that court life consisted of long dull spells interspersed with short periods of great excitement.

Only when the Queen's many royal duties were over and she could take her ease was it possible for the Maids to enjoy themselves with her. Today was not one of those days and the merry dance of the other evening seemed far away. Penelope was beginning to wonder, as she had done before she went to court, whether the honour which Castleford had done her in recommending her to be one of the Queen's Ladies in Waiting was an honour at all. He, though, was apparently content to be one of the many in attendance who rarely spoke or seemed to have any useful function.

Fortunately today's diplomatic meeting seemed to be a short one. Finally, the Queen waved her hand and all the men immediately around her stood back. She rose, and taking Cecil's arm, while gesticulating to the Spanish Ambassador to accompany them, walked to one of the tapestries on the far wall and began to discuss it vigorously. It was the signal for the rest of the company to chatter among themselves.

Oliver, with Jack Chancellor following him, came over to where the Maids still sat, for they could not rise until Kat Ashley gave them leave to do so. Both men bowed to them all. Penelope thought that Oliver looked more handsome than ever in one of his black and silver Italian suits, with a pearl in his ear and a ruff which would have rivalled a swan's feathers, so white it was. Jack looked quite commonplace beside him, although Alys Belsize's expression showed that she was as affected by Jack as Penelope was by Oliver.

'Ladies, I trust I see you well,' said Oliver, smiling at them all. 'Paris himself would have had great difficulty in deciding which of you to give the apple as the most beautiful of those present. He would have needed to carry a basket of them since you are all so worthy of the honour. Alas, I have not one apple with me!'

This fulsome compliment, with its learned reference to the Trojan prince Paris being given the task by the Gods of deciding which was the most beautiful of the three Roman goddesses, Juno, Minerva and Venus, set all the Maids laughing.

Penelope could not resist saying, 'Since, as we all know, Paris's apple is known as the Apple of Discord because it brought about the Trojan War, what catastrophe might be expected to follow from the distribution of a whole basket of them?'

This remark, which set all the maids—and Jack—laughing, did not dent Oliver's self-confidence. 'No catastrophe, Mistress Jermaine,' he said, bowing to her again, 'other than that to our enemies, who will be put to flight by the knowledge that our soldiers and sailors are supported by such a bevy of beauty.'

'Did you learn to talk like that in Italy, Master Woodville?' asked Janet, in the laughter which followed.

'Where else?' riposted Oliver grandly, 'but lovely though they are, the Italian signorinas cannot hold a candle to our Queen's Maids.' And his smile was for Penelope—or so she liked to believe.

Jack, who usually dominated any company he was in by his jests and japes, announced ruefully, 'How in the world do I follow such a gross piece of impudence, Woodville? You have quite set me down. The only fantastical offering which I can think of is scarcely fit for young ladies' ears.'

'Now how do you know that?' one of the Maids called to him, 'unless you tell it to us first and allow us to judge!' Jack's reply to this, to tell them one of Boccaccio's bawdier stories, brought on another great burst of laughter which resulted in Kat Ashley coming over to rebuke them for their bad behaviour.

'Ladies, you are making a great deal of unseemly noise,' she announced, before turning on Oliver and Jack who had obviously been the cause of it, but now it was her turn to be interrupted—and by the Queen's Grace, no less. Her Grace was apparently determined to discover what was causing all the mirth.

'After a morning in which I have endured the cares of State,' she announced, 'it pleases me to hear that my Maids, at least, are enjoying themselves. I wonder if you would care to share the jest with me. Mistress Jermaine, you will oblige.'

Penelope, all eyes on her, including Oliver's wickedly twinkling ones, would have given anything to be alone in her room with a good book. Instead she now had the task of not letting down herself, or the Maids, to say nothing of Oliver and Jack, by provoking the Queen to anger.

Inspiration struck. 'It was a most erudite jest from Master Woodville which provoked us into our somewhat unseemly mirth,' she began. 'Fresh from his travels in Italy he treated us to an elaborate compliment which turned on the legend concerning Paris and the three Goddesses.' And she proceeded to tell the Queen the details of it and the consequent ripostes to it, but carefully left out the last piece of bawdy contributed by Jack.

'A most learned cavalier, I agree,' said the Queen. 'You, sir, are obviously a splendid addition to m'lord

Robert's retinue. I commend you on your scholarship—although,' and she paused for a moment before going on, 'I am not entirely sure, Mistress Jermaine, that you told me the whole of the jest, given the noise and cheers with which the end of it was received by you all. So, I commend you also for your ready wit. Mistress Ashley, you may allow the Maids to rise and join in the general amusement which will precede dinner—they have been good long enough.'

'Oh, wise young Queen,' muttered Oliver in Penelope's ear when Kat, on her mistress's orders, gave her grudging permission to the Maids to enjoy themselves, 'and wise young Maid as well. Of one thing I am sure, that you were wise to censor Jack's jest, but I do believe that Her Grace would have enjoyed it. Now let us leave the others for Jack to entertain so that I may ask you if you are recovered from your late unhappy experience.'

He gave her his arm to hold before walking her over to one of the windows where they might be a little private without worrying Kat Ashley by completely disappearing from sight.

'I was shocked at first,' she told him, 'but I recovered very quickly, for after all, you saved me from the worst, for which I must thank you again. Only, when I saw him,' and she looked towards Castleford who stood at a little distance from them, staring at her, 'I felt a little faint, which is silly, because what can he do to me in a crowded room in the presence of Her Grace?'

Oliver nodded thoughtfully. 'True, but I am not surprised that the sight of him distresses you. I think that you would be wise not to venture out alone and to make sure that you always have a companion with you.'

Penelope looked earnestly at him. 'Would you think me foolish if I told you that I think that you ought to be careful, too? I did not like the way in which both Castleford and Bevis Frampton looked at you after you had rescued me.'

'Oh, I think that I can deal with Master Bevis, but Castleford, now, is another matter. I never liked the man, but I would not have thought that he would play such a scurvy trick on you—that was a real surprise. Yes, I suppose that after my encounter with him I, too, ought to be careful.'

'I wonder if I ought to warn Mary about his trickery and violence towards me,' Penelope said. 'I haven't done so far, because not only do I doubt that she would believe me if I did, but it would also mean revealing to her your part in my salvation—and thus possibly causing a scandal which would damage both of us if she talked of it.'

'I think that you are right to say nothing,' Oliver agreed, and then for a moment stood silent looking thoughtful. When he spoke his manner was grave and careful.

'You know,' he said slowly, 'I have just thought of something which I dismissed too lightly at the time and have not thought of since. When we visited

Dr Dee to ask him to forecast the most propitious day for the Queen to be crowned he tried some of his tricks on me—in fact, he singled me out most particularly. One of them had, I think, a rational explanation.

'But he also told me something else, something which he could not have inferred from anything I had said or done in his presence. He warned me that he saw danger all around me, and not only danger for me personally, but also to those whom I love because I had been exposed to an evil of which, he presumed, I might not be aware.

'I'm afraid that I laughed at him because I thought it likely that virtually everyone who frequents any court may be said to be in danger—according to which way the wind of state blows—and then I returned to find you in trouble, someone whom I have come to care for. I think that the commotion which followed drove Dee's words from my mind.'

'A lucky guess?' ventured Penelope.

'Who knows? But were I, by chance, to meet him when he brings his conclusions to the Queen and he should choose to warn me again, then I should be sure to take note of it. I can only hope and pray that my feelings for you have not, and will not, put you in danger from my unknown enemy.'

His feelings for her! And what were they? She knew quite well what her feelings for him were. In the beginning she had loved him with the love of a child who delighted to talk to him because he did not patronise her. Then, when they met again after his return from the Continent, her feelings for the handsome and gifted creature he had become had grown and blossomed until they had been transformed into an over-riding passion. The love of the mind and the love of the body had come together to create it. As a result merely to see him was to desire him, to touch him transformed her whole body. Every part of it was affected by him, including those parts which were not normally the subject of conversation! Were his feelings for her as powerful and as similar?

The eyes he turned on her were glowing. Perhaps that meant he did have feelings for her. Were her eyes glowing? The rest of her certainly was. When he told her that Dr Dee had warned him that those whom he loved might be in danger, was he also telling her obliquely that she was one of those whom he loved? If so, then her answer to him must demonstrate that she understood what he was telling her.

Penelope licked her lips. 'It is not your fault that I might be in danger—because of our feelings for one another,' she breathed. 'It is that of the unknown who threatens you—who may, or may not, be Castleford.'

'Or anyone else who thinks that I have done him a wrong. I cannot guess who that might be, for we are seldom aware of having wronged anyone—although we always know quite well who has wronged us!'

'How true that is! I had never thought of that before. It should make us careful of how we speak to others.'

'But not too careful, or we might never speak at all.'

Penelope began to laugh. 'Oh, I do love talking to you, Oliver,' she said impulsively, her own eyes glowing at him. 'Do you remember the old days when we sat by the brook in the sun and discussed everything from Socrates to Machiavelli?'

'Yes, but this morning I prefer to enjoy the new days.'

'So that you may remember them later?'

Oliver smiled at her. Did she know how much she had changed, and was still changing? Removed from Mary's influence she was flowering in the most delightful way. Those who said that blonde was always beautiful and that brown was always plain had not known Penelope. In some ways, she was better than beautiful. The humour in her face, the light in her eyes, the delicate twist of her lips when she spoke, the slender graceful body with its tiny delicate breasts...

To his astonishment Oliver found himself rapidly growing hard and he thanked the gods that the padded breeches he wore were cut in such a fashion that no one but himself could know of his uncomfortable, if pleasurable, condition.

Merely to look at Penelope is to desire her. Does she feel the same for me? If not, could she come to feel it?—and ought I to wish that she might, if in some way by being close to me she would find herself in danger from what Dee has called my unknown enemy?

On the other hand everyone, however powerful, has enemies, and the more powerful the greater the number of enemies, as Lord Robert is finding, and since I am growing powerful because he favours me, so I too must be accumulating enemies.

The thought was an unpleasant one and, for a moment, Oliver wished himself back in the safety of his relatively humble Leicestershire home—but only for a moment, since life at court was beginning to attract him more and more. The very danger in the air was enticing—so much so that it was almost like the ecstatic experience of love-making in its nature. He remembered an Italian friend at the court of Milan telling him that, and he had not believed him, but now he knew that he had been right.

Oliver shook his head. After being so wordy, he had now become unnaturally silent, which he feared might worry Penelope; but one of her many delights was that she did not feel it necessary to talk all the time—even though she loved talking. Yes, merely to be with her was enough—words might bring delight, but they could also spoil an intimate moment.

In any case, the Stewards were walking in, which told him that they would soon be called to dinner, so he must hope that the passion for her which held him in its thrall would not make walking too uncomfortable. Side by side, Penelope's hand on his arm, they processed into the dining room to sit at a little distance apart—something which allowed his unruly body to behave itself at last.

There he was assailed by two more problems, the first of which was that the old saw which said that those in love lost their appetite was coming true for him—and did he share that with Penelope, too? The second problem was an even trickier one: he had, most unfortunately, been placed next to m'lord Castleford, who glared daggers at him when the assembled company sat down after the obligatory prayer.

His missing appetite was not helped when, after they had been served with a meat broth, Castleford muttered at him, 'I would have a word with you when the meal is over, Woodville—and do not try to avoid me. It would not be wise.'

Now what further could Castleford have to say to him which would justify such a fiery look of hate? He looked around the room to discover that Bevis Frampton was not present but that Mary Jermaine was. She was seated among the Queen's Ladies in Waiting, far from Penelope or her future husband, something which, by her expression, did not best please her.

As dish followed dish, and all of them excellent, Oliver's mind was so occupied by what was happening both in front of, and behind, the scenes at court, that he could barely give his mind to it—let alone appreciate the salt beef, the mutton and the boiled

fowls which appeared before him. He had also become accustomed to using a fork in Italy and found
eating without one a messy business.

He was quite relieved when the last cold tarts and
syllabub had been disposed of, even though it meant
that he would have to listen to whatever Castleford
had to say to him. Even the sack and the hippocras
he had drunk could not reconcile him to that prospect.
Nor did it appear to cheer Castleford up, either, for
when the order was given for them to rise, he seized
Oliver by the elbow and dragged him into one of the
window embrasures.

'I would have you know, Woodville,' he began,
without ceremony, 'that I must advise you not to have
overmuch to do with either of the Jermaine sisters.
They are quite beyond your touch and you would be
wise to obey me in this matter—lest worse befall.
You may also count yourself fortunate that I did not
complain to your master, Lord Robert, of the manner
in which you behaved to me the other evening.'

'I am not one of your retainers, and shall therefore
speak to whom I please,' replied Oliver, controlling
himself with difficulty, 'and as for the other evening,
you are perhaps fortunate that I did not report *your*
unseemly conduct towards Mistress Penelope
Jermaine to the Queen's Grace. She is, after all, one
of her Maids of Honour, whose position ought to protect her from such insults as you were putting upon
her.'

Castleford's face turned purple. He was not accustomed to be contradicted by those whom he considered to be below him in station. Before he could say anything further, Oliver compounded his offence by bowing to him before showing him his back.

The insolence of the young swine! What were things coming to these days when a commoner like Woodville could speak in such a fashion to a peer of the realm! Only the knowledge that he would be the one in the wrong if he caused a scene in the presence of the Queen's Grace prevented him from following Woodville and assaulting him.

Oliver was looking for Penelope, and she, he soon discovered, was searching for him. Mary had come up to her once dinner was over and had issued her an ultimatum as well, after first berating her for being the cause of Castleford's changed behaviour to her.

'You are no sister of mine,' she said furiously, 'if, as I suspect, you are trying to turn Castleford against me. You are all that he ever talks about these days. I will not have it—and spare me wounded innocence. You have quite changed since you came to court—and not for the better.'

Mary's fury at Penelope was partly because although she no longer wished to become Castleford's wife, it would be one thing for her to find another suitor, but quite another if Castleford were to cast her off before she could cast him off!

Penelope stared at her, dumbstruck. Far from wishing to seduce Castleford away from Mary, she would be happy never to see or speak to the man again. That for some reason he had developed a passion for her was a mystery beyond her solving. Mary obviously knew nothing of his failed attempt to seduce *her*— nor, in view of her promise to Oliver, could she tell her of it, even to convince her sister of her own honesty.

'Do not trouble yourself,' she said gently. 'I do not even like him—and I never have done. I don't understand why our parents want you to marry him, unless they want an Earl in the family and wish to boast of their daughter, the Countess.'

'So you say—but I don't believe you. Just keep away from him.'

'With pleasure,' was all that Penelope could say to that, before, like Oliver, she took leave of her tormentor.

She was so distracted that when she finally reached him, he asked her, his voice tender, 'Is something wrong?'

'No,' she exclaimed, but whatever else he was Oliver was her friend and deserved more of an answer than that, so she said, 'I must not deceive you. It's Mary. She has accused me of trying to take Castleford away from her, and you of all people know what a sorry jest that accusation is.'

'Indeed, and I, too, have been given my orders by Castleford, as you have by your sister. He has just told me to have nothing to do with you—or Mary— lest worse befall. Have you any notion of what game they can be playing?'

'None, but whatever it is, I do not like it.'

What she did not add was, I do not like very much of what is happening at court. Everyone seems to speak with a double tongue. Does Lord Robert really love the Queen? Does she love him? Lord Robert, Master Cecil and the other great gentlemen and nobles dance around one another smiling, as though they are taking part in a continuous Galliard, but what they are thinking is often quite different from what they are saying.

Penelope could understand why the Queen had to be so careful with everyone. Now and again, when she was alone with her Maids, she often made remarks which showed how tiring it was to be the Queen's Grace—something which many might envy—when she knew that each word she said would be dissected and discussed by most of her hearers later. Words which might also be used against her.

'I think,' said Oliver gently, for he could see that Penelope was greatly troubled, 'that this proves that what I told you earlier was true. It really does behove both of us to go carefully in future. Dee spoke of possible unknown enemies, and we, alas, are now fully aware that we have at least a known one in m'lord Castleford.'

Penelope's answer was all that he expected of her. 'I am beginning to think that everyone connected with the court should go carefully—and that includes Lord Robert and Master Cecil, too, for who knows what the morrow might bring should Her Grace choose to marry a Catholic.'

They were silent after that. Both of them had friends and relatives who had lost their lives in the years since the late King Henry had broken with Rome. It was not only his Queens who had been sacrificed to his lust for power and a male heir, for even the most humble had walked in fear—and rightly.

Oliver, to bring a sparkle to her eyes again, decided to pass on to her some advice which a friend had offered him in Italy after Harry Grantly's sudden death had brought him low.

'We cannot change the past,' he told her, 'nor foresee the future, so we had best obey the old Latin motto, *Carpe diem*, or Seize the Day. In other words, we must enjoy what the present brings us for that is all we ever have. Today we dined in splendour, we have the monarch of our choice to rule over us, we enjoy youth and health, and you, my love, are beautiful. What more can we ask? To repine over the past is as bad as to fear the future. And that,' he added, with a smile, 'is my sermon for today concluded.'

'The Lord God knows why you should be handing out sermons,' remarked Jack, who had joined them in time to hear Oliver's last words. 'I get enough of them on Sundays and can do without them for the rest of the week. The news is that when Her Grace gives the word we are shortly to be entertained by a group of tumblers who do their tricks in time to music. Now that will be worth seeing. It is said that they are

Italians—saw you aught like it on your travels, Woodville?'

'Once, in Milan. They have many such acrobats there, as well as dancers and mimes of a skill I have never seen here.'

'Ah, but do they have the mummers and their plays that we do?' queried Jack.

'Yes, and masques and grand processions through the streets where men and women dance and sheep and oxen are roasted.'

'They say the weather is better there, too,' remarked Jack wistfully, 'but I wager that the women are no prettier,' and he waved a hand at Mary Jermaine, who was passing them in earnest conversation with Roger Temple—so earnest, indeed, that they had no eyes for anyone but each another and therefore ignored Jack's salutation.

So much for Mary's devotion to Castleford—if she ever possessed any—was Oliver's sardonic conclusion, and that being so, why should she badger Penelope about the man? Penelope was thinking the same thing. The Master of Ceremonies, however, now stopped all thinking by banging his staff on the ground and announcing the arrival of the tumblers, whose performance proved to be as spectacular as Jack had hoped.

In the applause and excitement which followed their act Penelope became separated from Oliver and, to her dismay, found that Castleford was bearing down on her, his face grim.

'Ah, Mistress Penelope, a word with you.'

'I had much rather not—even if it were to be only one word you offered me,' replied Penelope, trying to dodge around him.

'You would be wise to listen to me. I have an important message for you.'

There was no evading him without making a scene. As it was, curious eyes were staring at them.

'Very well, then, if you must. But I would prefer it to be one word only,' she told him hardily.

He took no notice of that.

'It concerns Master Woodville. If you are wise you will cease to encourage him in his pursuit of you, or speak to him more than the demands of your office under the Queen require. Otherwise…' He paused significantly.

'You have offered me more than the one word I asked of you,' replied Penelope, feeling less brave than she sounded, 'and the last one I heard I like the least of all. Otherwise…what?'

'Otherwise things might not go well with him— indeed, they might go so badly that *he* might not go at all or go in the worst sense of the word. It would be a pity to see such a fine young man cut down in his prime—and all because a young woman could not behave with common sense.'

Penelope knew exactly what he meant. He was threatening to have Oliver secretly killed if she continued to associate with him in any way. This was to be Castleford's revenge on him for rescuing her—that he would separate them. After that, he would renew his pursuit of her.

'I would also require you to be kind to me—which would calm my fears that you might be being kind to him.'

'And Mary? What part does my sister play in this plot which you are so busily hatching?'

'That is neither here nor there. She has never considered you—so why should you consider her?'

'Simply this. She is my sister, as Oliver Woodville is my good friend.'

He grinned foully at her after she said that. It was quite unlike the warm smile which Oliver had offered her. Penelope began to shiver—and tried not to let him be aware that he was frightening her with his threats.

'Your good friend, is he? Make him your bad friend and I might spare him—if that is how the fancy takes me—and mark me, do not try to warn him or speak to anyone of what I have just said. I would deny every word—and who would believe such as you before me?'

Penelope stared at him and tried to show him a bold front. She feared that he was speaking the truth when he threatened Oliver—but what would Oliver think of her if she suddenly dropped with him the friendly and loving manner which she had shown him since they had met again at Charter House?

He would think her light—or that she had found a new love—and what would that do to her—or to him?

'Do you truly mean what you say?' she managed at last.

'I always mean what I say,' he told her, grinning his foul grin again.

It was hopeless. Penelope felt as though something was dying inside her. On the other hand, how could Castleford possibly know if she did decide to tell Oliver of the threats which he had made to her? Could she risk his life knowing that if Oliver were to act so that Castleford was aware that she had warned him, it might result in the Earl doing his worst immediately?

The mere fact of being near the wicked wretch was making her feel dizzy. She must get away from him and try to find a quiet place where she might be able to think in peace and decide what to do for the best. What she dared not do was confide in anyone.

Above all, she must not show Castleford how much he had frightened her, for that would give him even more power over her. She must show him nothing, neither fear not defiance, simply bow and leave him, her face betraying none of her true feelings—nor of false ones, either. Just a simple passivity would be best. To add to her worries, if Dr Dee were right, Oliver was in great danger not only from Castleford, but also from someone unknown.

Besides that, there was Mary to consider, for she not betrothed to this monster who was pursuing her and threatening to murder Oliver, her one-time sweetheart?

So Penelope said nothing more, but bowed calmly and coolly as though bidding him a pleasant farewell, and walked away knowing that his eyes were boring into her back. She took care to follow a path which meant that she could return to the Maids' room without meeting Oliver.

For what could she say to him after what had just passed?

Chapter Six

Lord Robert was waiting on the Queen one morning, being required to attend yet another meeting of her Privy Council. Oliver and the rest of Lord Robert's Gentlemen were waiting for his chief secretary to arrive to inform them of their duties. They were passing the time by exchanging the latest gossip which was running around the court. Although some of it was serious, concerned with exactly what policies Elizabeth would set in train once the business of the Coronation was over, other lighter rumours were much discussed.

'I wonder,' said Oliver thoughtfully, 'exactly how many in Somerset House *are* hoping for a long and prosperous reign for the Queen.'

'I can tell you one who is not,' responded Sir Alaric Saville, 'and that's Castleford. Queen Mary's death was a grave blow for him, he's always been a major Catholic supporter. He's also desperately in need of a steady income and was expecting her to offer him some public appointment which he won't get from the present Queen. He's walking around with a gallows face on even if he has captured a pretty heiress for himself.'

'Oh, aye,' said Jack, 'and the word is that lately she's none too happy about marrying him—as who should know better than you, Temple—which perhaps explains Castleford's unhappy manner lately.' And he dug his friend familiarly in the ribs.

So, thought Oliver, it was true that Mary was favouring Temple these days—possibly because now that she was aware of her betrothed's preference for her sister she was more than willing to encourage another gallant. Certainly, he thought, she must think that young Temple might seem a better prospect for her than the morose wretch to whom she was betrothed, since he was not only rich, but also young and handsome and his father was the heir to an Earldom. Even her parents might be willing to accept him as a son-in-law rather than Castleford.

'One thing's certain,' said Jack, 'we none of us know where we really stand with the Queen—not even Lord Robert. Her Grace is having to go carefully and nothing is yet certain, other than that she's the old King's daughter and favours him in looks, aye, and in manner, too, occasionally.'

They were all agreeing about that when the Secretary came in and informed them that Lord Robert would not be requiring the services of any of his gentlemen that morning, but that he wished Master Oliver Woodville to attend on him in the afternoon. Tomorrow,' he ended, 'Lord Robert will require you all to be present in order to discuss the nature of the entertainments required over Christmas.'

So that was Oliver's day arranged—or rather his afternoon—which left his morning free of duties. He decided that he would try to find Penelope. He had become used to meeting her daily, but for some reason he had not seen her lately—possibly because both of them had been busy helping to organise the coming Coronation.

He had discovered where the Maids were housed and where they spent the day when they were not on duty with the Queen, so he walked in that direction, up the main staircase and along a gallery overlooking the Thames which led to a room from whence came the sound of someone playing the virginals. He entered it to find some of the Maids seated on cushions on the floor and the others on a bench which ran along the wall facing the windows. All of them were engaged in various forms of needlework. The Queen was not present.

The player entertaining them was Penelope: her embroidery frame was propped against one of the instrument's legs. She was singing a plaintive song. When she reached the end of it she let her hands fall on the keys and bowed her head for a moment.

Oliver walked towards her clapping his hands in applause and crying, 'Bravo!'

She swung round on her stool in order to face him and exclaimed, 'You!'

Oliver was surprised to find that her manner was such that it did not appear that she was particularly pleased to see him. Indeed, he would have sworn that the expression on her face and the tone of her voice betrayed something like dismay at his presence.

Penelope, regretting her shock at seeing Oliver so unexpectedly when she was still not sure what she ought to say to him about Castleford's threats, rose slowly from her seat and held out both hands to him in a belated welcome.

'Come, Oliver,' she said, 'Let us retire to the gallery away from the others. I have much to say to you.'

'And I to you. Am I right to suppose that you have been avoiding me for the last few days?'

There was nothing for it, but to tell him the truth.

'Yes,' she said simply, and then, 'I had good reason, Oliver.'

The resentment which he had felt when she had spoken to him so cursorily, as though he were a stranger and not Oliver whom she had come to love, and who already loved her, faded a little, even though she had confessed that she had been refusing to see him.

He followed her into the gallery where they sat, side by side, on a bench opposite a painting of the late King Edward VI. For a moment they both remained silent and constrained. Penelope, who knew exactly why she had been avoiding Oliver, was in some odd way the least troubled of the pair of them.

'Why?' Oliver asked abruptly. 'Tell me why have you been avoiding me. And for what reason.'

Now that they were together again Penelope lost all her doubts about the best course of action to take. 'Because the other night, after you and I had been speaking when dinner was over, Lord Castleford took me on one side and told me that unless I agreed to have nothing more to do with you he would arrange for you to be killed.'

'As bluntly as that?'

Penelope nodded, her eyes filling with tears. Ever since she had left Castleford on that horrid day she had tried not to cry, but seeing Oliver's beloved face again was too much for her.

'Yes,' she whispered, trying to blink her tears away. 'He left me in no doubt about his fell intent.'

All the natural desire which he felt to protect and care for a woman, and particularly a woman whom he loved, overcame Oliver, to the degree that he wanted to leave her immediately in order to seek Castleford out and punish him. That it was he whom Castleford had threatened counted as nothing against the distress which the vile wretch must have caused Penelope.

She saw his face change again and read it correctly. She said, the words tumbling out of her mouth, 'I kept away from you to give me time to make up my mind whether or not to tell you. It was difficult for me to decide what to do. It was a great temptation to me to avoid you forever, so that you would remain safe— and then it occurred to me that a man who could twice behave as he did towards me would not necessarily keep his word even if I did.'

Oliver's response was as simple as her original 'Yes' had been. 'I shall seek him out and kill him— for treating you so. He will never threaten anyone again.'

'No!' Penelope jumped to her feet and faced him. 'That was what I feared you might do—and why I have been avoiding you. You must not. The laws against fighting and killing in the royal precincts and around royal persons are condign. I would not have you executed on Tower Hill. Rather would I leave court and retire into private life, so that he can have no reason to harm you.'

Oliver rose and took her hands in his. 'I would do anything to him, anything, since he has chosen you as his innocent target, but you are right. It would be foolish of me to lose my life as a result of taking his. But where does that leave us? I cannot give you up, whatever the risk to me. The best thing would be for us to report his threats either to the Queen or to Lord Robert.'

Penelope shook her head. 'Who would believe us? He is greater than we are—as he told me at the time. It is my word against his.'

'His power came from being one of the late

Queen's advisers, but the new Queen will not favour him because he is so deeply Catholic.'

'Even so, he is a magnate, a member of the House of Lords, and we are nothing compared with him.'

Oliver knew that she was right, but it galled him to think of their impotence and that their lives depended on the whims of such as Castleford. He thought for a moment before answering her.

'We could pretend that we have quarrelled and parted, but try to meet in secret.'

'Which still leaves you at risk. Oh, I cannot do that, Oliver, I love you so.'

There, she had said it and if his face filled with joy, she knew that it left them in worse case than ever—compelled to deny publicly what they truly felt for one another.

'We have already been alone too long and gossip will surely follow,' she told him urgently, before he could say or do anything which might betray their deep feelings for one another to anyone who entered the gallery. 'Gossip which, when it reaches him, will inflame him even more.'

'No,' he said desperately, clutching at her hands to try to prevent her from leaving him, 'I cannot give you up, not now that we have found one another. We must try to meet in secret and while we are apart I must think what I ought to do to scotch this snake, even if I cannot kill it.'

He had never felt so helpless, so alone, not since Harry had died so cruelly in Italy. There friendship had been killed, and now love was like to be destroyed. He wanted to rail against God, or the Gods, since for the moment he did not know who or what he worshipped, except that they had let him down by allowing this.

In his pain it was the loss of Penelope which troubled him more than the threat to his life. Now he must drop his hands and let her go, but despite Castleford's threats he would not surrender her completely—he would, he must, find a way out of this dilemma.

So thinking, he watched her walk away from him, her head held high.

Bevis Frampton, who had been following Oliver around for some days, watched him leave the Maids' room and decided to visit it himself. He usually avoided the company of women, fearing that his lack of the obvious charms which fortunate creatures like Oliver Woodville and the late Harry Grantly possessed would lead to them ignoring him and passing him over. He had some small fortune and a few acres in Derbyshire, but they were not enough to enable him to marry an heiress—their parents wanted someone higher in the world than he was.

Nevertheless, ever since Alys Belsize had come to court he had found himself very attracted to her because she was so small and sweet, quite unlike the other young women, who were all bold-faced and given to staring at him unkindly. He had taken to following her around and speaking to her whenever he could.

Perhaps if he spoke kindly to her she would look favourably on him, might even agree to marry him if he ever dared to propose to her. This thought excited him so much that he forgot all about Oliver Woodville and his intended revenge on him and instead walked determinedly towards the Maids' room to try to further his acquaintance with her—if she were there, that was.

He was just about to enter it when he heard his name mentioned by that nasty trollop Janet Saville. He did not catch what she was saying about him but he heard every word the Maid who answered her said and each of those words cut him to the quick.

It was Alys Belsize speaking.

'Bevis Frampton my admirer,' she was exclaiming. 'The Lord God forbid. I do not like the way he looks at me. Don't tell me that it is admiration he is feeling for me. I do not want it, or him. You are not to tease me so. I'm sure I never have, and never will, offer him a word of encouragement.'

Bevis's love for her dropped dead and was succeeded instead by a feeling of intense hatred, made even worse by Janet going on to tease Alys by saying that if she were accused of being admired by Jack Chancellor she would sing quite a different song. He did not wait for Alys's answer but walked away as briskly as he could, painfully aware that the old saying that listeners never heard any good of themselves had come true in the worst possible way.

Never mind, he vowed that Mistress Belsize would pay for this cursory dismissal of him one day soon; and he added her name to the list of those whom he intended to punish. In the meantime he would keep careful watch on her in order to be ready for that happy day.

It was some time before Oliver arrived back at the quarters which he shared with Jack and Roger Temple. Jack was not there but Roger, already dressed to meet the Queen later, was busy writing a letter.

'There you are, Woodville. Lord Robert was asking for you a little while ago. Where the devil have you been?'

'I needed exercise. I have been walking in the gardens.'

This was no lie. He had been striding furiously about for the last hour pondering on what Penelope had told him. Finally he had decided that the best thing to do for the time being was to behave as though nothing had happened—which was going to be difficult.

Roger, accepting his explanation, said no more, while Oliver readied himself to report to Lord Robert. He found his master, splendidly dressed as usual, as though he were about to attend the finest reception which the court had to offer. Oliver sometimes wondered if he ever appeared dishevelled or troubled but decided that he didn't. He thought that Lord Robert had learned, in the dangerous days when he never knew whether or not he was to be executed on the morrow, that in order to live his life without giving way to despair he must never present a worried face or person to the world.

It was a lesson that he was going to have to learn himself.

Like Roger Temple Lord Robert was engaged in writing. He gestured with his quill at Oliver, silently bidding him to sit while he finished whatever task he was engaged in.

Once it was over he fixed Oliver with a stern eye before saying, 'Master Woodville, Sir Alaric told me that on the occasion of your visit to Dr Dee he took the trouble to speak to you personally about several things while ignoring the other members of our mission. Before he arrives I would be grateful if you would tell me of what he said—and how accurate his revelations were. It's not that I don't believe in him, but I would like to have some evidence of his powers before I take him in to see the Queen.'

Oliver found himself in something of a quandary. He could not tell Lord Robert the whole truth for that would mean admitting, that as Dr Dee had suggested, he had an enemy whom he might, or might not, know. Since he was now one of Lord Robert's trusted men his master would undoubtedly wish to know who that enemy could be. Alas, he could not tell him of Lord

Castleford's threat since he had no evidence to support this accusation, other than his, or Penelope's word, which might not be enough.

On the other hand he could tell him some of the truth—and no lies.

'Dr Dee told me that he knew that I had recently been to Italy—something which he could not easily have found out before I was one of the party which visited him. On the other hand I believe that he took the risk of guessing that because of my unseasonably brown face and my Italianate clothing. He next told me that I was in danger from an unknown enemy of whom I should be wary, for he intended to harm me if he could. That, of course was a statement which I could neither confirm nor deny. Perhaps,' and Oliver offered this as a guess as to why Dee should make such a claim, 'he believes that everyone connected with a court has a secret enemy—courts, as I found in France and Italy, being likely places for them.'

Lord Robert's laugh was a genuine one. 'You are shrewd, Master Woodville, as is Dr Dee. You could not hazard a guess yourself as to who your unknown enemy might be?'

Fortunately for Oliver he was able again to offer a partly truthful answer to this question. 'No, I have no notion of his identity, particularly since I have only been at court such a short time and from what Dr Dee said, it seems that he might have been plotting against me before I had arrived here.'

Lord Robert considered for a moment before giving a guarded reply.

'What you have told me proves nothing either way. Dee, however, has a great reputation as a necromancer and an astrologer. He is also, I understand, beginning work in an attempt to discover the Philosopher's Stone. Given his known reputation I feel that we must trust him—and that you, in particular, should take heed of his advice and go carefully. I do suggest, however, that when he arrives you engage him in conversation again and try to discover whether he can give you any hint as to who your secret enemy might be.

'Before I give you leave to go I must commend you on your facility in both reading and writing French and Italian. Do you have a similar command of Spanish?'

'I have not quite the same facility but I speak and write it well enough.'

'Excellent. You could, for my convenience—and I need not enlarge on this, I hope—give it out that your Spanish is non-existent. If this makes Feria and his staff careless when speaking their language in your presence—why, that would be all to the good, would it not?'

Oliver understood what his master was asking him to do. He bowed. 'Yes, m'lord, I quite understand you.'

He tried not to smile ruefully. It seemed that everyone around the Queen was determined to make him some sort of spy. First Cecil, and now Lord Robert, had put him in the business of being their ears and listening for treasonable talk engaged in when those using it thought that they were safe.

More than ever it behoved him to tread warily in the secret battlefield which surrounded his Queen.

If Penelope now had her own secrets to guard, she was also aware that those around her had theirs. After she had returned to the Maids' room she picked up her embroidery frame and began to work on it again. While she had been absent Alys Belsize had left by the other door and some of the Maids were giggling about her departure.

She had always avoided listening to gossip before, but now that she had been made harshly aware of the hidden life which went on in the court she decided that knowledge was power. The more she knew of what was going on, the better.

She leaned across to Janet Saville and said confidentially, 'Pray what is the joke that you should all laugh at Alys's leaving us?'

Janet, eyes dancing asked her, 'Do you really not know?'

Penelope shook her head.

'Then I shall not tell you. It will be a pretty task for you—to find out the truth without our help. All I can say is that you had best use your eyes and your ears.'

That, of course, offered no real assistance to her at all, Penelope thought aggrievedly.

'I believed you to be my friend.'

'Which is why I am setting you this puzzle. Solving a mystery will bring excitement into your life.'

Bring excitement into my life! Lord Castleford will make sure that I shall have plenty of that.

Aloud she saïd, 'I don't like mysteries.'

'Sometimes,' Janet replied, 'they are necessary.'

Penelope shrugged her shoulders and started to embroider as though her life depended on it—perhaps it did, although it was Oliver's life which had been threatened, not hers. Besides, it was none of her business what Alys was doing—unless it involved her own safety.

The general gossip was now about Dr Dee's visit and how that might affect the date of the Coronation. Penelope wondered whether Oliver would be meeting him again? And would Dee offer him any further information about his secret enemy if he did?

In the little world of the court, as in the greater world outside it, gaiety and pleasure went hand in hand with the more serious business of life. Oliver, in common with his fellows, worked hard in the day carrying out Lord Robert's orders, but by evening he joined in the revelry which grew increasingly hectic as Christmas neared. In order not to provoke Castleford he tried not to show an undue interest in Penelope, while she treated him as though he were merely one of the many gentlemen who paid mild court to her. Their problem was that life at court was lived in public and privacy was virtually non-existent.

Some, though, managed to achieve it, as Penelope was soon to discover. Janet's puzzle regarding Alys's occasional disappearances did not trouble her over-much, but nevertheless it pricked her interest because the other Maids' sniggers had betrayed that they knew what she was up to. She tried to dismiss it from her mind until one day she was sent by Kat Ashley to the quarters in which the sempstresses were busy making new clothes for the Maids in order to find out how soon it would be before they could be tried on.

In the warren of rooms and passages which made up Somerset House, most of which she had not visited before, Penelope became lost. More and more her journey was beginning to resemble the untangling of one of the mazes that were a feature of the gardens of all the palaces in which she had lived since becoming one of the Queen's Maids. Desperate to find someone who might help her, she opened a small door adjacent to the backstairs. The passage behind it simply led on to yet another door which was the entrance to an unfurnished room, little bigger than a closet, whose one window looked out on to a small court-yard.

At its far end was yet another door. She walked through it to discover that it led on to a very large room which was full of a mass of discarded furniture, including a battered oak sideboard and a rickety four-poster bed, minus its curtains, which occupied one corner.

It was not, however, the furniture which interested Penelope—if interest was the right word—but the two people on the bed and what they were engaged in. Their outer clothing scattered round the floor, Alys Belsize and Jack Chancellor were busy making violent, and noisy, love on it. So occupied were they, that they did not hear her enter—nor did they hear her retreat, her cheeks flaming.

Penelope had never before come across lovers enjoying themselves, but she was in no doubt of what she had seen. She now knew the reason for the knowing sniggers of the other Maids. One thing more she also knew, and that was that the passion which moved the pair on the bed was so strong that they were willing to risk everything in order to satisfy it. They must have felt safe to indulge themselves, here in a storeroom far away from the apartments where the powerful lived and worked.

She hurried away, her face scarlet, as she found herself unable to forget what she had just seen. What was more, now that she had met Oliver again and had fallen in love with him, a love which was returned, her own body's warm and strong response to the sight of Alys and Jack entwined together was telling, for the first time, to what lengths passion might lead those in its grip. For just one mad moment she had imagined herself there, on the bed with Oliver, while they explored each other's bodies.

One thing she was sure of, she would say nothing to the lovers or to Janet and the other Maids of what she had discovered. It was the lovers' secret and she would not gossip about it. She wondered whether Oliver knew how deeply Jack and Alys were involved, and decided that she would say nothing to him, either.

Certainly Kat Ashley could not be aware of how far Alys's friendship with Jack had gone, for if she had known she would immediately have punished Alys for her behaviour, and might even have ordered her to be banished from court. For Jack, however, there would be no punishment at all, and, not for the first time, Penelope wondered at the different standards of behaviour demanded of men and women.

Somehow she found her way back into the main building and at last reached the rooms where the sempstresses and embroiderers were working, to deliver her message and receive an answer, before returning, sadder and wiser, to Kat Ashley. She had eaten of the tree of knowledge, as Eve had done, and whether that was a good or a bad thing, she had yet to find out.

Chapter Seven

Lord Castleford was not used to being thwarted. The mere sight of Oliver Woodville made him feel sick. That Lord Robert had made something of a favourite of him galled him the more, and that the offspring of a mere country gentleman should be scaling the heights towards royal favour while he was condemned to be on the outer edge of it because of his Catholic persuasion also served to fuel his anger. The only consolation he possessed was that, according to his servants and spies, Woodville and Penelope Jermaine had never been seen in conversation together after he had threatened her with her lover's death if they continued their liaison.

Nevertheless, so long as this formidable opponent lived and breathed he did not feel safe. He would not use Frampton to dispose of him since, for some reason which he did not quite understand, he wanted Woodville's death to be of his own personal arranging—only that would give him true satisfaction. Consequently he ordered Bevis to watch Mary Jermaine in the hope that he could find incriminating evidence of a possible liaison between her and Roger Temple.

Late in the evening of the day on which Penelope had come across Jack and Alys making love, Castleford sent for one of his most faithful retainers and gave him his orders.

'Woodville is to be despatched—and promptly— but not in the precincts of Somerset House. Wait until he visits the city and do the deed then in such a way that some footpad will be blamed. Great will be your reward if you succeed.'

The man, who had been in Castleford's service since he was a boy, nodded his agreement: he was a man of few words.

'Understood, m'lord. It shall be done.'

'Good. I trust that you will arrange the matter soon.'

After that he could sleep more easily. Particularly since Bevis had told him that Mary and Roger were undoubtedly beginning to come to an understanding. He could use that knowledge as an excuse to throw the wench off and make an offer to her parents for the younger sister: an offer which he knew would not be refused.

That it might ruin Mary was, as he had told Penelope, neither here nor there.

* * *

Despite his intrigue with Alys, Jack was determined to seek other enjoyment in the stews of the City of London. He and a few friends decided to make up a party one evening in order to escape from the stuffy rectitude of Somerset House. He came upon Oliver when he had just returned from spending an hour with Lord Robert's secretary, going over some documents which had arrived from the Vatican, and invited him to join them that night.

'All work and no play…' he ended, since Oliver had always shown a marked lack of interest in such adventures.

'Makes Jack a dull boy, I know,' quoth Oliver with a grin, 'but since I am Oliver and not Jack, the saying does not apply.'

'Come, come,' retorted Jack, 'I'll be bound that you did not live a virtuous life when you were abroad.'

Well, that was true enough, but Oliver had not refound Penelope then, and to roister around London did not attract him.

'It's too cold to run about the city at night,' he said, and that was not totally a lie. After Italy he found England's climate grim.

'Oh, well,' said Jack with a shrug. 'Have it your way, but don't say that I never asked you.'

'No, indeed, but that should not stop you from enjoying yourself.'

'You may be sure that I shall,' was Jack's answer

to that—something which Oliver was to remember rather ruefully the next day.

He was, indeed, rueful that same evening when he discovered that his best and warmest cloak was missing. Not only that, it was a particularly splendid one with the arms of Sforza embroidered on its back and he valued it because it had been a present from one of the Milanese courtiers who had befriended him.

He immediately suspected that Jack had borrowed it without asking him for his permission. Jack's carelessness with other people's property was a by-word.

Oliver swallowed his annoyance, and after deciding that he would have a few hard words with his friend in the morning, he spent the evening reading Machiavelli's *Prince*, a book which he had acquired in Italy, marvelling at the man's understanding of the nature of political power and the stratagems used to grasp and keep it.

He was late in retiring to bed in the dormitory which he shared with some of the other members of Lord Robert's staff, but sleep came easily because the rest of his friends had joined Jack in his visit to London's night life.

He was not to sleep for long, though. Around one on the morning he was awoken by a noisy commotion, caused not by drunken revelry as he might have expected, but by the return of a sobered party whose experience of London's low life had been enlarged by an attack on one of their number.

'What the devil is wrong with you all?' he exclaimed, sitting up in bed and staring at the collection of glum night owls around him. 'Were all the stews closed that your faces are more fit for a funeral than a celebration of a night on the town?'

'You have almost the right of it about funerals,' Roger Temple told him heavily. 'Jack was attacked and badly wounded this evening. We had just left one of the taverns and were making for Moll Deighton's house when Jack fell behind a little—he had drunk rather heavily and was not very steady on his pins. The next thing we knew was that he gave a loud cry—and then was silent.

'Luckily I went to look for him, believing that he had fallen over, which he had, but not because of drink. Some thief had stabbed him in the back and made off with his purse. He had bled quite heavily, but by great good fortune was still living. We brought him back here in a cart belonging to Moll. At present he's in the apothecary's room being cared for. We have to hope that he will recover.'

Oliver sat up. He was sorry for Jack, of course he was, but he couldn't help wondering what had happened to his cloak. It wasn't long before he found out, since Roger was putting the torn and bloodied thing on the stool by Jack's bed, saying, 'I'm sorry, Oliver, but Jack borrowed your cloak this evening, and it will need a deal of mending—if it can be mended, that is. I wonder what made the thief pick on Jack—the splendour of the cloak, perhaps.'

Oliver nodded mutely at this. It was not until he

lay down again, waiting for troubled sleep to come, that something nudged at his brain which made him sit up sharply. Jack had been wearing *his* cloak, not his own, a cloak which most of the court knew of because it was so richly splendid. Castleford had threatened his life, and even though Oliver had been avoiding Penelope, might he not have decided to dispose of him all the same—most probably using some hireling?

Had the so-called thief stabbed Jack because, misled by the cloak, he believed that it was Oliver whom he was killing? The more he thought about it, the more likely it seemed that this might be the explanation for the attack. He could prove nothing either way, however, and given that he and Penelope had agreed to keep quiet about Castleford's threats, he could not speak of his suspicions to Temple and the others.

All that he could do was watch his own back—and be grateful that he had decided not to spend a night on the town with the others or he might be lying between life and death in the apothecary's room instead of poor Jack.

'You simpleton,' Castleford howled at his assassin, Taylor, when the news of Jack's assault ran round Somerset House. 'How could you have set upon the wrong man when the right one was alone in his quarters?'

'How was I to know that Chancellor had borrowed Woodville's cloak? I watched Lord Robert's men leave their rooms and there was that gaudy cloak of his among them. I wasn't to know that Chancellor had borrowed it.'

'Without permission!' Castleford roared at him, as though that were important. 'Now all's to do again, and next time it will be much harder. If two of Lord Robert's men are attacked, one after the other, it might start folks thinking.'

'There are other ways of despatching than that of the dagger,' whined his hearer. 'Trust me, I'll find another.'

'I did trust you—and what happened? You disposed of the wrong man. Fortunately for him they say that he's not likely to die, so I haven't his death upon my conscience—or yours. All I ask is that if you do try again you will succeed or it will be the worst for you.'

'Never fear, m'lord. The deed is done.'

'See that it is the next time.'

The assassin touched his forelock, and bowed servilely to his master before leaving.

Perhaps he ought to have used Frampton to despatch Woodville, after all: he doubted that he would have made such a stupid mistake as to attack the wrong man; but no, there was something about the fellow which he did not like. He could bully an underling like the one who had just left, but bullying Frampton was a different matter. Besides that, he did not want Frampton to know too much. There was no point in providing the man with an opportunity to gain a hold over him which carrying out an arranged murder might provide.

From something which Frampton had once said, he had gained the impression that he was engaged in plotting for others, too, not about murder, but about the best means of ensuring that the Queen did not marry Lord Robert, but some foreign Catholic prince instead. In certain lights that might be construed as treason and William Castleford was not quite ready to commit that yet.

'Sorry to ruin your cloak, old fellow,' whispered Jack to Oliver. 'Who'd have guessed that I should end up in the gutter, bleeding to death if Temple and the rest hadn't come back for me.'

'Don't worry about it,' Oliver told him. 'Did you get a look at the wretch who attacked you?'

'That's what everyone's been asking me, but, no. I didn't even know that someone was close behind me. I was just rolling merrily along when someone struck me a hard blow in the back, and then I was lying in the gutter where he promptly bent over me, cut my purse and fled with it. After that I didn't re-member anything until I woke up to find myself in bed here. You will forgive me over your cloak, won't you?'

'Of course; as you said, you weren't to know that you were going to be attacked.'

Jack nodded feebly. 'There is one thing that you can do for me, and that's tell Alys Belsize that I'm thinking of her. Perhaps you could even arrange for her to visit me.'

'I'll do what I can.'

'There's a good fellow.' Jack shut his eyes and fell silent. It was plain that he still felt very weak and that it might be some time before he was jolly Jack Chancellor again, if ever. A severe attack like this often changed a man. His family had been informed of what had happened and it had already been suggested that he should be sent home to recuperate once it was safe for him to travel.

Oliver met Penelope on the way to find Alys Belsize. His face lit up at the sight of her. She looked more beautiful than ever. There appeared to be no one about so he stopped to speak to her—to pass her by seemed an act against nature.

When he spoke, though, his speech and manner to her were formal since it was always possible that they were being spied on.

'Mistress Jermaine, I trust that I see you well.'

Her answer was a curtsey and a stiff smile. 'I am happy to say so, Master Woodville, and you look uncommon healthy, too.'

There was no help for it: the contrast of this cool exchange after their recent passionate conversations was so great that it set them both laughing. If Oliver thought that Penelope's eyes shone even more brightly than on their last meeting, Penelope thought that Oliver, in his new black and gold suit with its splendid cartwheel of a ruff, was handsomer than ever. Oliver's opinion of Penelope's gold and scarlet formal dress was equally admiring.

They both recovered from their mirth at the same time.

Penelope said, 'We really should not be laughing when poor Jack Chancellor is in such dire straits.'

'Not so dire as they were,' returned Oliver. 'He is recovering rapidly. He wishes me to remember him to Mistress Belsize. He's even hoping that she might be able to visit him.'

'No chance of that,' said Penelope. 'Kat Ashley would be sure to disapprove of one of the Maids visiting a young man in his bed.'

'Even if it were to comfort him because it is a bed of pain,' Oliver said.

'She would object most particularly to a visit to a man if he were on a bed of pain,' riposted Penelope. 'Things being as they are, who knows what might happen then?'

'Indeed,' replied Oliver, thinking that little Penelope was most definitely growing up, since by her joke it was clear she was aware that Jack and Alys had been meeting secretly. He wondered how she had found out.

'There is one rumour about the attack on Jack which interested me,' Penelope said, looking genuinely grave, 'which is that he was wearing your cloak. Is that true?'

'Alas, yes, and unfortunately it is too bloodstained to be restored.'

'I hope that you will not think me foolish,' Penelope said slowly, 'but I did wonder if the person who attacked Jack might have mistaken him for you—remembering Lord Castleford's threats. I know that we have done as he wished and have not met very often, but he might still think that he had nothing to lose by secretly having you killed. You will be careful, won't you?'

Oh, she had never looked more lovely than when she was so earnestly worrying about him.

'No,' he told her. 'I don't believe that you are foolish, because I thought of that, too. It made me most unhappy to think that Jack might have been injured because he was mistaken for me.'

Now wasn't that typical of Oliver's kindness—to worry about someone else? It was why Penelope loved him. There was an honesty about him which was lacking in most of the people she met about the court. Not that he was a fool, or too trusting, but the kind of deviousness which Bevis Frampton and Castleford engaged in was foreign to him.

Now why was she thinking of Bevis Frampton? Of course he had helped Castleford in his failed attempt to seduce her, but she hadn't seen him lately—was he still about the court?

'You look beautiful when you are thinking,' Oliver told her tenderly. 'Most men and women don't think at all, but you never seem to stop and it really becomes you.'

'I know that I ought to simper, or smirk, at you when you pay me compliments like that,' said Penelope, teasing him, 'but I suppose that thinking women don't simper.'

'And thank goodness for that,' returned Oliver. 'My preference is for a smile or a full-bodied laugh.'

'Which reminds me: I was thinking about Bevis Frampton just now, but I don't think that he's really the subject for a laugh of any kind.'

'Why Bevis?'

'Because he's Castleford's man and he helped to snare me—so I wondered if it were he who had stabbed poor Jack in the back.'

It was amazing how often they thought alike—two minds working as one. 'I thought that might be possible, too,' Oliver said, 'but when I—very cautiously—tried to find out where he was that night I discovered that after supper he had been gambling in the guard-room with some of the officers until the small hours and losing a lot of money to them on the way. It was one of the following morning's better jokes.'

'So, he did cause some laughter after all. I didn't really suppose it might be Bevis, but it was just as well for you to check.'

'And just as well for us both to be cautious. It's all very suspicious isn't it? You must be careful, too,

Penelope, I couldn't bear it if anything happened to you because of your friendship with me.'

'Yes, we must both be careful and therefore we ought to part now before anyone sees us together. Not that I want to leave you so soon, Oliver. Oh, I do miss you!'

This last sentence came out in a rush and, combined with the effect which seeing Penelope again after several days away from her had already had on Oliver, nearly overset his unsteady self-control.

'Oh, sweetheart, don't look and speak to me like that,' he exclaimed, 'if you want me to walk away from you! You are temptation itself. I can understand why Castleford is pursuing you, damn him.'

This was so heartfelt that it took all Penelope's resolution not to lean forward and kiss him on his warm cheek, but common sense prevailed. She curtseyed again, Oliver bowed, and they parted.

It was fortunate that they did. Castleford's man passed Penelope on the stairs, and shortly afterwards saw Oliver on his way to the Maids' rooms. He made a mental note to tell his master that they had almost certainly been meeting privily. It wouldn't do anything for his temper, but it might serve to make Castleford treat him more kindly if he knew that his man was keeping his eyes open for him.

So much was happening as the court prepared to move on to the palace of Whitehall, where they were to celebrate Christmas—yet another cause of a great deal of work—that after a few days the assault on Jack was almost forgotten.

One person who did not forget was Oliver's man, Gib. Shortly after the surgeon announced that Jack was recovering so rapidly that arrangements could be made for him to travel home, he sought out Oliver on one of the few occasions when he was alone, and said, 'A privy word with you, Master, if you please. Something is troubling me.'

'As many as you wish. I would not have you troubled,' said Oliver.

'There is an odd tale running round the kitchens,' Gib began carefully. 'They say that whoever stabbed Master Chancellor in the back probably thought by the cloak that he was stabbing you. Now, why should anyone want to kill you?'

'More to the point,' said Oliver gently, 'is how should some London cutpurse know that the cloak was mine?'

'Aye, and so I told the fool who passed the gossip on to me, whereat he winked at me, put his finger by his nose and said that it was common knowledge that it was not Master Chancellor who should have been attacked, but the courtier whose cloak he had borrowed.'

'And did your friend tell you who had paid this fellow to try to murder me?' asked Oliver.

Gib shook his head. 'Not so—it's supposed that it must have been one of the great ones round the court. Also it's generally agreed that it's a mystery as to

why anyone should wish to kill either you or Master
Chancellor. Have you made an enemy, sir? If so, I
would willingly help you to dispose of him or, if not,
to guard your back for you as much as I may. When
your father made me your man I promised him that I
would always look after you.'

Oliver already knew that very often servants and
retainers were more aware than their masters of what
was going on behind the scenes. Nevertheless, he was
surprised that this time, when it was plain that none
of his friends and superiors suspected that there was
anything strange about the attack on Jack, the servants
should be sure that there was.

No matter. There was no profit in pursuing this,
since servants' gossip, on its own, proved nothing—
although the Queen's mother, Anne Boleyn, had been
convicted of adultery and executed partly as a result
of their evidence. Evidence which was almost certainly tainted. He would not tell Penelope of it, even
though it supported his belief that he had been the
target, not Jack, and that Castleford was behind the
attack.

All that he could do for the moment was to tell Gib
to pass on any further news immediately and to watch
his own back.

When Penelope entered the Maids' room Alys
Belsize came running up to her.

'Have you any further news of Jack?' she asked

eagerly. Penelope thought she looked ill. Her face was wan and there were purple shadows under her eyes.

'Only what we already know: that he is recovering and will shortly be going home.'

Alys's lips quivered. 'He gave Oliver a message for me on the day after he was injured but since then I have heard nothing. Do you think that he will be going with us to Whitehall Palace before he's sent home? Perhaps I might be able to see him there.'

She hesitated, then said in a rush, 'That ugly little man Bevis Frampton has been following me about ever since Jack was hurt. He tried to console me once—he said something to me—I can't remember what, but it made me feel better. Oh, if I could only see Jack again just for a moment, he would know how to look after me and I shouldn't feel so ill all the time.'

Penelope hardly knew what to say. She was saved from having to answer by Kat Ashley coming in, saying briskly, 'Ladies, the Queen awaits you. Mistress Jermaine, the Queen has asked for you to be ready to play the virginals for her.'

Penelope curtseyed and Kat turned her attention on Alys, saying sharply, 'Mistress Belsize, are you feeling well? You look pale—and goodness me, I do believe that you're going to faint! Catch her, someone.'

It was Penelope who caught her. Alys, though small, was no light weight and it was with difficulty that she was able to lift her on to a settle. Janet ran off to find some water while Kat tut-tutted in the background, having done nothing herself, Penelope noticed acidly, to help in any way.

'What is the matter with the child?' she asked impatiently. 'She has been having one megrim after the other for the past week. Leave her, Mistress Saville, to recover while we go to attend on Her Grace.'

'Perhaps it's because she is unhappy over Jack's injury,' Janet whispered to Penelope while they filed into the Queen's room. 'She won't be better until he's completely recovered.'

Perhaps not then, Penelope thought, if he has to go home. Alys's wan face had disturbed her more than a little, for she could not help but remember what she had so recently discovered about her secret meetings with Jack. Was there more to her malaise than simple worry over his condition?

She tried not to let it trouble her while she played and sang the Queen's favourite ballads. The Queen had been told that Alys was unwell and had been sent off duty until she recovered. Later, when she had finished playing, Janet dragged her cushion over to where she sat, doing her everlasting embroidery—for so she was coming to think of it—and whispered, 'Do you really believe that Alys is pining for Jack?'

'She could be,' was all that Penelope could manage. Did the other Maids know how far Alys and Jack's passion had taken them? Was their giggling simply caused by the pair of them taking every opportunity to be together quite innocently, or did they suspect the truth: that they were lovers?

Well, it wasn't her business, except that if her suspicions were correct and Alys had become pregnant by Jack then it more than ever behoved her not to give way to her own growing passion for Oliver lest she, too, face ruin. Not that Oliver had ever directly tempted her, but every time they met she had this strong feeling that she wanted more from him than words and the slight contact of their hands—and by his expression he felt the same.

She could only hope that she was mistaken in thinking that Alys was breeding, but she could not help remembering what had happened to Joan, who had been her maidservant when she was a child. She had started to behave exactly like Alys: suddenly vomiting and fainting without warning. Not long afterwards she had been summarily dismissed. Puzzled, she had asked one of Joan's friends why, and had been told that it was because she had forgotten herself with one of the stable-lads.

Penelope had only been ten years old at the time, and had innocently asked, 'Forgotten herself—whatever does that mean?'

'You'll know when you grow up,' was all the answer she had been given, and, of course, when she did, she realised what Joan and the stable-lad must have been doing. Until Oliver had come back from the Continent she hadn't been able to understand how any woman could give way to a man, when the consequences for her might be so dreadful if she were unlucky enough to conceive a child out of wedlock, but each time they met she was learning more and more about the compulsions of passion.

She had little time for further worry about Alys, however, for later that afternoon she was favoured with a visit from her sister Mary. Although they were both in the Queen's service they rarely had the opportunity to meet one another, and now that they had it was plain that Mary had not come in friendship.

'How many men do you wish to have dangling after you?' she demanded of Penelope, once they were alone together in a small room leading off from the Great Hall, where the other Maids could not overhear their conversation.

'Isn't it enough that you now have Oliver Woodville, but that you must snare my future husband as well? Not only does he spend his time with me complaining that I am not more like you, but I found this under my pillow when I retired to my bed last night,' and she thrust a grubby scrap of paper at Penelope.

'Beware, Mistress,' was written on it in a florid hand, 'your sweet sister and your husband are meeting secretly to devise plans which will see him rid of you. Her interest in Woodville is false, designed to deceive you as to her true intent—take care of what you eat and drink—from your well-wisher.'

Penelope, disgusted, tossed the paper on to the floor. 'Who sent you this lie? And how can you believe it?'

Mary bent to pick the paper up before hissing at

her, 'Lie, you say? Do you dare deny that you are secretly meeting my betrothed husband?'

'I dare deny it because I am speaking the truth.'

'Then tell me this. If you are not lying, how is it that I have had a peculiar malaise lately—a malaise which has caused me to vomit more than once? The apothecary thinks that I must have eaten or drunk poison by mistake. Was it a mistake—or was it put in my food deliberately? I know that Castleford often sneaks away these days, but even that creature of his, Frampton, does not know where he goes to—or so he tells me.'

'Well, he does not visit me because I do not like him and do not wish to be either his lover or his wife. I detest him, and have refused to listen to his pleas of love for me. If he says otherwise, he is lying.'

'I have asked him and he says that he has been meeting you secretly since you are more pleasant to talk to than I am. Deny that, if you dare?'

Now this was all mysterious enough—for who might want to poison Mary, unless it were Castleford if he wished to marry her sister instead? But why would Castleford send Mary a letter which would incriminate him and his supposed lover: it would be a stupid thing to do. Was it possible that there was a third man involved—someone who hated all three of them?

This was too fanciful a notion to entertain, for who could that person be?

'Of course I deny it,' Penelope said at last, 'and I

am astonished that you should believe such a thing of me. I detested the man before he became betrothed to you, but once he was I was always coldly civil to him. I cannot imagine why he should find me attractive or why he should think that I might be attracted to him. I have twice told him nay, but he will not believe that I mean what I say. What's more, I can only wonder that you still wish to marry a man who treats you so scurvily by trying to woo your sister—and may possibly be poisoning you.'

Mary sat down—so far she had remained standing—and burst into tears.

'I wish that I thought that you were telling me the truth,' she said pathetically, 'but he is so insistent. What's more, who can have sent me this letter?'

'Now that I do not know, nor can I hazard a guess,' Penelope replied, feeling sorry for Mary for the first time. 'I only know that I have no wish to hurt you: I wish you nothing but well.'

One odd thing about her sister's story troubled her a little, and that was that some of the symptoms of her illness were similar to those from which Alys Belsize was suffering. She could not believe, knowing Mary well, that she had lain with Roger Temple and become pregnant—she was too hard-headed for that, unlike gentle and tender Alys.

'I will try to believe you,' said Mary slowly, 'but who can the friend be who has sent me this letter?'

'A friend!' exclaimed Penelope. 'Why should you believe that it is a friend who has sent you this letter?

A friend would not wish to cause you such distress by being so mysterious.'

She said as much later to Oliver after Mary had left her, not now quite so sure that Penelope was betraying her, but still desperately unhappy. In view of Castleford's threats to him over his friendship with her, she thought that he ought to be told of this latest piece of news.

'I am surprised that Castleford has the time to meet so many people clandestinely,' was Oliver's immediate exclamation. 'The rumour running round is that he is secretly plotting with Feria and some other Catholic sympathisers to try to blacken Lord Robert's reputation in such a way that he will no longer be able to make an offer for the Queen's hand—and now this! He can scarcely have time to sleep!'

'It is not a matter for joking, Oliver,' said Penelope reproachfully. 'Mary's distress is real, and though we have never been close friends Castleford's behaviour is ensuring that now we are not friends at all. Except that when she left me just now she was kinder to me than she has been since she broke with you and agreed to be betrothed to him—something which I think that she is coming to regret now that she has met Roger Temple.'

'You say that she has an unexplained illness. Forgive me for suggesting this, but do you suspect that she and Temple have become more than friends?'

'No, I don't think so: Mary is not the sort to give way to passion.'

For the first time in their sober conversation Oliver offered her a smile.

'Dear Penelope,' he said, 'I fear that we are all of the sort to give way to passion. I doubt that your sister is an exception—though I tend to agree with you.'

'Well, *we* haven't,' said Penelope spiritedly, and then added a rider '—at least, not yet.'

Oliver's shout of laughter at this might have been heard outside in the Strand.

'Oh, Penelope my darling, you give me hope!'

Of what, he did not tell her: he did not need to.

'The strangest thing of all though,' said Penelope, still worried, 'is who can have sent Mary the letter? Can it possibly be true that Castleford is trying to poison her?'

'If everyone who had fits and heavy vomiting because of eating bad food was thought to have been poisoned we should be in worse case than Rome was at the time of the Borgias,' was Oliver's answer to that. 'After all, Alys Belsize is similarly afflicted and no one can be wanting to poison her!'

So Oliver obviously did not know of the true nature of Alys's secret meetings with Jack Chancellor. She debated whether to tell him, but decided against it. She had always disliked gossiping and she had no wish to blacken Alys's—or Jack's—reputation needlessly.

And what about her own? Here she was, secreted with Oliver in one of the empty alcoves at Somerset House which had been provided for the beautiful statues which the Queen had been unable to afford when she was simply the poverty-stricken Princess Elizabeth.

It was time to move on. If Castleford were truly wicked enough to attempt to murder Mary, then he was likely to be equally ruthless where Oliver was concerned, since he considered him to be one of his enemies.

She said so. Her reward was not only a look of love, but a kiss, a chaste one, on her cheek. Visitors from France and Italy were always remarking on how freely and openly the English kissed one another. To her surprise Penelope found herself asking Oliver, once he had stepped back again, whether he had found on his travels that it was true that on the Continent they kissed less often.

'In public yes,' he told her, his eyes sparkling wickedly, 'but I believe that, in private, there is very little difference between us. Would you say that, half-hidden here, we are in public, or in private? Now that is a fine distinction for scholars to debate.'

'I suppose that the answer might be that our position is neither one thing nor the other. Unfortunately we have no time to debate it, either. If Kat Ashley found me here, alone with you, I should never hear the last of it. She considers all courtiers under the age of seventy to be wicked would-be seducers of her girls.'

'Well, I know one of her girls I would like to seduce,' was Oliver's riposte to that, while naughty

Penelope widened her eyes and said in return, 'You do? And pray who may that be, Master Woodville?'

His reply was to lean forward and kiss her briskly on the lips before retreating again with the words, 'Now, that should help you guess, my sweet hussy, and you are, as usual, right. We should part on the instant. Lord Robert awaits me and Her Grace's dragon awaits you. *Au revoir*, as the French say.'

It would be a painful retreat for him in more ways than one. That last kiss on her lips had undone him. To be with her was sweet torment, as was being away from her, and by her behaviour she felt the same way about him.

Oh, if only they were a cook's boy and an apprentice sempstress they would be able to enjoy themselves to their heart's content. If matters went awry they would simply tie the knot at double speed and the world would wag on. But for those, like the pair of them, who lived in high places, discretion was all, or ruin awaited. Not so much for the gentleman— although Oliver had no mind to become known as a despoiler of virgins even if by doing so he would largely escape punishment—but the lady who surrendered her chastity surrendered everything.

Chapter Eight

Jack Chancellor recovered rapidly from his injury. Fortunately for him, nothing vital had been affected and the family coach had been sent to carry him home as soon as he was fit to travel. It was, it seemed, unlikely that he would return to Lord Robert's service. In his absence his family were trying to arrange a marriage for him with the daughter and heiress of a neighbouring landowner, and he was expected to settle down and learn the management of both of the estates which would one day be his.

He had sent a letter of farewell to Alys which was given to her after his departure. Her behaviour on reading it had been stoic, but later in the day, after dinner, she had suffered her worst attack of vomiting yet. She wandered about Somerset House looking frail and ill—all of which was put down to Jack's desertion.

Penelope, between semi-secret meetings with

Oliver and the demands of the Queen with whom she was reading the classics, was busier than ever until one evening, not long before the court was due to travel to Whitehall Palace, Kat Ashley bustled up to her, exclaiming, 'Mistress Jermaine, have you come across Alys Belsize lately? No one has seen her since early morning. I know that she has taken lately to hiding herself away, but she has never been missing for so long before.'

Penelope shook her head. 'No, madam, I have been with the Queen all morning and this afternoon I have been busy embroidering a scarf for my new gown.'

Kat sighed. 'She was such a good child until recently. You are sure that you have no notion of where she might be?'

Penelope was about to say no when a sudden, unwelcome, thought struck her. It was an unwelcome thought, because if she were to tell Kat of Alys's and Jack's use of the room where unwanted furniture was kept, her mistress might not be best pleased with her for having known this and not reported it.

She decided that it might be best to say nothing at all. If she were wrong she would look a fool, and a malicious fool at that. The sensible thing would be to visit the room herself, find out whether Alys was hiding there and tell her that her disappearances had been noticed and that Kat Ashley was far from happy about them.

Kat sighed again, 'Oh, well, she is sure to turn up when it is time for bed. You seemed to be one of her friends so I thought that you might know what she is doing, but if you don't…'

More than ever, Penelope thought, when the disturbed Kat had left her, it was essential that she visited the room again. The only thing was that she had forgotten where it was. All that she could do was try to retrace her steps again and hope that they would not lead her astray. In the end, after some wrong turnings, she at last discovered the door to the room which Alys and Jack had used for their rendezvous.

She opened it, to find Alys lying on the bed.

It was also Oliver's day to find things. He had been sent on yet another errand for Lord Robert, which involved him passing the rooms which Castleford occupied. On an impulse he decided to pay him a visit. Penelope's account of Mary and her letter had disturbed him more than he had allowed her to know. His suspicions of Castleford were heightened by Lord Robert having discovered that he was actively plotting with the Spanish Ambassador to blacken his name so that it would be impossible for him to marry the Queen.

Oliver was not sure what he would say to the man when he found him. As it happened, Castleford was not present but his underling, Bevis Frampton, was. A footman led him into a room which was a cross between a library and a study, where Bevis was busily engaged in rummaging through one of the drawers in Castleford's desk. As usual when Oliver saw him, the hairs on the back of his neck bristled, just like those of Caesar's, the dog he had owned as a boy, whenever he saw anyone he disliked. The sense of something wrong was strong in him.

After all, why was Bevis meddling with what must be Castleford's private papers? On hearing Oliver enter he had turned to smile greasily at him. 'Ah, Woodville, since m'lord is absent, what may I do for you?'

'Nothing,' returned Oliver briefly. 'It is Lord Castleford to whom I wish to speak.'

'You may leave a message with me,' offered Bevis, staring hard at him.

Now Oliver had no wish at all to leave a message with Bevis, but suddenly and astonishingly, from nowhere, it seemed, he heard himself saying, almost without his willing it, 'Simply this, inform him that I take no note of his threats against me, but should he pursue Mistress Penelope Jermaine further, I shall take action against him which he will not like.'

'Oh, yes,' murmured Bevis, turning his face away, 'I do understand you, Woodville, and be sure I shall pass on your message.'

Oliver shook his head to clear it. What, in the devil's name, had impelled him to say that? And to Bevis, of all people? The less he knew of Oliver's intentions the better—and now he had given himself away.

No matter, if he had been a fool, it was his own fault. He would tell Penelope of what he had done and urge her to be as careful as he intended to be, and as he had not been just now. He concluded his business for Lord Robert and went to find her.

Penelope's first horrified thought was that Alys was dead: she lay on the bed without moving, her face grey. She had a little glass phial clutched in her hand. Suddenly she opened her eyes to stare dreamily at Penelope, before offering her a weak smile.

'Do not worry,' she said. 'I shall be better soon. My good angel promised me that and he has been so kind to me that I do not think that he is lying.' Her eyes closed again and her breathing slowed perceptibly.

She might not yet be dead, but it was plain to Penelope that she was in great danger—and whatever did she mean by 'her good angel'? She leaned forward and shook Alys until her eyes slowly opened.

'Don't do that,' she whispered, 'Let me sleep. I was so happy. I was dreaming that I was with Jack, and, as my good angel has promised me, all will be well with me again.'

'Your good angel!' exclaimed Penelope fiercely. 'Who is he? What did he give you, Alys, that has made you like to die? Tell me, and I will go to find help.'

'Something. I don't know. I only know that it tastes nice and when I drink it all my worries disappear.' She offered the bottle to Penelope. 'There's a little left. Would you like to drink some of it so that you may be happy, too?'

'No,' Penelope exclaimed, snatching the bottle from her. 'Lie there, and try not to go to sleep.'

'But I want to sleep,' Alys protested. 'I like sleeping because I forget things and he told me that when I wake up I shall be with Jack and our baby: he said so, more than once.'

'He…he…he…' choked Penelope in exasperation. There was nothing for it but that she must leave at once in order to find help for poor Alys, since there was nothing in the room which would be of the slightest assistance.

The phial clutched in her hand, she hurried towards the Queen's quarters. All the way there, running through her brain, was that Alys's malaise had indeed been caused by her having conceived Jack's baby— and what did Alys mean when she babbled about an angel who had helped her and whom she called 'he'? Who could the 'he' be? And had he given her the phial which was making her sleep? It certainly wasn't Jack. Her illness had begun after he had been attacked. Not that it mattered at the moment: her first duty must be to try to save Alys from what looked like certain death.

Afterwards would be the time to discover who her unknown accomplice could be.

Oliver had almost reached the Maids' quarters when he saw Penelope running towards him, her face white. She stopped to gasp at him, 'Well met, Oliver, I am sure that you will know what to do…' She could say no more, for her fear for Alys, and her dash through Somerset House, had left her short of breath.

It was obvious to Oliver that something was very wrong. One of the things he loved most about Penelope was her calm control, and to find her shaking and distraught told him that the matter must be serious indeed. What troubled him the most was that she was clutching a small glass phial to her bosom.

'What is it, dear girl?' he asked her. 'Are you ill…?'

He got no further. Penelope panted at him, 'No, not I, it's Alys. She may be dying at this moment so we have no time to waste. I'll tell you everything if you'll come with me to try to find the Queen's physician.'

She was so distressed that Oliver thought it best to obey her without question, and by the time they reached the Queen's rooms she had poured out the whole sad story to him.

What followed next was like something out of a nightmare. The physician was found, Kat Ashley informed and a party, which was sufficiently small enough to ensure that as few as possible knew of Alys's misfortune, hurriedly followed Penelope to the room where Alys lay, still breathing, but only just. It was made up of the physician, the physician's boy and Oliver, there to act as a messenger if one were needed.

Alys still lay, motionless, on the bed. The mask of

death, the physician later said, was already beginning to settle on her face.

He immediately told Penelope to help Alys to sit up. She tried to resist both Penelope and the physician, but her struggles were ineffectual.

'I want to sleep,' she cried, 'my angel said that I must sleep.'

'No,' said the physician who had fetched from his satchel a small glass drinking vessel and a blue bottle. 'If you sleep you will die. From what Mistress Jermaine has told me, you have drunk poison. Who gave you this?' He held up the phial which Penelope had taken from her. 'And do you know what is in it?'

'My spirit, my good angel, he gave it to me. He said that it would help me. I know not what it is.' Her voice had sunk to little more than a whisper.

'Not so, Mistress, this will not help you. I believe that he may have given you a potion which causes a sleep which leads to death. I fear that we must make you vomit this venom from your stomach before it completes its fell work. Hold the basin which my boy will give you steady before her, Mistress Jermaine, so that after she has drunk this strong draught her stomach's contents will void themselves into it of their own accord.' So saying, he poured liquid from the blue bottle into the glass vessel and held it to Alys's mouth.

'Drink, mistress, drink,' he bade her, 'and God willing, you will be well again.'

She fought him and tried to push him away, until

the physician pinched her nose tightly while he forced the liquid into her mouth and down her throat so that she was compelled to empty the glass, willy nilly.

Nothing happened for a moment until suddenly, Alys gave a harsh cry and, as the physician had promised, was convulsed with a spasm of vomiting so violent that at the end of it she fell back on to the bed, her face more ghastly white than ever.

'Oh,' cried Penelope, 'she is dying after all.'

'Nay,' said the physician calmly, 'she will feel worse, and then better. The desire to sleep will leave her. When she is a little better Master Woodville will carry her to a room near to my office where she may be assisted to recover further. There is one question, Mistress Belsize, which I must ask you straightway. Mistress Jermaine believes from what she has observed and what you have told her today, that you may be with child. Is that true?'

Alys, whose colour was slowly returning, said faintly, 'Yes.'

'Did you take this potion so that you might miscarry?'

Weak though she was, Alys, reared up and shouted, 'No, no, he gave it to me so that I might reach a state of grace where I would be happy with Jack and the baby.'

'He? This *he* of whom you speak gave you poison which was like to kill you if Mistress Jermaine had not acted with such commendable despatch. Tell me the name of the man who tried to kill you.'

Alys looked away from him. 'I don't know his name. He is a spirit, he comes to me by night and day and helps me. He soothes me. I don't believe that my spirit friend meant to harm me.'

The physician sighed. 'She wanders in her mind. This often happens when poison has been drunk.'

He turned towards Oliver and Penelope, who had put down the bowl which she had been carrying: the boy who looked after the physician's equipment placed a towel over it so that his master might examine its contents later.

'Sir and madam, know you aught which might help us to find this man, this would-be murderer who has so deceived this poor child?'

They shook their heads. Penelope, who much to Oliver's admiration had remained remarkably composed throughout this whole dreadful business, said earnestly, 'If I did, I would tell you, but Alys has never said anything which might help us to identify him.'

'Then it must remain a mystery. A spirit, forsooth! I hear that that fellow Dee converses with spirits who advise him daily, but I am a plain man and the only spirits of which I have knowledge are those animal spirits which relate to the body.'

He was a breath of fresh air, was he not? Penelope, who had been feeling low as a consequence of what had happened that afternoon, suddenly felt better, even though she knew, by Oliver's expression, that he had taken note that she had said nothing to anyone, including him, of Alys's possibly being with child until she had been found at death's door.

Well, she would cross that bridge when she came to it. Meantime she was cursing Jack, who had led Alys into sin and who had so thoughtlessly disappeared from her life without troubling to see her, sending her only a brief letter.

Oliver was thinking the same thing and said so to Penelope later, after he had carried Alys to the bed which had been prepared for her.

'I had not thought it of him,' he said, 'first to seduce such a young maiden and then to leave her so carelessly, except that it may be that he did not know that she was with child. How came you, Penelope, to know of their amour?'

'By chance,' she told him. 'I came on them one day, not long before Jack was injured, in the room where I found her today. They did not see me.'

'And you said nothing of this to anyone, not even to me? They were…on the bed together?'

'Yes,' she told him, as she had hoped she would never have need to do.

There was some reproach in his voice when he murmured, 'Did you not trust me?'

Penelope hesitated. 'It was not that, Oliver, believe me, but I knew not what to do, or say, for the best. There was only my word, after all, and Alys has always been kind to me. I was relieved when Jack left, for it removed temptation from her. When she began to ail, I started to fear that she might be with child. I was not sure to whom I owed a duty. Was it very wrong of me?'

Oliver scarcely knew how to answer her. He could understand how difficult it had been for her to decide what she ought to do for the best. More than that, in some odd way, however much it hurt him to learn that that she had not spoken to him of it, it made him admire her the more. Most women would have gone tattling and giggling around once they had discovered the guilty pair at their games, only too happy to spread scandal abroad and shame them.

But not Penelope: she had held her tongue, and when Alys had disappeared she had gone to find her. After that she had promptly fetched the physician in order to try to save her, although she knew that she might be in trouble herself with Kat Ashley and the Queen for not telling them of Jack and Alys's behaviour. Her own behaviour, once she had found Alys so near death, had been exemplary.

Suddenly her face crumpled. 'Oh, Oliver, if only I had told someone earlier, Alys might have been saved from what happened today. She might not have turned to this spirit she spoke of so often. She called him *he*—but who can he be? The only man I ever saw her with was Jack. After Jack was injured she started to hide herself away and couldn't be found when she was required to carry out her duties. Was it then that she met this so-called spirit? After all, someone gave her the potion which so nearly killed her. It's a mystery and I don't like mysteries.'

She began to sob quietly. Oliver, overcome with pity for her, took her in his arms.

'Hush, my darling. Don't cry. It's not your fault that Alys and Jack misbehaved, nor that Alys became entangled with a supposed spirit. I understand how difficult it was for you to tell anyone.'

After all, she had been but an innocent young girl, tenderly nurtured, when she came to court, however clever she was, and now she had been introduced to the harsher side of life and he could see that it must have been a shock for her.

She looked up at him, her glorious eyes drenched in tears. 'You do? I fear me that Kat Ashley will not be so kind. I'm sorry now that I didn't tell you.'

Oliver nodded. 'I know, a trouble shared is a trouble halved, but reflect that in the end you helped to save Alys.'

How kind he was and how comforting were the strong arms which held her. They stood entwined together for a moment, forgetting that they might be seen—and become the cause of yet another scandal. It was Oliver who acted first, releasing her and stepping back, saying gently, 'We must part to carry out our own duties.'

Penelope offered him a watery smile.

'Yes, and my first duty must be to report immediately to Mistress Ashley on what has passed—and learn what my punishment will be. I know that Alys will be banished from the court, but I don't think that I shall be quite so harshly treated.'

'The stocks, perhaps,' said Oliver with a smile.

Penelope laughed a little at that. He found it a blessed sound, for it showed that she was recovering her normal good spirits again.

'Nothing quite so severe, but severe enough, no doubt. I will tell you later.'

Oliver watched her go. Her step was lighter now. She had leaned heavily against him after they had left Alys in the physician's care, and his urge to protect her had never been so strong. So powerful was it that it temporarily extinguished the desire for her which merely being in her presence always created.

He sighed, and made his way towards Lord Robert, to whom he must reveal not only result of the journey on which he had been sent, but also the sad story of Jack and Alys's intrigue and its near-tragic consequences.

No, Kat Ashley was not best pleased when Penelope finally told her the truth about Jack and Alys's affair and that Alys was now recovering in the physician's room.

'The silly girl is with child, you say—hence her minor vomitings and general low health?'

'Yes.'

'You did not think to tell me of her misbehaviour with John Chancellor?' It was typical of Kat that she never called him Jack.

'I was not sure what I ought to do.'

'For that matter,' Kat admitted frankly, '*I* am not

sure what I ought to do with you, either. I must inform
Her Grace of all that has passed and, no doubt, she
will wish to decide your fate. She will not be best
pleased at such a scandal occurring while we are preparing for her to be crowned, but we may be lucky
enough to keep the whole wretched business a secret.'

She sighed, 'You will go to the Maids' dormitory
at once and stay there until you are sent for. I shall
speak to the Queen as soon as she has finished con-
sulting with Master Cecil.'

The Queen! It was going to be the Queen who
passed judgement on her! Penelope, naturally very
worried, could not decide whether this was a good or
a bad thing. Fortunately she did not have long to wait.
Kat herself came to fetch her, for the less everyone
knew about this potential scandal the better, although
to keep it a total secret might be impossible.

The Queen was alone, seated at the virginals. She
was playing a most melancholy tune and did not
break off straightway when she and Kat entered. The
tune slowly meandered to its end, whereupon she rose
from her stool and walked to her chair of state where
she sat for a moment, her chin propped on her hand,
staring at the pair of them.

She had seldom looked more majestic, or as Kat
told Penelope later, more like her late father, King
Henry VIII. He, too, had possessed the same shrewd
assessing glare.

After a moment she nodded at Kat, and said, 'You

may leave us, Kat, I wish to speak to Mistress Jermaine alone.'

Kat thinned her lips at this, but had no choice other than to curtsey and retire. The Queen now turned her glare on Penelope, who quaked internally wondering what was coming.

'I have been listening to what Mistress Ashley has told me of your behaviour. I would now like to hear your account of it.'

Penelope swallowed. 'Everything, Your Grace? This is not a short story I have to tell you.'

'No matter. Pray begin.'

As succinctly as she could, Penelope recited everything which had happened since she had found Jack and Alys together on the bed in the store room, all the way up to the moment when Oliver had carried Alys to the physician's quarters.

The Queen's glare grew no warmer. Her first question related to Alys's claim that she had been helped by a spirit.

'Do you believe that?' she asked.

'I neither believe, nor disbelieve it,' Penelope said, 'since there is no evidence to prove anything either way. I think that Alys believes it—but that proves nothing.'

Her Grace nodded, without speaking, and her hard glare softened a little when she asked her next question.

'Mistress Ashley says that until you fetched my physician you told no one of what you had found out—even when Mistress Belsize was taken ill. Is this true?'

'Yes, Your Grace.'

The Queen leaned back in her chair. 'No one. Not even Master Oliver Woodville? Now, I do find that surprising.'

'Nevertheless,' Penelope retorted, thinking later that she must have been mad to be quite so bold with the late King's daughter, 'surprising or not, that is the truth. I had no mind to spread wanton tittle-tattle about Your Grace's court until the matter took on a more serious aspect and Mistress Belsize's life proved to be in danger. More than that, I had no real proof that she was with child, only my intuition.'

The Queen resumed her earlier position, chin on hand, and stared at Penelope for what seemed to her victim to be forever.

And then she began to laugh. 'Of all of my Maids you are, perhaps, the last whom I might have expected to be as discreet as I should always wish them to be. You are the youngest, the least experienced in court life of them all—but you are a woman after my own heart. You kept quiet when it was of no matter, and then you acted when it was. In that you have behaved as I would always wish to behave myself. I would like to offer you an honour similar to the Order of the Garter, but alas, since you are a woman, I do not have one to bestow on you.

'No matter. I believe that Mistress Ashley would have wished me to dismiss you at once, but that fate is reserved for Mistress Belsize. You will retain your post, and my respect, so long as you continue to maintain your discreet behaviour—which must extend to the details of this meeting with me. That is all. You may return to your usual duties, but not before you have played on the virginals for me. Music is the most soothing thing I know, and I trust that it will sooth you as it has often soothed me. Play me something merry to lighten both our hearts.'

Outside, waiting for a suitably chastened Penelope Jermaine to emerge, Kat Ashley was astonished to hear the sound of music. The tune being played was a jolly one and whether it was mistress or maid performing, she could not tell. It was not quite what she had expected at the end of a misbehaving Maid of Honour's interview with her royal mistress!

Penelope did as she was bid and told no one of what had really happened during her meeting with the Queen—not even Oliver.

'She was very much her father's daughter,' she informed him later, 'but she reserved her greatest strictures for poor Alys and her foolish behaviour.'

Now that was to say everything and yet say nothing, and had the Queen heard her, she would have known that she had discovered—and in some sense, helped to create—an apt pupil, able to behave as carefully as she had done in those difficult days when her half-sister had been Queen. Penelope was privately astonished at her own devious behaviour. She was sorry that she was unable to tell Oliver the truth, but she had promised the Queen that she would remain discreet and she always tried to keep her word, however difficult that might be.

She was even more discreet with Mary—and many others—on the evening before they all left for Whitehall Palace, when the whole court was present at a dance which was to celebrate the Queen's last night at the home which had been hers before she had inherited the Crown.

Oliver had persuaded Penelope—although she had needed little persuasion—that they ought not to pander to Castleford's desire to control them by avoiding one another. On the contrary, they should show him that they would do as they pleased and be together as often as they wished.

They danced the Galliard—but now Penelope had become used to it, and was delighted when Oliver competed with the other young men as to who could toss their partner the highest. They were all, she noted with some amusement, careful not to throw them any higher than Lord Robert threw the Queen when they danced together.

Mary had been partnering Roger Temple. Castleford had not offered to lead her out once. He had tried to reach Penelope to ask her to dance with him, but every time that he walked towards her the carefully watching Oliver had seized her hand and they had disappeared into the crowd, or into one of the anterooms filled with people busy eating and drinking. Penelope sometimes wondered how much all this entertainment was costing and where the money was coming from—particularly since a fortune was being spent on decorating the city in preparation for the Coronation.

Oliver had once told her that the Treasury was virtually empty, but no one would think so by the way money was being thrown about. There was something frantic in everyone's enjoyment. After the miserable days of Mary's reign, when there had been repeated burnings of Protestants at Smithfield and Calais had been lost, the thought that there was a new, young and handsome Queen on the throne was an invigorating one.

It was impossible to avoid Mary and Castleford for ever, though, and it was Mary who cornered them first.

'So, you are with your other cavalier tonight, I see,' she began unkindly, glaring at the pair of them rather as the Queen had glared at Penelope.

'My other cavalier?' retorted Penelope. 'So far as I know I only have one.' And she smiled at Oliver, who was content to remain silent. He thought that Penelope was well able to defend herself.

'You know perfectly well whom I mean,' was Mary's answer to that. 'Castleford has been avoiding me all night, and by his behaviour he has been trying to find you.'

'Well, I have been avoiding him—but not too successfully, I fear, for here he comes.'

It would be impossible for them to escape him this time, thought Oliver resignedly. The anteroom was too crowded and Castleford too determined to corner them.

Mary was the first to speak. 'You have come to ask me to dance the Pavan with you,' she said, turning her glare into a smile.

'No, indeed,' he told her, his manner cold. 'Not until you dismiss that follower of yours and behave yourself as a virtuous woman should. I have come to ask Mistress Penelope to honour me with her hand.'

Mary resumed her glare. It was now directed at her unloving betrothed. Penelope inclined her head, and murmured, her voice as low as she could make it so that none might overhear her.

'No, m'lord, I cannot accept your invitation, as I have told you before. Your place on the dance floor is with my sister, not with me.'

Oliver nodded his head and said, almost in a whisper, 'Bravo.'

Mary's response was to toss her head, turn her glare on Penelope and hiss, 'I do not require you to defend me, sister. I am quite capable of speaking on my own behalf.'

It took all Penelope's resolution not to say, 'But to little effect, sister, so far as I can judge.' Instead she remained silent, to hear Castleford snarl at Mary, 'I might wish to have more of your company, Madam, if your tongue was less nasty. You may leave us, and if you try to argue with me again I shall announce publicly, this very evening, that I intend to cast you off because of your loose behaviour with young Temple—so retire to your dormitory at once if you do not wish me to ruin you tonight.'

Three of the party fell silent on hearing these cruel words. Mary's glare disappeared, to be replaced by silent tears. Penelope felt so sorry for her sister that she had to stop herself from telling Castleford exactly what she thought of him and his behaviour to Mary— which would, given the Queen's recent advice, be quite the worst thing she could do.

Her head drooping, Mary walked away, compelled into apparent obedience. Castleford turned back to Penelope and, ignoring Oliver, said, 'Now will you consent to dance with me, Mistress Jermaine? As you may note I am preparing to rid myself of my encumbrance in order to make you my wife.'

The man was mad! He must be, to expect her to partner him after treating her sister so brutally. Penelope controlled herself and made the only reply she could: 'No, m'lord, I must repeat my first refusal to dance with you.'

It was Castleford's turn to glare at her. 'Oh, I see in what quarter the wind sits. It is this fellow of whom you are enamoured.' He waved at Oliver. 'Rest assured, madam, that you will not be enamoured of him long unless you do as I ask. The price of his life is your consent to marry me. I have not forgotten what I have so recently told the pair of you.'

Oliver spoke at last.

'I am constrained by the rules which govern those of us who live and work in the court from calling you to immediate account for the manner in which you have spoken to both the Jermaine sisters and to myself. I may, however, inform Lord Robert Dudley of your threats and ask him to have you banished from the precincts of the court because of your untoward behaviour.'

'And who will Lord Robert believe if you do—and I deny everything—or tell him that you threatened me first?'

'There were witnesses, m'lord. They heard what you said.'

'Two women—and what is their word worth?'

'A woman is our Queen.'

'And would that she were not. Mark you, I would deny saying that, too. And so we reach nonplus—where neither of us has the advantage.'

There was no gainsaying that, and Penelope began to understand the wisdom of the Queen in stressing the need for discretion—but discretion could not help them here. Castleford was a magnate, whose word was law wherever he went. If he did succeed in having Oliver murdered there was a faint possibility were he stupid enough to be careless and leave sufficient evidence behind, that he might be tried in the House of Lords by his peers—but who knew what their verdict might be?

Oliver, endeavouring not to surrender to Castleford's blackmail of them—for that was what it was—said, 'Nevertheless, m'lord, you have threatened us and I assure you that we shall not oblige you in any way, by obeying you as a result.'

'And does Mistress Penelope Jermaine agree with you…young fellow?'

Doubtless 'young fellow' was meant to demean Oliver, although Castleford must have thought that he had won the argument, even though Penelope did not speak, but simply took Oliver's hand and nodded agreement with him.

'So be it, then. Defy me and take the consequences.'

He strode away.

Once he had disappeared into the crowd Penelope turned to Oliver.

'No,' she said breathlessly, 'you are not to defy him. I will not have you put your life in danger by continuing to be seen with me. We must part, if only for a time until this wretched business has ended.'

'That would mean he wins twice over—he disgraces your sister and deprives us of one another.'

'Better to give way to him, than that you should lose your life. Chance may give us the opportunity to turn the tables on him—or in his mad pride he may do something stupid and play into our hands, as the gamblers say. Until then, let us be discreet. We may contrive to meet in private, but must avoid one another in public.'

She was talking sense, he knew she was, but a great fear overcame Oliver—not for his own safety, but a fear of losing Penelope, possibly to another man. He had never thought that a woman would come to mean so much to him. There was also the worry that if Castleford succeeded in ridding himself of Mary and offered to marry her sister instead, her parents would use their power over her to compel her to accept him.

He wanted to lift her up and carry her away, to discover a place to hide where Castleford could not find them; but this was the stuff of fairy tales, or of the romances of Boccaccio which he had read in Italy: behaviour which would not be possible in the harsh world of Elizabeth's England.

'I would not give you up,' he said fiercely, 'not for a king's ransom.'

'Nor shall you. Think: this may only be for a little while.'

'Little or long, it is too much.'

There was one thing of which Penelope could not tell him: her conversation with the Queen. The Queen trusted her, and if Castleford were stupid enough to do anything which she could take to the Queen as direct evidence of his villainy, she thought that the Queen would believe her and move against him.

It was a faint hope, if hope it were, but, bound by her promise to Her Grace, she could not tell Oliver anything of this.

Oliver saw Penelope's face working. He longed to take her in his arms and kiss away her troubles, but that was a foolish thought, too, here in this room where none were private. No, she had the right of it.

They ought to appear to give way to Castleford's demands—except that Oliver had learned enough from his time abroad in Europe's courts, and now his stay in England's, that even if they obeyed him and seemed to part, Castleford would yet contrive to have him killed.

'Dead men tell no tales,' the proverb said, and Castleford might feel safer if Oliver Woodville did not walk the earth.

'Sweeting,' he said softly, 'I hear you and I will obey you, I would not have you live in fear for me. Trust me, in one way or another we shall contrive to meet. I would not have him destroy everything which lies between us.'

'Nor I, but we must not be foolish. If, in her youth, the Queen could walk a narrow path to save herself from ruin then we must be able to do the same. I shall leave you now—and you must not follow me.'

The parting smile Penelope gave him was bittersweet. With it she offered him a light curtsey and walked away, to be lost in the richly dressed crowd, to become someone whom he might see only in passing, and if it were breaking his heart, then she, by her expression when she left him, was breaking hers.

Chapter Nine

It was the hardest thing that she had ever done. To send Oliver away, to part from him, was like losing her second self. The only thing which gave her any form of consolation was that if she had agreed to join him in defying Castleford she might be in danger of losing him for ever, instead of for just a short time. It was a faint hope, for, like Oliver, she feared Castleford's spite, and that even parting from him was no guarantee that his life would be saved.

Unhappily, they were both right. Castleford's rage at the sight of them together was such that, even though he saw Penelope walking alone into the room where dancing had begun again, he determined that if he could not have her, then Woodville should not. His first effort at disposing of him had failed, but a second attempt might be more successful.

As for Mary Jermaine, he would have her watched by Bevis in the hope that he might find some evidence

which would enable him to cast her off. Even when
Woodville entered the ballroom and made no effort
to join Penelope, his anger was not abated. It was too
late. They should have done as he wished when he
had first threatened them.

It was, perhaps, fortunate for the lovers that the
business of moving the court to Whitehall Palace was
such an overwhelming task that they had little time
to think of anything else. They were to spend
Christmas there and preparations for the final festivities were already in train.

Alys had been sent home, and it was to be expected
that it would be the last that they heard of her.
Penelope missed her. Until she had become with child
there had been a sweet-natured gaiety about her such
as Penelope had never before encountered. In truth,
she was the first woman friend whom she had ever
had.

She had said as much to Oliver immediately after
he had joined her in helping Alys.

'I am so sorry that I shall probably never know
what happens to her and Jack's child, and that he will
never know that he is to become a father.'

Oliver had said nothing to her at the time, but on
the afternoon of the day they arrived at Whitehall
Palace she found that someone had thrust a letter into
the bag in which she kept her embroidery silks.

It was from Oliver.

In it he told her that he had written to Jack of
Alys's illness, that she was with child, presumably by

him, and had been sent home. 'I thought that he ought to know,' he had ended. And then, 'I miss you.'

That was all.

It had to be enough: any pleasure which Penelope might have felt at the celebration of Christmas and the coming Coronation was quite diminished. At first Mary refused to speak to her. She walked by with her nose in the air: gossip had it that Roger Temple was greatly distressed because she had broken with him. Could that be true, or were he and Mary dissembling as she and Oliver were? She wondered where he was and what he was doing.

Oliver was hard at work. Dissembling, both with Penelope and his fellow courtiers, seemed to have become a major part of his life and thoughts, and the Christmas celebrations, to which he had looked forward, had lost their attraction for him now that he could no longer share them with her.

In the middle of all this, on the court's first day at Whitehall Dr Dee arrived. He had completed the Queen's horoscope, and had also decided on the most propitious date for her Coronation.

Oliver was amused to find that Dee was greeted by Lord Robert almost as though he were the Ambassador of a foreign power. Before the party got down to the main business of the day, compliments were exchanged on both sides. Dee was asked when he had last broken his fast and on his answering that it had been early that morning, food and drink were brought in and the whole company engaged in idle conversation.

By now Oliver was cynical enough to grasp that this show of concern was an attempt to loosen Dee's tongue, but, if so, it was a failure. Dee ate and drank sparingly. He was talking to Sir Alaric when, looking over his shoulder, he saw Oliver and motioned with his hand for him to come over to them.

Oliver, remembering Lord Robert's instruction, obeyed him immediately. Dee continued his conversation with Sir Alaric for some minutes before turning to Oliver and saying, 'Ah, the young man with the secret enemy. How fare you, sir? Has he yet moved against you?'

'He may have done, but so far I've no real evidence of anything untoward,' was Oliver's answer. 'But if you have any further news for me of who he is and how he is likely to act, I should be most grateful if you would tell me of it.'

Dee shook his handsome head. 'Alas, my spirits are silent on that point. In this case it is his intent of which they speak—his identity they have not revealed.'

Oliver pounced on this answer, but kept his outward manner cool. 'But that is further news, Doctor Dee, is it not? For you have told me that it is a man I must fear and not a woman, which certainly lessens the number of persons of whom I must be wary.'

Sir Alaric, who did not share the common view that Dee possessed remarkable powers, believing that his conjuring extended only to the artful juggling of words rather than to the calling up of spirits, smirked behind his hand at this. He unknowingly echoed Lord Robert's view that Master Oliver Woodville was a shrewd fellow, fit for advancement.

Dee was not daunted by Oliver's remark. He smiled mysteriously, shook his head, and said, 'You must understand that there is undoubtedly a powerful reason why my spirits have decided that you are not to have further information: a reason which may be as good as it appears to be bad.'

'I am most happy to hear that,' replied Oliver, speaking in a double tongue which had Sir Alaric privately amused again. He decided not to bait Dee further, since he was more than ever convinced that Dee's original prophecy to him had been made on the basis that all men and women at court had secret enemies so it was quite safe for him to make such a statement.

In any case Dee had finished with him, the light meal had ended, too, and the company rapidly proceeded to the main business of the meeting, which was to learn of Dee's proposed date for the Queen's Coronation based on the position of the stars on that day. It was, he told them, 15 January, and so he would inform the Queen on the morrow.

The only problem with Dee's date—which the Queen immediately accepted—was that it was so soon that all the preparations for it had to go ahead faster than ever. The sempstresses, tailors, and cobblers making the elaborate robes for the Queen and her court, and all those who were arranging the various processions involved, as well as making sure that Westminster Abbey was suitably decorated so that the actual ceremony would be of the utmost splendour, were hard put to finish their work in time.

Cecil privately grumbled at the cost of it all, though conceding that it was necessary if the world was to be convinced that Elizabeth would be a great and worthy sovereign. Lord Robert, on the other hand, was even more determined than the Queen that everything should be as fine and expensive as possible. He and his men were to be equipped and accoutred in a manner fit for the installation of a potent monarch.

Elizabeth was setting a good example to her subjects in beginning her reign by working harder than any of her predecessors. She consulted her ministers and advisers daily. It was, she told Cecil privately, necessary for her to learn the art of being a good ruler as soon as possible if she were to be successful in achieving her dream of making England a great power again. It was this as much as her dislike of his Catholicism which was making her refuse to accept King Philip of Spain's proposal. If she were to marry him England's interests would inevitably become subordinate to those of the great Spanish Empire.

Her firm conviction that this ultimate goal would not be accomplished if the internal religious war be-

tween Catholic and Protestant was not resolved by
one means or another was so strong that it influenced
the lives of all her subjects. Her determination that
England should be efficiently ruled meant that she
insisted that all her ministers and immediate attendants should work as hard as she did.

So it was that after yet another long day with Lord
Robert, who was becoming more and more demanding the nearer the Coronation loomed, Oliver found
it tedious to dress himself in his finery to spend another evening without Penelope, even if it was
Christmas Eve. Nevertheless he was expected, as one
of Lord Robert's most trusted men, to make an appearance at the evening's frolics.

Only duty saw him putting on his best black and
silver Italian suit. He had discarded his large cartwheel ruff in favour of a small oval one because he
found it less constricting when he was dancing—not
that, without Penelope, he intended to do much of
that. Gib had come in to help him dress, and if he
noted the lack of enthusiasm which his master was
showing by delaying his preparations for the evening
until all the other gentlemen had left, he made no
comment on his master's unusual behaviour.

He was ready at last, looking as fine as he had done
in Italy where all the ladies had made a great fuss of
the handsome man from far-off England, but not feeling at all as happy. To compensate for the fact that
he had been somewhat short with the faithful Gib, he

pressed a groat into his hand and made for the grand stairway.

He was so late that no one was about. He had just reached the turn of the stairs when he thought that he heard someone behind him, but before he could look to see who it might be he felt a hand on his back give him a violent shove.

His balance suddenly, and surprisingly, gone, Oliver began to fall. To save himself he clutched at one of the elaborately wrought wooden banisters, but unfortunately he could only break his fall a little, not prevent it. Down he went, arriving at the bottom half-stunned, to lie there for a moment before he recovered enough to wonder whether he had Castleford to thank for this attempt to kill him. Only chance—or luck— had saved him from a broken neck or back.

Whether he had broken any other limbs he had yet to find out.

It was in the middle of the celebrations that evening, when the Great Hall had been cleared after supper and boisterous games were being played, that Mary at last came over to speak to Penelope. The company was engaged in one of the most riotous games of them all, called Hoodman Blind, known to the commonalty as Blind Man's Buff. It was a game which Penelope thought was merely an excuse for men and women to romp amorously together in a public place after a manner usually forbidden to them.

'A word with you, sister, if you please,' Mary demanded in her most domineering manner.

Or even if I don't please, no doubt! But Penelope said aloud, 'If that is what you wish.'

Mary sniffed. 'Have you noticed that that nasty little creature, Bevis Frampton has been following me around? I keep meeting him in the oddest places. Has he been troubling you? Or Oliver?'

'I haven't seen him lately, no. I had heard that he's no longer part of Lord Castleford's retinue.'

'Whether he is or not, I fear that he may be trying to get back into favour with his late master again by following me. I have written to Father and Mother begging them to release me from my betrothal to Castleford. I have now no wish to marry him. I deeply regret that I sent Oliver away when he returned from Europe, but since he has become so obsessed with you I doubt whether he will want me back—although I haven't seen you with him since we left Somerset House. Besides, I have Roger now. We are meeting secretly so that Castleford may not have an excuse to cast me off, before I rid myself of him. I have not been feeling so ill lately and have received no more warning letters.'

Well, that was frank, was it not? Her appointment as one of the Queen's Ladies in Waiting had only served to increase Mary's belief that everything in the world should be subject to her whims and fancies. To find, quite suddenly, that life was not so obliging as she might have hoped, had soured a temper which had never been very sweet.

Her manner to Penelope had consequently become more poisonous than ever. 'Has your cavalier acquired a new sweetheart?' she asked nastily. 'He doesn't seem to be here tonight. I wonder if he is sighing over another fair one somewhere else. I'm told that many of the younger men are celebrating Christmas in the City. They find the royal celebrations a little lacking in spice.'

'I've no notion where he is,' said Penelope, trying not to sound disappointed, 'but for the last two days our duties have kept us so busy that we have not found time to do anything else.'

Mary's answer to that was, 'Pish,' and 'I must not stay here gossiping with you any longer, Castleford would not like it and while I care nothing for his opinion I have no wish to cross him more than I need.'

While they had been talking a commotion had occurred that was even noisier than the game of Hoodman Blind, which showed no sign of drawing to an end.

Roger Temple had just entered and was talking urgently to Lord Robert, who rose from his seat by the Queen after speaking to her for a moment. He and several of his followers—except for Roger—left the chamber, but not before the possible cause of the excitement had stirred speculation and debate.

'Something must be wrong,' Mary said. 'I wonder what it is?'

Penelope was struck by a sudden dreadful thought. Oliver was not present at the party, which, as one of Lord Robert's men, he had undoubtedly been ordered to attend. Was it possible that Lord Castleford had carried out his threat to kill him—or was she starting at shadows?

Mary might not wish to be seen with Roger Temple, but there was no reason why she should not ask him what all the fuss was about. Penelope liked Roger, who was one of the kinder young men about the court, and thought that he would make a better husband for Mary than Castleford.

Roger, for his part, liked Penelope. He thought that Oliver Woodville was a lucky fellow to have gained her affection, and his pursuit of Mary was partly because she was Penelope's sister. Tonight Penelope, although more richly dressed than he had ever seen her before, had been looking worried—but he had put that down to Oliver's absence.

And now he had news for her which would only serve to deepen her troubled expression. Before she could ask him what was wrong, he gently took her by the arm and drew her to one side.

'I am sorry to be the bearer of ill tidings,' he said, 'but there is nothing for it. A few moments ago I found Master Woodville lying dazed at the bottom of the main staircase.

'No,' he exclaimed, when Penelope put her hand

before her mouth to stifle a cry, 'do not fear the worst. By the mercy of God when he became fully conscious it was plain that he has not been badly injured. He has no broken bones, but is merely shaken and heavily bruised. It seems that he broke his fall by catching at the banisters on the way down. The physician has been sent for, although there is not much which he can do for him, other than prescribe a soothing potion.

'I will tell you the truth of the matter because I believe you to be discreet and that you will neither tattle nor gossip to others of what Oliver told me. He said that his fall was not an accident. He was, without warning, struck hard from behind at the turn of the stairs. Of course, there was no one about when I found him immediately after his fall.

'This is a grievous business, because Master Woodville is not a man to engage in fantasies. Although he does not wish, at the moment, for Lord Robert, or the Queen, to be told that his fall might be the result of an attack, they ought to be informed of his accident immediately. Lord Robert has gone to interview him—he is famous for taking great care of all his men.'

It was Castleford—or one of his men—who had done this, of course it was, but Penelope could not say so. She tried not to do anything foolish like faint or scream, but could not prevent herself from shivering.

'Come,' said Roger, who could see how distressed

she was, although she was valiantly trying not to show it. 'Sit down and I will fetch your sister to look after you.'

Penelope began to say, 'No,' for the last person she wanted with her was Mary, but she could not say so to kind Roger. Fortunately Mary had disappeared into the mêlé around the game of Hoodman Blind and it was Janet Saville whom he brought over to her.

'Master Temple tells me that you are distressed because Master Woodville has had a bruising fall down the main staircase. He says that you are not to worry overmuch and that he will bring us a draught of sack—white wine is a great restorative.'

'You are both being very kind,' said Penelope gratefully, 'seeing that I am being rather foolish.'

'By no means,' Janet told her. 'It is only natural that you should be distressed at harm coming to Master Woodville. I believe that you have known him since you were children together.'

Penelope nodded agreement and when Roger arrived with the sack drank it gratefully, even though the shivering fit which had overcome her had ended. Lord Robert had returned to his seat by the Queen and was laughing and talking with her, which did not please—for a variety of different reasons—a large number of those present.

It was quite plain to Penelope that Roger had not told Janet that Oliver had been deliberately pushed down the stairs, nor had he said anything of it to Mary, who came up to her a little later, loudly commiserating with her on Oliver's fall. She wondered whether Oliver had told Roger of Castleford's threats, which made it very possible that he was responsible for the attack on him—but she thought that that was most unlikely. By one means or another she must contrive to meet him soon. She could not bear to think of him being alone and hurt.

A little later, after Roger had persuaded her to join in one of the country dances which were being played, Oliver came in. His face was grey above his fine new black and silver suit, which had long-paned breeches reaching to just below the knee. He told her later how fortunate it had been that he had decided to wear not his new large cartwheel ruff, but a little oval one—to which he attributed his ability to break his fall: the cartwheel one would have made it impossible.

By then most of the court, including the Queen, knew of his accident, and that he had been ordered to tell her of it in person since it had taken place on royal premises, where anyone convicted of causing injury or death was almost certain to be tried and executed. On his way to where she sat, still talking animatedly to Lord Robert, Oliver came near enough to Penelope for her to see the great bruise on his forehead which had caused his confusion after his fall and which had made him unable to move for some little time after it.

Oliver himself was painfully aware of the excitement his mishap had caused. He had not told Roger who he suspected of attacking him, but the question he now had to ask himself was, ought he to tell the Queen the truth—that he had been pushed?

He could only imagine the excitement which that blunt statement would cause, whereas if he merely said that he must have stumbled, little would follow: the whole incident would be a mere ten minutes' wonder. It was useless for him to wish that he had recovered his senses earlier and returned to his quarters before Roger had found him, so that no one would have known of his misadventure.

Too late to worry about that now. He bowed to Her Grace and, having decided that he would shade the truth rather than tell a direct lie, said, in response to her kind enquiry as to how his accident could have happened, 'Alas, madam, I fell into a stupor when I reached the bottom of the staircase and I was so fuddled when I recovered from it that I have no clear understanding of how I came to find myself there. I only knew that everything happened very suddenly.'

He thanked God that the Queen seemed to accept this as a reasonable explanation.

'And do you feel fully recovered now, Master Woodville?'

'Not quite,' he told her, relieved that this time he could offer her the complete truth, 'I am still somewhat disturbed in my mind and body but the physician has assured me that it will soon pass and that I shall be able to fulfil my duties in the morning.'

'I am well pleased to hear that, Master Woodville.

Lord Robert tells me that you are a hard and willing worker and I should not like to lose your services when there is still so much to do before I am crowned.'

Well, that was good news at any rate, although not quite worth being pushed downstairs to find out! What he really wanted to do was to talk to Penelope as soon as possible and assure her that he was not severely injured.

Instead the Queen kept him for several minutes more, asking him about his tour of Europe. She ended by saying, 'I would dearly like to embark on such a trip myself one day, but unless my royal duties make it diplomatically possible, it is sure to be denied me.' After which she offered him her shapely royal hand to kiss. It was as trim and orderly as the rest of her person, and the gems on it were as dazzling as the many others which she was sporting, on her head, in her ears, around her neck and dangling from her waist.

And that was the paraph, the formal signing off which ended an interview as a letter was similarly concluded with both a written and a pictorial flourish. He bowed again, backed away and looked around for Penelope—and to hell with Lord Castleford and his warnings: he had survived two attempts on his life and, by God, he'd be damned if the wretch's threats would stop him from talking publicly to the woman he loved.

There she was with Janet Saville, her face as pale

as his, and God be thanked that her vinegar-faced
sister was not with her. It was not his usual practice
to use the Deity's name so often and so carelessly,
but his first dull reaction to what had almost been
done to him had been succeeded by a fierce determination not to allow such a cur as Castleford to rule
his life.

By the time he reached Penelope he was in a fine
old state of boiling rage, so that when she murmured,
'Oh, Oliver, I am so happy to see you are able to
attend the festivities tonight after surviving such a
dreadful accident,' he growled at her, 'No accident,
alas, and no thanks to Castleford. I was deliberately
pushed down the stairs—and who could have done it
but either he or one of his minions? I have told no
one but you and Roger Temple that it was not an
accident.'

Castleford had tried to kill him and, thanks be to
God, he had failed, but he would almost certainly try
again.

'But why?' she exclaimed. 'We have been avoiding
each other ever since he threatened us.'

'Dear heart,' he said, and however much it sad-
dened him that her colour had fled and her lips had
begun to tremble after he had finished speaking he
could not help but be happy that they were the outward and visible signs that she loved him, 'they were
but a few days lost. Nevertheless it shows us that
however we behave, whether we meet or not, he
means to kill me. That being so, why should we avoid

one another? Let us capture the fleeting hour together and defy both him and chance. By attacking me so soon he has made it possible for us to be together again, for there is little point in our remaining apart if I am still in danger if we are apart.'

'But that is sophistry,' Penelope said, 'not truth, merely a semblance of it—and yet…and yet…'

'And yet,' finished Oliver for her, 'let us enjoy the time we may share if we ignore his threats and thank the kind gods that I have survived so that we might find one another again. Come with me, I know a place where we may be secret and need fear neither Castleford nor interruption.'

'Yes!' began Penelope joyfully, and then she was stricken with a memory of Alys lying white-faced and betrayed on the bed. 'But we must be discreet, not fall from one peril into another.'

Oliver took her meaning. 'Sweeting, much though I wish to be your true lover, yet I will be careful with you. I would not have you end as Alys has done. I love you too much for that.'

So he, too, had thought of Alys. Very well, she would do as he wished and what would happen, would happen. She *must* trust him, because if she could not, then that might mean that she did not truly love him. Oh, what with their love, and the danger which it had brought them, it was enough to turn a poor girl's brain! She, who had never thought that a man would find her lovable, was now being pursued by two men: one a man of honour and the other, his opposite! It was Mary, the admired sister, the pride of her mother and father, who was alone and rejected.

If the latter thought gave her no pleasure and even the first one was bitter-sweet because of Castleford's wickedness, she still had Oliver—and must pray that her trust in him was not misplaced. So thinking, she took his offered hand and left the room with him. Another boisterous game of Hide and Seek had begun and no one but Bevis Frampton, standing half-hidden in an alcove, saw them go, secretly following them to discover what their destination might be.

The room which Oliver had found was small and away from the main galleries, and like the one which Alys and Jack had used was part of an unused connecting suite. It was called the Flemish Room because there were Flemish tapestries on the walls showing incidents in the life of Odysseus. A round table with a tessellated top stood in its centre, and a black and gold lacquered cabinet, and a settle placed beneath the tapestry depicting Odysseus's temptation by the nymph Calypso on her island, made up the rest of its furnishings.

'Oh, it's beautiful,' breathed Penelope when they entered. It was quite unlike the squalid scene of poor Alys's seduction. 'Does no one know of it?'

'Apparently not,' Oliver told her, leading her to the settle where they sat down, side by side. 'It is not near to any of the state rooms. I found it quite by accident yesterday when we arrived here: one of the footmen told me that its small size means that it is rarely used. Most people are enjoying the revels too much to want to desert them.'

Penelope thought of the huge rooms where she had spent the day. Rooms so large that the frescos Holbein had painted of the late King Henry VIII and his family were giant things. They were all quite unlike this quiet bower. The only thing that troubled her was whether she would be able to resist Oliver if he wished to take her into the realms of love which Jack and Alys—and possibly her sister Mary—had wandered into.

She turned her great shining eyes on him—and nearly undid all of Oliver's virtuous resolutions. He had told himself that when he and Penelope were at last far away from the noise and bustle of the court, this beautiful room and its holy quiet would serve to keep him from temptation, from doing with Penelope what he so longed to do: make love to her.

Alas for him: she seemed to grow more attractive every day. The shy girl whom he had met when he had first returned from his travels was gradually turning into a beauty beyond compare. He could only wonder that she had chosen him from all the young men around the Queen to give her heart to.

He said hoarsely, 'Oh, Penelope, you are temptation itself. Give me one kiss, but one kiss, and make me so eternally happy that I shall not pursue you further, lest I dishonour you.'

She could not refuse him. She turned her face towards him, shining with the innocence which even finding Jack and Alys together had not breached. He took it into his two hands and kissed her gently on the mouth, even though his whole body was quivering with desire to do more. To behave himself was to court discomfort, but behave himself he would.

The tender kiss with which he began was rapidly transformed. The charming eagerness with which Penelope at first received it changed into something much more passionate. When at last he lifted his mouth away, she gave a little moan of sheer delight, which merely served to fuel his passion the more, particularly when she put up her hands to pull his head down so that he might kiss her again. Despite his determination to go slowly with her, he found it impossible to refuse to satisfy her wishes, and he immediately found her lips again, aye and her tongue which he stroked with his when he had coaxed her mouth open so that he might enjoy her the more.

What Oliver did not quite understand was that to the novice in love which Penelope was, the reaction of her own body, of her own senses, was both strong and surprising. The second kiss, so satisfactory at first by reason of its increased passion, suddenly became not enough; during it her whole body had shivered with a previously unknown delight. Yet she wanted more than that, more of him, but what that more was, she did not know. Afterwards, when they had parted, she remembered her brief sight of Jack and Alys's bodies intertwined on the bed and understood that they had wanted—and achieved—whatever it was that she, unknowingly, had also desired.

Once the kiss had ended Oliver did not take his head away as he had done the first time. Instead he transferred his attention to her neck, kissing his way slowly up the right side of it to her ear—which he nibbled at gently, so that her whole body quivered and throbbed with delight.

Oliver was the first to pull away again—it was one of the hardest things that he had ever done, but to go on would be to risk both their honours, for he might find himself unable to stop. Already his own body was crying out for fulfillment and its being denied was causing him physical pain. His love was a virgin and he must not defile her virginity: to do so would mean that he was acting through mere lust, not true love.

'No,' he said hoarsely. 'No more, not now. We have defied the devil who seeks to destroy us and that must be enough.'

Penelope, her eyes dazed, her mouth swollen and her body one vast ache beneath its stiff and formal clothing, murmured, 'Oh, I had not thought that a kiss could be so sweet.'

This straightforward expression of her pleasure almost unmanned Oliver, but pride in his honour kept him resolute. He, too, had memories of poor desperate Alys and he would try not to do anything which would reduce Penelope to the ruin to which love had led her.

'We must not stay longer,' he told her. 'Lest some-one else comes and finds our version of Arcadia—and discovers us enjoying it.'

Penelope understood what he was saying to her of Arcadia—that magic and innocent land where only happy beings dwelt, and nodded her head. Hand in hand they left the Flemish Room, where the lovers knew at last that they were truly meant to be one—but might not yet achieve that blessed state.

Oliver's supposed accident created little of a stir after the first news of it. The courtiers were too busy exhausting themselves by playing and dancing until long after the midnight hour had struck. On the other hand there were those who learned of it and became immediately thoughtful. One of them was the Queen's Secretary of State, Master Cecil. Early on Christmas Day Oliver encountered him by chance—or was it by chance?—on his way to Lord Robert's rooms.

'Well met, young Woodville. I am of a mind to have words with you,' said the great man. 'I hear that you have had an accident from which, fortunately, you suffered no lasting harm. I had no notion that the front stairs were so dangerous: not dangerous enough to kill you, but that was your great good luck, I am sure,' and he beamed benevolently at his hearer.

Now what in Hades is all this about? wondered Oliver. He was about to speak when Cecil leaned forward and said confidentially, 'Good luck follows you round, it seems. There was that business of Jack

Chancellor being attacked in the City when he was wearing your cloak. Fate was kind, I take it, that you were not the one carousing on the town that night.'

He leaned forward confidentially, wagging a finger at Oliver. 'The adage has it that similar events come in threes—I would not dare to wager what piece of great good luck will save your life next time.'

Oliver tried to look bewildered—which did not deceive the great man at all. 'Oh, I dare swear, sir, that the two events were not connected.'

'Dare you? I think that you dare a lot. I gather that Dee told you that you were to beware of a secret enemy—now who may that be?'

'Since the enemy is secret I know not his name. I believe that the good doctor was drawing a bow at random.'

A shrewd young man, then, as many said. 'Besides that, I wonder whether you have thought of what I asked you—about keeping your eyes and ears open to detect Her Grace's enemies. Could your man be also one of her secret enemies?'

A new problem for Oliver! Should he tell Cecil that it was Castleford who wished to kill him—and that because of a woman, and not the secrets of the State. On the other hand he could set Cecil on Castleford and perhaps lose an enemy in doing so, by telling him the gossip that Castleford was plotting with Feria over a Spanish marriage. Except that Cecil probably knew of it already.

No, he would keep quiet and indulge in a little

more verbal fencing. 'If I were to hear—or over-hear—aught which might damage the security of our realm, then I would, of course, inform you of it at once, sir. I had heard that the Spanish Ambassador was not best pleased that he had not been given lodgings in the palace of Whitehall as he had expected—but I believe that you must have been made aware of his dissatisfaction already.'

'Well spoken,' was Cecil's answer to that—and why, he thought, was he sure that the handsome young man before him was not betraying everything he knew. He was certain, from what his informants had told him, that it might be Castleford who was behind the attempts on young Woodville's life, but not, they believed, because of any plotting either of them were engaged in. Some complication over the Jermaine sisters was the problem.

It was, he conceded wryly, rare to meet a young man of such discretion. Oh yes, Master Woodville had an old head on his shoulders and would go far in life if he continued as he had begun.

Oliver had bowed in recognition of what he thought were Cecil's last words, but they were not quite the last, for, 'Remember me to your father when you next write to, or see him,' he ended. 'You may tell him that Lord Robert Dudley is not the only man who thinks highly of you and your undoubted abilities.'

So someone had informed Cecil that his fall was not an accident, and even before that the shrewd fox—or one of his spies—had told him of the likeli-

hood that Jack had been attacked by mistake. The
court was similar in nature to a collection of vast spider's webs and a man had to be careful lest, like the
fly, he became entangled and dying in their filaments,
the prey of the creatures who had spun them.

Christmas Day at Whitehall Palace, once the service in the Royal Chapel had ended, was the merriest
it had been for many years. No one would ever have
called the late Queen merry, and her predecessor and
half-brother, King Edward VI, had not lived long
enough to stamp his authority on his reign.

The Palace had been decorated with boughs of
holly, ivy and laurel; the Yule Log had been brought
in; there was food and drink in abundance and music
reigned everywhere. The new Queen's passion for it
was as great as that of her father. He had been a
skilled performer who had composed his own music
and the words which often went with it.

Even Christmas Day, however, could not stop the
bickering which went on among the different religious factions. The Archbishop of York had refused
to crown the Queen because of her leanings towards
Protestantism, and it was only with the greatest mis-
givings that Bishop Oglethorpe of Carlisle agreed to
officiate in his place. Not only that, but the gossips
were given something to chew over when the Bishop
refused to accept the Queen's orders that he was not
to elevate the host: as a consequence of which she
walked out of the Mass once the Gospel had ended,

taking her retinue with her in order to show her displeasure.

Not that that was allowed to diminish, or mar, the
day's merriment, but there was something feverish
about it, Oliver thought. It was as though many feared
that the long and murderous years which had elapsed
since King Henry VIII had broken with Rome had
not yet ended, but might continue into the new reign,
so that one ought to take one's pleasure while one
could.

In the afternoon, after a long and lavish dinner
which had Master Cecil secretly lamenting the cost
of this whole wretched business, country dancing began instead of those stately measures which the court
usually favoured.

Penelope, seated in one of the windows, watched
the Queen take Lord Robert on to the floor of the
Presence Chamber to be followed by half the court,
including her sister Mary and Roger Temple, now her
constant companion. Fortunately Castleford did not
appear to be present, which meant that she would not
suffer from his unwanted advances.

To her great joy Oliver came over to her, his hand
extended, saying formally, 'Mistress Jermaine, will
you do me the honour of joining me in the dance?'

'With pleasure, Master Woodville,' and they
walked on to the floor to join in dancing—or more
accurately, romping—Sellenger's Round to the music
of psalter, pipes, drums, a harp and a clavichord.
Penelope had seen boisterous Christmas celebrations

before, but nothing quite so wild as this one which was being held in a palace. She was quite out of breath once the music ended, but not so much that she could not gasp her thanks to Oliver for asking her to join him.

'A drink, then,' he ordered, 'so that you shall be ready to sport with me again—in our little refuge, perhaps.'

Penelope, her eyes shining, agreed to that, too, and joined the rest of the men and women celebrating the birth of Christ in a stable by enjoying themselves in a Palace—as she remarked to Oliver once they had taken their goblets of sack and walked towards the hearth where the Yule Log, or one of its successors, was still burning.

They toasted the Log, Christmas and the coming Coronation before they slipped away to the Flemish Room, to celebrate in their own way—although Penelope's chastity and Oliver's resolution not to breach it were to be sorely tested.

Upstairs Lord Castleford was being dressed by his valet, Jenkins. He had drunk too freely on Christmas Eve, and almost worse than that, he was feeling unhappy because Oliver Woodville still walked the earth. The man must have the luck of the devil to survive not one, but two, attempts on his life—he would have to make sure that the third would prove more successful. Once he was gone for good, then

Penelope Jermaine would find it difficult to resist his advances.

He had already written to her parents asking that she should replace Mary as his bride, since he much preferred her to her elder sister. He would be only too happy to agree to a somewhat diminished dower for Penelope in order to appease any anger they might feel over Mary's rejection. Besides, once they learned that that ass, Temple, was after her, they would find a fair exchange to be no robbery, or so he hoped.

He had just sent his man away and was preparing to leave to join in the Christmas games when a man entered by the door to the backstairs and whined, 'M'lord,' at him.

'You,' he exclaimed, 'what are you doing here? I thought that I had turned you off.'

'A mistake, m'lord, don't you think?' riposted his unwanted guest. 'I wouldn't have made the mistakes over young Woodville which the fools you employed did.'

That this was true annoyed Castleford more than a little.

'Nevertheless, I have done with you. Be off,' he ordered brusquely.

'Oh, no, you haven't,' snarled his intruder. He moved forward, raised the dagger which he had been hiding behind his back, and drove it upward into Castleford's heart after the fashion he had learned in Italy.

Castleford dropped like a stone, the dagger still in him.

His murderer laughed down at him. 'No one takes me lightly, you fool,' he said triumphantly, which was Castleford's only true epitaph.

And then he left, by the door through which he had come.

Chapter Ten

By the time that Oliver and Penelope returned from the Flemish Room the court was playing Blind Man's Buff again—although many of the older, more sober and weary, servants of the Queen had adjourned to smaller rooms in order to play at cards and dice. The Queen herself, together with her Maids of Honour and most of the younger courtiers, was enjoying to the full the beginning of the Twelve Days celebrations.

It was shortly after they had finished playing Blind Man's Buff that Whitehall Palace saw a repetition of the drama of the night before, although at first the news was kept hidden from the revellers when Castleford's agitated valet approached Master Cecil and began talking rapidly to him.

One of William Cecil's great accomplishments was that he rarely allowed any emotion he might feel to write itself on his face. He remained expressionless while he thanked the valet before slowly making his way to where his royal mistress sat. Once there he bowed and spoke solemnly to her. Like him the Queen's manner gave no hint of the gravity of that which she was hearing.

'I have sad news for Your Grace, I fear. The fellow who has just spoken to me is—or rather was—Lord Castleford's valet. He told me that he believed that Lord Castleford had joined the Christmas celebrations some time ago, but when, a moment since, he went to his room to work there he discovered that his master was lying dead on the floor, a dagger in his heart. I have told him to say nothing to anyone of this until I give him permission.'

Elizabeth nodded her head and said, 'I commend you, Master Cecil, for your common sense. It would not be well done to bruit his death—or rather his murder—abroad in the midst of our Christmas celebrations. If you can find any way in which this sad news can be delayed from becoming known until tomorrow I shall be eternally grateful to you.'

'That is my feeling, too, Your Grace. I shall send the valet back to his room with one of my most reliable men, who will begin the work of trying to discover who has done this foul deed and who will arrange matters so that Castleford's servants do not leave his rooms until morning.'

The Queen nodded again, as though they were having some kind of gossiping conversation. 'You may take any action you please. I know that you will always do what is for the best for me and my country.

Neither of us wants or needs a scandal of this nature to mar Christmas Day.'

Cecil bowed. 'I must leave you for a little while I arrange matters, but I shall return as soon as possible. Gossip we shall have in plenty on the morrow, but we must avoid it today.'

'Stabbed to death in the Italian mode, with the blade entering upwards,' said the burly man, one Jasper Morton, who had gone upstairs with the valet to inspect the body. Fortunately the valet had not touched it. He pulled from Castleford's breast the dagger which had killed him and was inspecting it carefully. It was a finely made long-bladed stiletto with a tiny lion's head on the end of its hilt.

'The dagger was made in Italy, too,' he announced to the white-faced servant. 'Have you ever seen it before?'

'No, sir. M'lord was not a great lover of weapons.'

The burly man looked keenly at him. 'It is not his then? His murderer brought it here, intending to kill him with it? Had he any enemies, look you? Anyone who might have wished to murder him?'

The valet, still dazed by finding his master dead, shook his head.

'Oh, all men have enemies, sir, but few wish to kill them after such a fashion. Except,' and then he stopped, 'I see no harm, sir, in telling you this, but he was not fond of Master Oliver Woodville, one of Lord Robert Dudley's men. The servants' gossip was that they had a private violent encounter which m'lord lost—something to do with the sister of the lady to whom he was betrothed. After that he is supposed to have sworn that Master Woodville would pay for his presumption.

'For the truth of the matter I suggest that you might speak to Master Bevis Frampton, one of the gentlemen about the court. He was m'lord's man until he turned him off recently, and might know something which would help you.'

'Um... Turned him off, did he? Could Master Frampton hold a grievance against him?'

The valet laughed. 'So strong as to murder him? Lord no, sir. He's a little sprat of a man, humble as you please, wouldn't hurt a fly. Master Woodville, now, is a powerful fellow. He has lately been travelling in Italy, they say.'

'And the dagger is Italian.' The burly man was thinking of a recent saying, 'An Englishman Italianate is the devil incarnate.' Could it be that Master Woodville had turned into a devil incarnate? It would not hurt to question him—and Frampton—in the morning.

'I do not mean to accuse Master Woodville,' said the valet, suddenly anxious. 'I know nought to his discredit. Twas but gossip I spoke of.'

'But gossip can be useful,' smiled the burly man. 'Do not fret yourself overmuch. I shall be questioning many. Be sure of that.'

He was lying. The only two whom he might wish

to question so far were the two of whom the valet had spoken. His master wanted this matter over and done with quickly and, God willing, one or the other of them might be able to provide him with that requirement.

Morning came and Master Bevis Frampton was not easily found. Morton finally ran him down in a room used as an offshoot of the library. The valet had been right about him. He was a little scrap of a fellow with a grovelling, frightened manner and was just about the least likely assassin anyone could imagine.

The burly man came to the point briskly. 'I am Jasper Morton, one of Master Cecil's men. Know you that your late master, the Earl of Castleford, has been murdered?'

Bevis Frampton's yellow face turned grey.

'Murdered, you say? Not I. Who did such a dreadful thing?'

'That is what Master Cecil wishes me to discover. You know of no one who might wish to kill him? If you do, pray tell me. The sentence will be harsh for such an act committed in a royal palace—death by the executioner's axe on Tower Hill.'

Master Frampton's face turned greyer still. Morton thought that he was about to faint. 'My late Master had very few enemies—other than scaly Protestants who disliked him for being Catholic, but I don't think that they would go so far as to kill him for that.'

He paused, began to speak again, but shook his head and said, 'No, I think not...' His voice trailed away.

Jasper Morton was suddenly a bloodhound on the trail. 'What is it, sir? Have you remembered something, or someone? If so, pray tell me of it.'

Bevis hung his head. 'I know that m'lord was at odds with Master Oliver Woodville, one of Lord Robert's men. But surely he would have no reason to kill him. After all, they never met until after Master Woodville and I returned from touring the Continent together.'

'The Continent, say you? On these travels did you visit Italy?'

'Oh, aye, a beauteous place, but too bloodthirsty for me, I fear, and dangerous, too. Our other companion, Master Harry Grantly, died there of the Roman fever.'

'Did either you or Woodville buy a dagger in Italy and bring it back with you?'

Bevis gave the most artistic shiver. 'A dagger, you say? Not I, I have no love, or need, of arms, being but a frail creature as you see.'

'Did Woodville? Bring back a dagger?'

'Let me think. Aye, I believe he did. Not a dagger, a stiletto—a nasty thing with a long thin blade.' The shiver which accompanied this true statement was more artistic than ever.

'Was there aught about it which you might remember?'

'Let me think. Yes, it was very beautiful, with an

animal's head decorating the end of the hilt. I can't remember exactly which animal. Master Woodville was very proud of it. It was one of a pair made specially for him. Was a stiletto used to kill m'lord?'

Jasper Morton made no answer to that. Instead he inspected the wretched creature before him and turned towards the door. Except that he did not immediately reach it, twisting round to ask, 'What was the trouble between m'lord and Master Woodville of which you spoke?'

Bevis cracked his knuckles agitatedly. 'Oh, something about the Jermaine sisters. M'lord was contracted to marry the elder one, Mistress Mary, but he grew tired of her and wanted her younger sister, Mistress Penelope, instead. Master Woodville was the young lady's suitor and he and m'lord quarrelled over her. I remember that on one occasion Master Woodville threatened m'lord...' His voice died away. 'I would not like to get him into any trouble as a consequence of anything I may have said to you.'

'Do not fret, sir. I have my duty to do and there are many further questions which I may have to ask others.'

Which was another lie, but apart from his ability to ferret out the truth in such affairs as these, Jasper Morton and the truth seldom met. A useful lie could be a most potent weapon—but not as potent as Master Woodville's lion-headed stiletto, which had most probably ended up in Lord Castleford's breast. After all, it was unlikely that there were two of them who had found a home in the Palace of Whitehall.

Bevis Frampton was hugging himself after Jasper Morton had left. Two birds down with one shot, he told himself gleefully. Now let Master high and mighty Woodville talk himself out of that!

Oliver was descending the palace stairs, taking the greatest care while he did so. Two falls would be one too many. He had just reached the entrance hall when a burly man approached him.

'You have been pointed out to me as Master Oliver Woodville, sir. Is that true?'

'Yes, I am Oliver Woodville. What may I do for you?'

Young Master Woodville certainly did not look like an assassin, but then, neither did Lord Castleford's valet, nor Master Bevis Frampton.

'I would wish to have a word with you, sir, on a grave matter. Is there a nearby room where we may speak in private?'

He was using *sir* to Oliver because he was so obviously a fine gentleman, carefully and beautifully dressed, with an open manner which contrasted well with Master Frampton's furtive one. Jasper Morton, however, was experienced enough to know that it did not necessarily tell a wise man anything of his true nature.

Oliver, staring at the man mountain opposite to him, was wondering what in the world necessitated a

private room, but all he said was, 'Follow me,' and
led the way down a long gallery. A room opened off
it at the end where they might talk unseen. He waved
towards a bench before a window saying, 'Pray be
seated, sir.'

His courtesy was so marked that it almost upset
Cecil's agent. It seemed wrong to be questioning him
on suspicion of having murdered a fellow courtier.
Nevertheless he had his duty to do, and quickly.
Master Cecil wanted this business concluded as soon
as possible.

'My name is Jasper Morton. I am one of Master
Cecil's men and he has sent me on this errand. I believe that you know Lord Castleford. If he is a friend
of yours then it is my sad task to inform you that last
evening his valet found him dead in his room. He had
been murdered. The matter has not yet been made
public, as both Her Majesty and Master Cecil do not
wish anything to mar either the Christmas celebrations or the coming Coronation.'

Something had to be said. Oliver said it.

'I am sorry to hear of his untimely death and of its
manner. I cannot say that I knew him very well.'

He did not add, but what is this to do with me? For
some reason he thought that it might not be wise.

'So I understand. I believe that you have recently
been at odds with him. Is this true?'

'Yes. We had occasion to differ over my friendship
with Mistress Penelope Jermaine.'

Morton looked wise and said nothing for a moment

or two. Oliver began to rise. 'Is that all, Master Morton? That I am acquainted with Lord Castleford? So are many other courtiers.'

'Not yet, sir. I believe that you have recently travelled on the Continent and visited Italy while you were there. Is that true?'

Oliver sat down again. 'Yes, although I do not understand what my travels have to do with Lord Castleford's murder.'

'A moment, sir. While you were in Italy did you buy any weapons—a sword, for example?'

'I bought a rapier and a matching stiletto. Italian workmanship is very fine.'

'So I understand. Would you show them to me, sir?'

Oliver stared at him and knew instantly why the request had been made. Castleford must have been killed with either a rapier or a stiletto of Italian origin—and Morton must have discovered that he had bought such a pair in Italy. The most likely person to have told him must be Bevis Frampton—but it would be easy for him to prove that he had not murdered Castleford.

He rose. 'Come with me, Master Morton. I will show you what I brought back with me from Italy. I think that you, too, will find them very fine.'

He was so much in command of himself, so unlike Frampton or the valet, that Morton could not help but admire him. He must have guessed how Castleford had been murdered, but he was giving nothing away.

He followed Master Woodville up the stairs, and down yet another long gallery. A large room opened off it at the far end.

'This dormitory for Lord Robert's men is my temporary home, Master Morton, while the court is at Whitehall Palace—and here are the two chests which contain my possessions,' Oliver told him.

He opened the second, larger, finely ornamented one and after a few seconds spent rummaging in it fetched out a rapier of such dangerous elegance as Master Morton had not seen before. Oliver handed it to him, saying, 'I bought this first and then the matching dagger—which is somewhere at the bottom of this chest, I believe.'

Morton took the rapier and duly admired it, and the tiny lion's head on its hilt. 'And have you, sir, used the rapier and dagger in a duel?'

Oliver, on his knees, still rummaging, said, 'Not yet, Master Morton, and if I am honest I hope that I may never have occasion to. I have practised with the foils often, though.'

He straightened up. He had been so sure that a moment's work would serve to produce both sword and dagger, but he was now convinced that the dagger was not there. And if it were the weapon which had been used to dispose of Castleford, where the devil did that leave him? Under suspicion for his murder, doubtless.

'I should,' he said, over his shoulder, 'be deceiving you, Master Morton, if I failed to tell you that I cannot find my dagger. It must have been stolen, or mislaid. I will call my servant, Gib, to ask if he knows where it might be.'

'Pray do so, Master Woodville. His evidence may be most important.'

Gib, fortunately, was soon found. He knew nothing of the dagger and was surprised that it was not to be found in its proper place.

'So,' said Morton, looking thoughtful. 'I wonder if this dagger, which I am carrying on my person, although not in its proper sheath, is yours, Master Woodville? I found it in Lord Castleford's heart.'

He drew the dagger, the stiletto with the lion's head, which Oliver recognised immediately as the one which he had bought in Florence, the one which, taken from its rightful place, had been used to kill his enemy.

Oliver took it and examined it, although he did not need to: it was so obviously his. He looked hard at Morton, who was smiling as though he knew that he had found his murderer. He now had to be careful what he said.

'I am supposed to be so stupid that I would not only kill m'lord, but would do so with a weapon which would immediately incriminate me. That would indeed brand me a fool.'

'Perhaps so, sir, but even clever men do foolish things when their blood is hot. M'lord was killed some time during the festival on the evening of Christmas Day. Where were you then?'

'Why, where everyone else was. In the Great Hall sharing in the Yule-tide festivities.'

'You were seen there?'

Oliver thought of the happy crowd in the Great Hall, many flown with drink and intent only on their own enjoyment.

And then he thought of something else.

Fairly early on that night, he and Penelope had withdrawn to the Flemish Room so that they might be alone. At first they had merely talked, and then, against all the rules which they had made for themselves, their hot blood, as Morton had called it, had taken over.

They had begun by holding hands and kissing, well aware that at any moment they might be interrupted, and equally well aware not only of the scandal which might follow, but of the ruin of Penelope's reputation—even if consummation had never been reached. Alas, where love and lovemaking are concerned, reason has a habit of flying out of the window, the victim of the body's demands.

From kissing Penelope on the lips and then the cheek, Oliver had allowed his mouth to travel down her neck and bosom to the point where a faint mauve cleft signalled the beginning of the breasts which her tight bodice hid from sight.

It was not enough for either of them. Penelope moaned and writhed as her body responded ever more rapturously to each kiss Oliver gifted her with. More, she wanted more, and the very tenderness with which he was treating her contributed to her body's growing demand for fulfillment.

As for Oliver, he not only swore internally against his own constricting clothes, but also at Penelope's, which denied him access to the treasures which they covered. Oh, to caress those hidden delights: her breasts, her…her everything. What joy would then be sure to follow.

He tried to lift her skirts, but their sheer weight defied him. He was in prison and could not get out of it, but love has many ways by which its end may be achieved and Penelope was allowing him to achieve it, for she was lost in a dream of love and was offering him no resistance. Together they had almost reached the point where they would follow Jack and Alys's bad example when prolonged frustration took its toll on Oliver.

He drew away from her. He had no notion of how long they had been enjoying themselves in the Flemish Room, and their chances of being discovered were growing with each minute that passed. Not only that, he had no wish to ruin Penelope for a moment's snatched and difficult pleasure.

'Come, my love,' he said. 'It is time we joined the others again,' and when she looked at him, her eyes dazed, and tried to hold him to her again, he shook his head before helping her to smooth her dishevelled skirts and restore her bodice to its previous modest position.

So this was what passion led to, if one abandoned

one's self to it. Penelope did not know whether she was glad or sorry that Oliver had checked himself at the last fence of all. Like him, walking back into the gaiety outside, she was silent, reliving again those last few hectic moments.

Shortly after they had parted for the night, Oliver and young Temple had gone to bed, tired by the day's excesses. Penelope was thus the only person who could bear witness that it had been impossible for him to have murdered Castleford. But the thought of destroying Penelope's reputation by asking her to confess that they had been alone together for a large part of the evening was repugnant to him.

He could only imagine Kat Ashley's reaction to the news that one of the Maids of Honour had been closeted with a young man for so long. She would undoubtedly assume that the worst had happened—and so it nearly had.

'Most surely,' was all that he could reply to Morton's question.

His hesitation had been noticed, though, and Morton had drawn his own conclusions.

Oliver exclaimed spiritedly, 'Come man, you cannot, in all honesty, be so foolish as to believe that I murdered Lord Castleford?'

Morton raised the dagger which Oliver had handed back to him.

'I have to consider what this silent witness has to tell me. I must also inform my master of what I have discovered this morning. It will be for him to decide what action to take. In the meantime I trust that you will not leave the Palace.'

'Since I have committed no wrong, I shall have no need to. In the meantime, I suggest that you try to discover any other who might wish to see Lord Castleford dead.'

'That, sir, I will do before I report to my master,' and Morton bowed and left him.

Cecil was questioning Morton.

'Master Woodville, you say. And this is his dagger?'

'So he admits. It was missing from the chest where he keeps it. He says that he was present at the celebrations which were taking place at the time of Lord Castleford's death, but offered me no name of anyone who saw him there. Besides that, according to Bevis Frampton, lately one of Castleford's gentlemen, he and Castleford had quarrelled recently over a matter involving the Jermaine sisters.'

'He was certainly present early in the evening,' said Cecil thoughtfully, 'because I saw him then. I could not vouch for his being there later, though. I must confess that I cannot see young Woodville stabbing a man to death in secret: he has always struck me as a man of honour.'

'It was his dagger that did the deed.'

'You say that he immediately took you to the chest where he said it was stored. He showed no hesitation then?'

'None, sir: which might have been bravado.'

'Not like the man I know.'

'What action do I take now, sir?'

'Continue to question others. Later, I myself will interview young Woodville. It may be his dagger, but I am not certain that it was his hand which held it. I shall announce the news of Castleford's murder after that—we must not delay longer lest we, too, fall into suspicion of having caused it. One thing before you go. This Frampton fellow—may we trust his report that Castleford and Woodville had quarrelled?'

'I think so. On the other hand it seems a small matter for which to commit murder.'

'Smaller things than that have ended in death and despite; nevertheless I am inclined to agree with you. And the valet, what of him?'

'He, too, must be considered, but those who saw him soon after he found his master's body have sworn that he was greatly distressed. It seems that he suffers from a strange disorder: the sight of blood sets him first fainting and then vomiting, which renders it unlikely that he would carry out an act which made heavy bleeding inevitable.'

'That is a strong argument for his innocence, but, nevertheless, we must include him in our considerations. Continue with your enquiries and when you have anything material to tell me, return to me at once.'

After Morton had gone, William Cecil stared at the fire so busily burning in the hearth. It was not simply because Oliver Woodville was the son of an old friend that he doubted that he had killed Castleford, it was also that he could see no profit for him from such an act.

The motive could scarcely be revenge. Woodville had recently spent some time abroad and had not encountered Castleford until he had come to court. Never mind, he would send for the young man immediately and harry him a little himself.

Oliver knew that he had not heard the last of this business with Castleford, so he was not surprised when a messenger arrived ordering him to go immediately to Master Cecil's rooms.

Cecil was as friendly as ever. 'Sit, young man,' he bade him. 'What is this tale I have been hearing about Castleford's death and missing daggers? I would wish you to give me your explanation of this wretched business.'

'I have no explanation, sir. The first I knew of the matter was when your man Morton arrived and began to question me about it. He spoke of the dagger which had killed m'lord and asked to see mine. I found it to be missing and when Morton showed me the one used to murder Lord Castleford, I knew that it *was* mine. I also believe that, seeing that it was in a room accessible to all, it could easily have been stolen— and then used for its fell purpose.'

'So it was indeed your dagger which killed him?'

'Yes, but as I said, I was not holding it. I was in

the Great Hall at the time when Morton thought that the deed had been done. I had no reason to kill Lord Castleford, although I must admit that I did not like the man. He bullied my childhood friend, Mary Jermaine, to whom he was betrothed, most unmercifully and was very ungallant to her sister.'

'Um,' said Cecil thoughtfully, 'that scarce seems cause for murder. I saw you earlier in the evening, but have you friends who could vouch for your presence there later?'

'I retired early to our dormitory with Master Roger Temple.'

'But before that?' smiled Cecil.

'I spoke to many: I cannot remember whom.'

'And joined in the country dancing, perhaps?'

No need to lie now, the truth would serve. 'Yes, with Mistress Penelope Jermaine.'

'That was when I saw you,' agreed Cecil. He thought that the whole business was neither here nor there. To try to convict Master Woodville because of the dagger would be difficult as a result of the ease with which it could have been stolen. He must let Woodville go free—for the moment.

'It would be helpful in proving your innocence,' he finally said, 'if you could remember someone to whom you spoke in the Great Hall between the time when Lord Castleford's valet left him, still alive, and the time in which he returned to find him dead. Such a witness would end the matter, so far as you are concerned, once and for all.'

Oliver knew that no one in the Great Hall could have seen him after he had danced Sellenger's Round with Penelope until he had emerged from the Flemish Room on his own to find Roger Temple and retire for the night. To cite Penelope as the proof of his innocence would save him immediately, but he had no wish to do that if he could possibly avoid it.

He left Cecil's rooms with a heavy heart and a further warning that he was not to leave the Palace for the time being. He had no doubt that Morton believed in his guilt but that Cecil was not fully convinced of it. What puzzled him was not only who could have murdered Castleford, but what his motive could possibly have been.

Chapter Eleven

When Castleford's murder was at last made public by Cecil after his interview with Oliver, Mary Jermaine thought that it was her duty to mourn him as loudly and publicly as possible. When Kat Ashley sent for her and told her the dreadful news, she gave a loud cry and swooned, recovering only to begin the most desperate sobbing. What she was really thinking was, 'Now Penelope shall not have him,' for she found it difficult to believe that her sister would not have wished to marry such a powerful magnate as Castleford had been.

The fact that it had happened on a day when all the world and the court were celebrating the birth of Christ inevitably caused the most excited gossip. It was generally agreed that Castleford had been a dull stick—and such creatures did not usually die so dramatically.

Penelope, called on by Kat Ashley to comfort her

sister, told herself that she, at least, did not need comforting. She was sorry that the man was dead, but not sorry that he was no longer alive to persecute her and Oliver. She wondered where Oliver was, since she wanted to share with him the relief of knowing that they were no longer at risk from Castleford's spite.

After leaving Cecil, Oliver had returned to his quarters to carry out his duties as one of Lord Robert's men. Lord Robert had immediately handed him a large pile of foreign correspondence which needed, he said, to be translated immediately. To Oliver's surprise when he left him he found Bevis Frampton in the ante-room waiting to see his master.

Bevis, looking more servile and downtrodden than ever, bobbed his head at him, looking sideways while he did so.

'I suppose you wonder why I am here,' he offered.

Oliver supposed nothing of the kind. He had no interest in Bevis and it wouldn't trouble him if he never saw the man again: his presence brought back too many unhappy memories. Nevertheless he said, as offhandedly as he could, 'I would guess that you are on an errand of some kind.'

'Of some kind, yes. I am here to offer my services to Lord Robert. I have the command of several languages, as you know, and a wide knowledge of European affairs.'

Oliver forbore to reply that Lord Robert was already using him for that purpose. He was also of the opinion that m'lord would not want such a cringing creature as part of his retinue. Instead he replied, for want of something else to say, since Bevis was obviously expecting an answer from him, 'I suppose Lord Castleford's death has left you needing further employment.'

Bevis shook his head. 'Not so, we had already parted company—after a friendly fashion, you understand. M'lord was already reshaping his staff because of his coming marriage to Mistress Jermaine. His murder was a sad business, was it not? It is to be hoped that they soon find the miscreant who slew him. Some fellow of Cecil's came to me asking me for my advice, but, alas, I could not help him since I had left m'lord's service before his sad death.'

Fortunately, m'lord's steward appearing and calling for Master Frampton to be ushered into Lord Robert's presence saved Oliver from answering. He would have bet good money that it was Bevis who had gossiped to Morton of his fracas with Castleford over Penelope—which would have set that determined bloodhound on his trail. Working feverishly, to satisfy Lord Robert's demands, he decided that he must see Penelope as soon as possible—which, he feared, would be no earlier than the evening's celebrations.

In all this major political discussion Castleford's murder, for the moment, took second place; nor was it allowed to cast a shadow over the celebrations of the Twelve Days of Christmas. No one, other than a few who saw him as one of the leaders of the Catholic interest, had greatly liked him—indeed, it would have been fair to say that he had no real friend at court. General opinion, ignorant of his affliction, held that it was probably the valet who had slain him, since Castleford was known to be a cruel and abusive master. Consequently jollity and licence continued to reign supreme after supper was over.

It was Penelope who found Oliver on the following evening. For once her sister was not present to provoke her—she was still publicly mourning Castleford as though she were his bereaved widow and Roger Temple had never existed: in private she had sent him a letter saying that, sad though Castleford's death was, it had freed her to follow her heart. It was to be expected that she would retire from the court and go to her family home, there to mourn her loss.

It was some time before Penelope saw Oliver. For once Lord Robert's immediate retinue were late in joining the revels and she, who was not usually impatient, found herself chafing intolerably at the delay. Worse than that, she could not refuse to join the dance with Roger Temple when he came over to her to ask her anxiously how Mary was faring before begging her to partner him in the Galliard.

The dance seemed to last forever and only the knowledge that she was helping Roger to forget his worries over Mary enabled Penelope to continue to the end of it. It was impossible for her to forget how much she needed to talk to Oliver, who was standing near to Lord Robert, looking stern.

At last the dance ended: during it, Lord Robert told the young men behind him that they might now join in the fun. Oliver immediately looked around for Penelope and walked over to where she stood talking to Roger. They spoke briefly of Castleford's murder and of Mary's distress and her coming departure, of which Oliver had not yet heard, before Roger left them together to find a partner for the next dance.

'There is no privacy in a court,' were Penelope's first words, 'but I need to talk to you. Fortunately we may do so here since the noise tonight is so great that if we are careful no one will overhear us.'

Oliver nodded agreement to this.

'Dear Oliver, I have been fretting all day, ever since I first heard that Lord Castleford was dead. I am not cruel enough to say that the news pleased me, but I did think that now he was gone we could walk safely together once more. What also pleases me is that he must have been slain when we were together in the Flemish Room, so that no one could accuse you of being his murderer.'

What to say to her? That I have already been half-accused and am confined to Whitehall Palace while I remain under suspicion. More than that, she must not bruit abroad that she and I were alone together for a long time in the Flemish Room lest her reputation be quite ruined.

He told her so. 'My love, I dare not leave the Hall with you tonight lest we may be watched and followed, but to say too much here might be dangerous, however great the noise. I must, however, beg of you not to tell anyone that we visited the Flemish Room together on the night of Castleford's death. Think of what Kat Ashley and the others would make of it—especially after the scandal concerning Alys and Jack.'

Anxiety rode on Penelope's face. 'Dearest Oliver, I should do so only if it became necessary to clear you of any suspicion of having a hand in his death. Then I should be compelled to bear witness that we were alone together—but surely no one can believe that you killed him?'

'To some extent, we are all under suspicion. One of Master Cecil's most trusted men is asking questions of everyone who knew Lord Castleford. He might even question you, or Mary. Besides that, Bevis Frampton was a witness to the altercation between Castleford and me when he had lured you to his rooms and would probably delight in telling of it.'

Penelope placed an earnest hand on his arm.

'But if I know that we were alone, and will so swear, then it is useless for this man to question you at all, for I can straightway prove you innocent.'

Oliver shook his head. 'No, you must keep quiet and hope that Cecil's ferret finds the true murderer, so that your evidence may not be necessary.'

'But suppose he doesn't—what then?'

'Then I would still wish you to say nothing—unless by some ill fortune I am accused of his murder, and then, only then, would I agree to your coming forward to bear witness to my innocence.'

In all his considerations of what would follow the news of Castleford's murder, Oliver had forgotten how shrewd Penelope was, and that she would immediately grasp that she could prove his innocence, even before any accusation were made. Even then, however, her evidence might be considered dubious because of her love for him.

He would tell her nothing of what had passed between him, Morton and Cecil, nor that it was his dagger which had been used to kill Castleford, for the less she knew, the better.

'We must not needlessly compromise your honour,' he told her gently.

'My honour,' she scoffed back at him. 'Of what worth is that—set against your life?'

There was no answer he could make to this frank statement from the woman he loved, and who loved him, so he remained silent until the dance ended. Once it was over and the noise had abated a little, they both strove to try to look as though they had not a care in the world, wondering how many present were practising a similar deception.

If Cecil had hoped that gossip concerning Castleford's slaying could be kept to a minimum, he was soon to be proved wrong. The rumours sprang from nowhere and were soon merrily making the rounds.

Mostly they concerned Oliver Woodville and the strong possibility that he was the murderer. It was said that he and Castleford had come to blows, that they had disagreed about the Jermaine sisters—to one of whom Castleford was betrothed and the other, the younger, being the *amoroso* of young Woodville, whose dagger had been used to kill Castleford. The more the story was repeated the stranger it grew.

Mary, having behaved more like Castleford's widow than his betrothed, found that she would be unable to return to the court until his funeral was over, much to her annoyance. The Queen and Kat Ashley were adamant that it would be improper for her to rejoin the revelry. Her only consolation was that now Roger Temple could ask her parents for her hand. Lord Robert made a point of raising the matter with Oliver on the day after he had been interviewed by Cecil.

'This business of you and Castleford, Woodville, is there any truth in it?' Now this was blunt, especially coming from a man usually given to the most polite and courtly speech.

Oliver answered him in the same straightforward manner, saying, 'In part only: it is true that I disputed with him on one occasion, and that someone stole my dagger in order to kill him, but I give you my word that I am innocent of his murder.'

Lord Robert studied him for some moments before remarking, still in his severe mode, 'I believe you to be a man of honour, Master Woodville, and so I accept your word, but I understand that Master Cecil has questioned you and asked you not to leave Whitehall Palace until he gives you permission.'

Oliver bowed agreement again.

'He wishes to make further enquiries and has required all those connected with Lord Castleford to remain in attendance here, so he is in no way making an exception of me. I think that he considers that if I had wished to murder m'lord I would not have been fool enough to use my own dagger, unique in design, and to have compounded my folly by leaving the dagger behind.'

'And so I told him,' said Lord Robert, who naturally had no wish for one of his gentlemen to be proved a criminal by his great rival. 'Of course, you understand that Master Cecil cannot act on our word alone. He will continue to look for proof, either of your guilt or of another's. Until then I support all his decisions regarding you and any other who might be involved.'

Oliver bowed. He had expected nothing else. He waited for Lord Robert to give him permission to leave, but his master had not yet finished with him.

'One more thing. I understand that you were a particular friend of Master Jack Chancellor's. This morning I received a letter from him. He has recovered from his wound, but has decided not to return to court. He further informs me that he is to marry Mistress Alys Belsize. He has also sent a letter to be delivered to you, which I hereby give you. I must also

inform you that I have invited Dr Dee to court on the
29th of December. He will become part of my family
until the Queen's Coronation is over.'

Oliver took the letter. So he would never see careless and jolly Jack again, but at least he had this last
message from him. Once in his own room he opened
it. As he had expected the letter was not a long one.

'Oliver, my friend,' Jack wrote in an unclerkly
hand—scholarship had never one of his great virtues.
'I shall be sorry not to rejoin you, but my bout with
death has had a strange effect on me. My father never
wished me to go to court. He would have preferred
me to stay in the country and learn how to manage
the estates which I shall one day inherit. To my surprise since I have returned home I find that it is now
my wish, too. I have no desire to return to court. I
thank you for writing to me of Alys and her coming
child. With my parents' permission and to my great
joy we are to be married in a week and my fond hope
is that one day you will visit us. Your old friend, Jack
Chancellor.'

So Jack was settling down on his family's acres—
with Alys—and with her large dowry, which must
have reconciled his family to this hasty marriage. He
must tell Penelope of this happy turn of events. She
would be relieved to learn that Alys had not been
abandoned. Now all that remained was for him to
hope that like jolly Jack, who had now been transformed into apparently sober Jack, he would achieve
his salvation, too.

* * *

Someone else was thinking of him, but only with hate. The someone sat, a small grey spider, but none the less dangerous for all that, in the centre of his giant web. Matters, alas, were not going as smoothly as he wished. Certainly not as smoothly as similar intrigues he had read of in the tales of Messer Boccaccio.

First he had not succeeded as he had wished with Alys Belsize. And now, by rights, Oliver Woodville should be on his way to Tower Hill, and not as an honoured member of the Queen's court, but being led towards the headsman's axe. Instead he seemed to have become one of Fortune's favourites so that the powerful evidence which tied him to Castleford's murder, his one success, was being ignored.

To ensure his doom events needed a little push in the right direction, and if killing Castleford had served only one end and not two, as he had intended, then another stratagem might have to be employed. It mattered not why and how Oliver Woodville met his deserved death so long as he met it and soon.

Something smells rotten, Cecil told himself after listening to Morton's latest report. It was too pat, and when young Woodville had told him that he would have been a fool to use his own, easily identifiable, dagger to do the deed, he was inclined to agree with him. On the other hand a really clever man might have tried a double stratagem by using his dagger and then disclaiming the deed for precisely the reasons which Woodville had used in his interview with him.

He sighed and flung down the quill pen which he had been using to list a series of possible reasons for Castleford being disposed of. The sigh was also because he was asking himself why he should try very hard to track the murderer of such a man down.

That cock wouldn't fight, however much he might like it to. Castleford had been an important Catholic magnate, and not to put too much effort into finding and punishing the man who had killed him might cause many to allege that the new Queen's government was quite happy to see Catholics murdered—and that would never do.

He picked up one of the notes he had made while Morton had been speaking and saw that he had again interviewed the man Frampton. This time Frampton had produced some more evidence which might prove that Woodville had excellent reasons for hating Castleford. It seemed that he had been informally betrothed to Mary Jermaine before he travelled to the Continent with Frampton and young Harry Grantly, only to find on his return that she was now officially betrothed to Castleford.

After that Woodville seemed to be content to befriend the younger sister, Penelope, except that Castleford rapidly tired of Mary and turned his attention to her—leaving Woodville losing yet another of the Jermaine sisters to him, hence the murder. To Cecil this all seemed very thin and not at all like the

Oliver Woodville whom he thought that he knew—although that wasn't evidence, either.

He had asked Morton to investigate the Jermaine business further and at the same time to look at Frampton a little harder. He had left Castleford's service recently—had he been turned away? Was he a sound man financially, or did losing his place in Castleford's family leave him in difficulties? It was probably not wise for Morton to dismiss him as a possible suspect. After all, he had known of Woodville's distinctive rapier and dagger and could therefore have stolen the dagger—so he, too, would bear investigation.

And what of the valet? Had he not been too easily dismissed as the possible culprit because of his supposed violent aversion to the sight of blood? Impatiently he flung down his pen again, leaving a string of blots on the sheet of paper before him. He swore at them: God knew that he had enough to do with a demanding mistress who worked him night and day, with the constant moving from palace to palace, with the Tower to visit again before the Coronation, without him having to be troubled by the murder of an unpleasant nonentity like Castleford!

So far Cecil had carved a successful career for himself through tricky and dangerous times by trusting in his instincts, and those instincts were now telling him that something strange was going on in the new Queen's court. Alys Belsize's odd story about a spirit giving her a potion so that she might meet her love again, but which had been designed to kill her, Oliver Woodville being pushed downstairs, now followed by an attempt to implicate him in a murder which he had probably not committed, were all alike in being mysteries.

William Cecil did not like mysteries. He was a hard, pragmatic man and he particularly did not like this recent outbreak of them. One thing he was sure of: there must be someone behind them, working for some unknown end whose purpose he could not guess. He was also sure of something else: sooner or later, to relieve the heavy burden of work he was beginning to shoulder, he would be compelled to appoint a new officer of the Crown. That officer's duties would not only be to investigate possible conspiracies against the Queen, but also such oddities as these which might affect England's security.

This, however, was for the future: for the present it was his responsibility.

'What's this about Oliver being Castleford's murderer?' demanded Mary of Penelope, who was paying her a visit. 'Why should he murder Castleford? I know that they did not like one another, but surely that is not a good reason for suspecting him?'

'They say that it was Oliver's dagger which was used to kill him, but I shall never believe that Oliver would ever do such a thing.'

'Nor I,' said Mary fervently. 'Someone must have stolen it.'

'The problem is,' said Penelope sadly, 'that if so, who could hate Oliver so much that he stole his dagger in order to kill Castleford, knowing that suspicion would then fall on him? Oliver is not the kind of man to make enemies easily—on the contrary. He was patient, even with Castleford when he behaved so badly to the pair of us.'

'True,' said Mary, 'One thing is encouraging, though, and that is that he has not been arrested.'

Penelope thought ruefully that it was a sad thing that it had taken Castleford's murder to renew their sisterly regard, before she told Mary of another hopeful development.

'The Coroner's inquest is not being held until after the Coronation is over. Master Cecil and the Queen are agreed that it would not be wise to have such a dismal event take place at a time when happiness at her crowning should reign supreme.'

Like Oliver, Penelope believed that Cecil had advised this delay in the hope that the mystery of Castleford's death might be solved before the inquest, thus preventing the Coroner from finding Oliver guilty of murdering Castleford simply because of the presence of his dagger.

'Since I was betrothed to Castleford I am being condemned to miss all the joys of Christmas and the Coronation,' Mary complained just before Penelope left her to wait on the Queen. 'My only consolation is that father is looking favourably at Roger's pro-

posal that we should marry as soon as decently possible after Lord Castleford's funeral.'

There was nothing that Penelope could say which
would comfort her sister, who had seen herself as one
of the main celebrants of the Coronation and then the
court. She could have pointed out that Oliver, being
the main suspect, was in a much worse case than she
was, but tactfully decided to keep quiet.

As she said to Oliver when she met him that evening after supper just before the games and dancing
began again, 'I feel so sorry for her, but had she not
deserted you and agreed to marry Castleford, she
would still be here, enjoying herself.'

'It may be ungallant of me,' said Oliver fervently,
'but I am so glad that she did. I had no notion of her
real nature, being blinded by her beauty, and I would
never have met my true love. I was saved from a
marriage doomed to unhappiness. I could not have
believed that two sisters could be so different.'

'Nevertheless…' began Penelope, remembering
Mary's sad face and her dashed hopes.

'Nevertheless nothing,' retorted Oliver. 'She never
showed any kindness to you when she was prospering
so it is truly noble of you to grieve for her. And why
should she be unhappy? Temple wishes to marry her,
so she has exchanged a bad man for a good one! Her
behaviour makes me even more content that I have
settled for the younger, not the older, sister. And if
you look at me like that I cannot answer for my good
behaviour. It is becoming more and more difficult for

me to be near you these days without having impure thoughts.'

'Then perhaps I ought not to be near you,' replied Penelope, demurely but naughtily. 'I would not like it to be thought that I am tempting you into sin.'

'If to love you is to sin, then I am sinning whether you are near me or not,' was Oliver's answer to that. 'The musicians are beginning to play a measure for the Pavan, which dance is enough to cool anyone's blood—even mine.'

'That being so,' said Penelope, 'here is my hand and we will both bid temptation flee, for I must confess that I am as bad as you are. The devil whispers in my ear whenever we are together.'

The stately dance ended and they retired to stand before one of the room's long windows. Presently a Steward, carrying a long white staff, came up to them to ask Master Woodville to accompany him to the Queen, who wished to speak to him.

They looked at one another. Penelope whispered, 'Go with God,' for like Oliver she feared that this might be the prelude to his arrest—to be done unostentatiously in order to avoid gossip just as the next dance was beginning.

Lord Robert was in his usual seat, Master Cecil sat on the opposite side to him. They were just below the Queen, whose chair was in the centre of a small dais. She was, as usual, magnificently dressed, and despite having nothing openly masculine about her, her appearance, as always, reminded everyone of her father,

King Henry VIII. It was her expression of command, perhaps, coupled with her red-gold hair and her penetrating eyes.

Oliver bowed to her. He was dismally resigned to try to endure whatever might happen to him.

'Master Woodville,' she began, 'I have conferred with both Lord Robert and Master Cecil about the murder of Lord Castleford. It seems, that although your dagger was used to kill him, they neither of them believe, without further evidence of your guilt, that it was you who used it. It was, I understand, stored in an unlocked chest in an unlocked room. This, together with your previous good character, has caused them to advise me not to have you charged with his murder until further investigations have been set in train. For the present, though, you must not leave the precincts of the court until the matter is resolved.'

She turned to Master Cecil. 'I understand that he has already given you his word of honour over this matter.'

Cecil agreed that Oliver had.

'That is all, then, Master Woodville. You may thank your God that you have powerful friends at court and that they have given me strong evidence of your previous good behaviour. You may leave me now.'

It was, thought Oliver, offering Her Grace his farewell bow, ironic that Lord Robert and William Cecil should have reached agreement on something, even if it was only over the treatment of lowly Oliver

Woodville! England might yet prosper under the three of them.

Penelope watched him walk back towards her, his face impassive. So, he was not to be summarily arrested—yet.

'What had Her Grace to say to you?' she asked as coolly as she could, so that none watching them might know how disturbed she was.

As briefly as he could, he told her.

'You are free for the present then, after a fashion—but they must still suspect you.'

'After a fashion, as you say, yes.'

'That being so, you must allow me to speak to Master Cecil, to tell him that we were alone together in the Flemish Room at the time and thus prove your innocence beyond a doubt.'

'Not yet,' he told her, 'You must not risk your reputation yet. They are still investigating the matter.'

Penelope stared at him horror-struck. 'Oliver,' she said at last. 'You must allow me to be the best judge of this. I cannot sleep easily at night, knowing that this shadow lies over you and that I can remove it.'

'You gave me your word,' was all he said.

'Then I take it back. As you love me, do not deny me.'

What could he say to her? He had fallen in love with her as much because of her strong mind and her dauntlessness as for any other of her many attributes, and because she might be going to exercise these qualities for his benefit he could not complain because she was intent on doing so. His fear that she might lose her reputation if she told the truth might rule him, but it did not rule her.

He bowed his head.

'It must be as you wish,' he said at last.

'Which will not be now,' she told him, not triumphing over him as he gave way to her, 'but when I deem the time to be right.'

'You may suffer for it,' he told her.

'That is as may be. Think rather of what *you* might suffer if I keep quiet. Once you are arrested your guilt will already have been proved in the eyes of the law and you will be immediately imprisoned and tortured, whereupon one of two things must follow. The dreadful pain you will suffer will either cause you confess to having killed Castleford when you have not, and you will be executed on Tower Hill, or you may die in agony rather than confess to a lie. I cannot bear to think of leaving you in this dreadful position. What is my lost reputation worth, compared with your inevitable and terrible death?'

'Even so,' he told her, 'my honour demands that you keep quiet.'

'For the time being, only,' she said. 'Now ask me to dance with you. They are playing the music for the Galliard and I would have you rival Lord Robert when he tosses up the Queen.'

What could he say to her but yes? However much it might grieve him that she would not bend to his will, and however much it seemed to him that she was usurping his right as a man of honour, if truth were told, he could do no other than allow her to act as she thought best. That it should be the man, not the woman, who made the decisions for them both was another thing which stuck in his craw, but he could not in all conscience be openly angry with her when she was trying to save him.

Hand in hand they walked on to the floor: the cavalier who was honour bound to die if need be to preserve his love's reputation and his gallant sweetheart who was equally willing to sacrifice her good name so long as it freed him from the prospect of execution on Tower Hill, which lay in wait for all who were convicted of killing in the precincts of the court.

Chapter Twelve

How could it all have gone so wrong! He had laid his plans most carefully, nothing left to chance. Who could possibly have guessed that both Lord Robert and Cecil would find it difficult to believe that Oliver Woodville could be a murderer, and that they would then influence the Queen so that no action was taken against him. Worse than that, Cecil's man—and another of Lord Robert's—had started sniffing suspiciously around him, so he must take instant action before by some mischance they might begin to question the circumstances of Harry Grantly's death.

Well, he would see that one day the Queen would suffer for that, but in the meantime he would have to devise a new stratagem to make sure that Oliver Woodville paid for all the slights which he and Harry Grantly had put upon him on their tour of the Continent. That these slights were imaginary, the misinterpretations of the small-minded creature he was, envious of two handsome young men of better birth than he, was beyond his understanding. His crooked view of the world simply told him that the sooner the remaining one of the precious pair was out of it, the better.

And then he thought of the valet. The valet who had pushed Oliver Woodville downstairs at his Lord's behest. He deserved to die, too, did he not, for failing to kill him and thus leaving him with the task instead and the difficult business of creating a false explanation of his whereabouts on the night of the murder? One advantage was that the valet was a weak-minded fool, just like the Belsize woman and the guards. It would be as easy with him, as with her, to use his hard-won talents to persuade the wretch to do that which he would never do in his right mind.

He must be quick, though, before those carrion crows came round to question him again. After all, as one of them had slyly insinuated when interrogating him, he was the only person who knew of Woodville's distinctive weaponry, was he not?

Yes, speed was essential. The valet, together with Castleford's other servants, was waiting at the palace for the arrival of his cousin, the heir: he would be on his trail within the hour, and then, as the Blessed Julian of Norwich had said, 'All will be well and all manner of things shall be well.'

His mind had become so twisted that he saw nothing wrong in invoking a pure-minded saint to help him in his wickedness. He would have been pleased had he known of a conversation between Cecil and Lord Robert on the next day.

Lord Robert had called on his rival for the Queen's favour immediately after he had broken his fast. Cecil met him with his usual courtesy, refraining from asking what it was that brought m'lord to him with such urgency. He had not long to wait until he found out.

'It is plain,' Lord Robert began, 'that this business of charging Castleford's murderer is dragging on, which is a great pity. That the suspected man is a member of my household reflects badly on me, and since there is little evidence of anyone else being involved I do not wish to have half the court whispering behind my back that because he is a favourite of mine nothing is being done to bring Woodville to justice. It is even being suggested that I have brought undue influence to bear on the Queen not to have him charged and arrested. I must confess that I like the young man and find it difficult to believe that he is a murderer, but my reputation is at stake here.'

'I see your point,' returned Cecil gravely, 'and I, too, am in some difficulty over this matter. To some extent he has been a protégé of mine also, but I fear that if nothing further emerges then I shall have to give the order for him to be arrested and questioned with the utmost severity—if only to stave off any suggestion that I had a hand in Castleford's murder.'

'We are of a mind, then,' said Lord Robert. He was not completely pleased with Cecil's answer. He had hoped that Cecil might demur and he could then pose

as an upright courtier who would even see a friend
of his arrested to maintain justice and truth, however
much it pained him to bring it about.

Cecil nodded. 'Which is as well,' he remarked,
'since we are both servants of the Queen's Grace and
must not be seen to evade the true course of justice.'

He was quite aware of Lord Robert's ploy, but, as
usual, betrayed no knowledge of it in anything he
said—or didn't say, for that matter.

It was thus fortunate that Penelope did not delay in
her mission to try to clear Oliver's name. At whatever
cost to her, she must try to save him from the clutches
of the law, regardless of his belief that her honour
must be preserved at all costs. She sometimes thought
that men's obsession with their honour was one of
their greatest mistakes. What was the use of preserv-
ing her own honour if by doing so she allowed him
to be consigned to the scaffold? That surely was an
even greater breach of honour, and if that was what
men would call the argument of a weak woman, then
so be it.

More than that, from all that she had seen of her
new Queen she would understand what she was about
to do, for had she not managed, through a series of
contrivances, to inherit a crown, and Penelope for one
was sure that no misunderstandings about the nature
of honour had been allowed to stand in her way.

Besides, she was tired of people smiling sideways
at her and asking her if it were true that Oliver had
done the deed, as so many about the court were hint-

ing, nay, saying. So she took herself off to where Master Cecil was lodged, not fully grasping that that other shrewd survivor through difficult and dangerous times would approve of her decision.

She was kept kicking her heels in an ante-room for some time. It seemed that Master Cecil was very busy: too busy to waste time rushing to interview a mere Maid of Honour, even if she had told his Steward that the matter was both urgent and important.

Finally the Steward reappeared and led her into the great man's presence.

'Yes, Mistress Jermaine, what is it you want with me?' he asked her without preamble—doubtless his way of telling her that he was doing her a great favour by seeing her at all.

Penelope went immediately to the point, never mind that he might think her bold by so doing. 'It is about the matter of Lord Castleford's death,' she told him. 'All the gossip is that you suspect Master Woodville of having murdered him. I have come to tell you that I can prove, beyond a peradventure, that he did not.'

'Can you, Mistress Jermaine? Now how do you propose to do that?'

'It happened on the first night when we played the Twelve Days games. Early in the revelry Master Woodville and I left the Great Hall. He took me to the little Flemish Room—of which you may know— and we remained there until just before the festivities ended. He did not leave me during that time in which I understand that Lord Castleford must have been murdered. Before that he was present in the Hall with Master Temple, taking part in the opening games. Thus it was impossible for him to have committed the murder.'

There! It was out at last, and what could Master Cecil think but that she was a loose doxy—just like Alys—who had slipped away with her lover so that they might enjoy themselves playing Cupid's games in peace.

He had put his chin in his steepled hands and was leaning forward to inspect her as though this was the first time he had seen her.

'Say you so, Mistress?' he came out with at last.

'Aye, so I do, and would swear it on oath before a Justice, a Coroner or in a Court of Law if it were required of me.'

'You understand that in claiming that you were alone together for so long you are putting your reputation for virtue at risk?'

'Yes, but what is the loss of that as against the risk that Master Woodville will lose his life if I do not tell the truth,' she told him, as she had previously told Oliver.

He nodded, as though he understood her reasoning.

'There is one problem with your story, though,' he said. 'It is some days since Lord Castleford was murdered and Master Woodville came under suspicion. Many men—and most lawyers—would ask why, this being so, he did not tell me that he was with you, and wish to know why you did not come forward with your story until this afternoon.'

'Are *you* asking me to answer that question, sir?' Penelope knew that she was being bold again, behaving as a man would and not as a woman was supposed to. But if the Queen could take the place of a man and behave like one, then so could she.

'Yes, I am asking you that.'

'It is because Master Woodville's sense of honour would not allow my honour, my reputation for virtue, to be put at risk. For this reason and this reason only, he would not tell you and forbade me to. For a time I agreed to say nothing, but since it appears to me that he is now in danger of being arrested, tried and condemned for something which I can prove he could not have done, I must speak out.'

'I have to point out to you that by delaying you may have risked being unable to save him and the loss of your reputation as well.'

Oh, he was well named the fox was he not? And she, what was she but a young vixen for daring to cross verbal swords with him?

'Yes, I understand that and regret it, but I love Master Woodville dearly and did not wish to disobey him until it seemed that by not coming forward I might be putting him in mortal danger.'

Cecil regarded Penelope in silence for a few moments. She tried not to let it distress her, although she was beginning to fear that either he did not believe her, or, as he had said, she had taken too long to tell her tale.

'You see, my dear Miss Jermaine,' he said at last, 'Many will say that you have invented this story in order to save Master Woodville and that, therefore, there is not a word of truth in it.'

'But it *is* the truth, Master Cecil. You must believe me. As I have already told you, I am willing to swear to it on oath if it should prove necessary.'

'Dear child,' he said, suddenly kind, '*I* may believe you, but you may have to convince those who do not know you, or Master Woodville, and where my word counts for no more than that of any other man, least of all those who will question him in the torture chamber should he be arrested. Nevertheless I will interview him at once and question him again: he will need to confirm your evidence. In the meantime I shall say nothing of what you have told me, other than to those who are trying to discover the truth of the matter. In the meantime I must ask you not to meet or speak to Master Woodville until I have interviewed him.'

It was over—at least for the time being. She had done what she could to save Oliver and if it were not enough, then it was not for the want of trying. Penelope rose and left behind a man who could not but admire her steadfastness and her intellect. His Queen was not the only remarkable woman in England, was Cecil's last thought.

* * *

Oliver knew at once why Cecil had sent for him again—and so soon. Penelope must have been to see him to tell him of their secret tryst.

Cecil did not keep him waiting. His expression was grim and he came straight to the point of the meeting. 'Why did you not tell me earlier of what Mistress Jermaine has told me so lately?'

Oliver hesitated for a moment—only for Cecil to pounce on him. 'Come, come, Master Woodville, the question is a simple one. No embroidery is needed, no beating about bushes. Tell me, in your own words, what she has just told me. Questions of honour have flown out of the window in the face of truth—if Mistress Jermaine was speaking the truth, that is.'

'If you are referring to the night of Lord Castleford's murder then I am to suppose that she informed you that we spent the majority of it, together and alone, in the Flemish Room. I love and respect Mistress Jermaine, I hope to make her my wife. I would not do anything which might dishonour her, nor did I that night. I asked her not to tell you, or anyone else, that which might save me, because I would not have her dishonoured, the centre of un-pleasant gossip, together with ruin and disgrace as a consequence.'

'Very noble of you,' remarked Cecil nastily. 'A better feat of nobility would have been not to have lured her into the Flemish Room—although, on the other hand, since you did, and if you are both speaking the truth, you may have saved yourself from the headsman.'

'At the price of her reputation,' returned Oliver stiffly, 'and we are neither of us liars.'

The man opposite to him sighed. 'We are all ready to lie to save ourselves from a dishonourable death and so a jury might decide here. But since Mistress Jermaine swears that she came to me of her own accord and without your knowledge, the truth, or not, of your story must lie on the table, and you may walk free, although only in Whitehall while my investigations continue. Her evidence will remain a secret until the time when I hand my findings to her Grace. After that—well, who knows what after that may bring. You may go—for the time being.'

Once Oliver had departed, Cecil laid his weary head on his hands. Why was he so sure that something about this business stank to heaven? That there was more to it than met the simple, enquiring eye? He could only hope that as the old saying had it, Truth will out.

The valet proved to be as easy meat as Bevis could have hoped. When he took him on one side and asked him for some information regarding his late master, Jenkins glared suspiciously at him and mumbled, 'What for?'

He smiled at him, holding Jenkins's eyes with his own so fiercely that Jenkins looked away, and then, as though under compulsion, looked back at him again. 'I believe,' he said earnestly, 'that he was a cruel, unfair master: at least he was when I was part of his family.'

'Oh, aye, I know that—and you know that already.'

Still holding the other man's eyes, he said, smiling as though at a joke, 'Angry with you, was he, for not having killed Woodville when you pushed him down-stairs—at his orders?'

'That he was. Mind, I'd warned him that it was a chancy thing, not sure to finish him off, but he still threatened to turn me away when he survived—so I swore at him and said that if he did I'd peach on him over Woodville's fall—and where would he be then? I hated the pair of them, that I did—mostly Woodville for saving himself when he fell. I'd have been rich if he'd died from it—or so m'lord had promised.'

'So you would. How would you like to be revenged on Woodville for managing to survive, and Castleford for embroiling you with him?'

'I would if it were possible.'

'Then listen to me, but first look me in the eye so that you may remember all that I tell you.'

Jenkins duly did as he was bid. Something about the man before him, whom he had dismissed as a crawling runt of a fellow, was so powerful that for a moment he felt that he was drowning. Afterwards he was to remember little or nothing of what was said to him, only that it was his good angel who was help-ing him to gain his revenge on all those who thought themselves his betters. Time, indeed, seemed to have stopped. He had no recollection of anything that was said after he had done as he was bid. It was as though he had been dreaming, but like most dreams it faded when he awoke and time started again.

Whereupon Jenkins blinked, and said, 'That is all?' But what the all was he did not know. He possessed no memory of his new friend telling him shortly before he awoke that he was no longer sick at the sight of blood and that when he next heard the magic name Azazel, he would carry out the instructions which he had just been given.

'That all is quite enough, don't you think?' smiled his new friend, and pressed a coin in his hand, saying, 'As a token of my friendship.'

Bemused, Jenkins looked at the coin, and wondered why he had been given it. He had done nothing to earn it, but a man was a fool who looked a gift horse in the mouth.

'So Master Cecil is not going to inform the Queen immediately about our spending the evening of Castleford's death alone in the Flemish Room?'

Annoyed though he was that Penelope had defied his wishes by going to Cecil and telling him of their tryst in the Flemish Room, Oliver could not be other than grateful for what she had done for him. She had almost certainly saved him from eventual arrest and a painful death, and it would be the mark of a cur for him to reproach her for her bravery in facing possible ruin.

'Not yet,' he replied to her worried question, 'but sooner or later you may be sure that our secret will be out. If something happens which proves beyond a doubt that I was not the murderer, then nothing will be said, but otherwise—' He shrugged his shoulders.

Penelope looked through the windows at the sleet which was falling outside. 'I am not hopeful,' she said, 'there are few secrets in a court. I am sure that one of Cecil's or Lord Robert's men will say something which will betray us and I shall have Kat Ashley charging at me as though we were facing one another in the tilt-yard. As for what the Queen might say…' She shuddered.

'So we are not yet out of the woods,' finished Oliver, 'as I warned you.'

'No,' retorted Penelope smartly, 'but I don't think that we are quite so deep inside them. We must ask the Lord for a miracle. Or hope that Master Cecil's men will discover the truth. I thought, from Master Cecil's manner, that he is growing impatient with the whole business. The most hopeful sign is that no action will be taken before the Coronation, which gives them more time to question other possible suspects.'

'Such as the valet and Master Frampton,' added Oliver. 'Castleford turned him off, you know.'

'And in the meantime, we watch and wait.' She paused before saying, 'You know, Oliver, there is something else of which I ought to have spoken to Master Cecil, but I thought that he might consider me a foolish woman if I raised the matter.'

She stopped again and looked at him, her great eyes solemn, the shining hint of tears in them, something which had the contrary effects of both arousing him and angering him. The first, arousing him because she never looked more beautiful, or desirable than when she offered him their full glory, and the second, angering him because the tears were there for him and his predicament. It was wrong that she should be so troubled and that he should be unable to dispel her fears.

'What was it, my darling? What should you have said?'

'That it seems very strange that first someone should have tried to kill you and then, almost immediately afterwards, Lord Castleford should have been murdered. Is it possible that the two things are connected?'

'No!' he exclaimed, and then more slowly, 'Perhaps. Are you saying that we were attacked by the same enemy? How could that be?'

Penelope sat down on one of the benches which lined the walls of the gallery in which they were seated. People were coming and going, but none made any attempt to stop and speak to them—possibly because Oliver, under suspicion of murder, was not the kind of man to befriend, if one were ambitious, that was.

'I don't know,' she said. 'What puzzles me is who such an enemy could be? What seems plain to me is that by making it appear that you murdered Lord

Castleford, the real culprit was making sure that one way or another you were to die—first on the stairs and when that failed, on the scaffold.'

Oliver stared at her in amazement. 'My dearest girl, I think it a pity that women cannot hold any office, other than that of the monarch. You would make a splendid addition to Master Cecil's household. On the other hand such a suggestion smacks more of Messer Boccaccio's romances than of our everyday life.'

'I haven't read Messer Boccaccio, because I have little Italian, but I have heard that they are based on things which actually happened, and if we think of what has passed here, at the English court, since King Henry divorced his first Queen, then what I have suggested is not really very remarkable.'

'True,' said Oliver, 'and I think it a pity that you did not tell Master Cecil of this. Would you agree to my writing him a letter setting out this possibility?'

'Indeed, although I have no proof to offer to support my suggestion.'

'That is of no matter. Now that you have pointed it out it is most strange that both events should involve me. I must think carefully of who, and what, may lie behind them. I have a mind to grasp at any straw which might save me from Tower Hill and you have, I believe, offered me more than a straw.'

And then, his eyes shining, he leaned forward to say hoarsely to her, 'By my troth, dear heart, I have never before felt such a burning desire to kiss you, nay, to take you to bed and prove my love to you.

As soon as this wretched business is over and I am truly a free man again—please God—I shall ask your parents for your hand in marriage. For the present, though, we must wait.'

Penelope, careless of who might be watching them, took his hand in hers, and stroked it, saying, 'Fie on you, Oliver! You have not yet asked me if I wish to marry you. Is that not the usual custom between a man and his maid at such times?' Her words were reproachful, but the look which she gave him was mischievous.

'Tease me not, wench,' was all the answer she got, with a smiling shake of his head. 'The honourable man asks the parents first.'

'And you are nothing if not honourable, as I well know—since you put your life at risk by refusing to allow me to tell Cecil of our tryst before I became convinced that my duty to you bade me do that.'

Oliver looked around. No one seemed to be interested in them, or looking their way, so quickly, surreptitiously, he loosened her hand from his and kissed hers tenderly. Their secret watcher ground his teeth at the sight. Enjoy her while you may, for your time is not long now, he swore to himself.

All unaware that evil lurked so near them, Oliver whispered to Penelope, 'You have known since before we heard of Castleford's murder how much I love you and wish to make you mine. Oh, it is sweet torture for us to be together and I not allowed to prove my love.'

'Torture for me also,' said Penelope, gently disengaging her hand from his. 'Now we must part—to meet again soon, I trust.'

How many more times must she watch him leave her, before they could meet and be together without any man, or woman, saying them nay? Would that blessed time ever come, or were they to be like the doomed lovers in the tales she had read? Pray God that might not be so.

Later that day Cecil read Oliver's letter setting out what Penelope had suggested to him. He acknowledged that, overburdened with the cares of state, he had not fully recognised a possible relationship between the two events involving young Woodville. Penelope and Oliver had agreed not to tell Cecil of their suspicion that Jack Chancellor had been attacked because he had been wearing Oliver's cloak. They feared that he would think them run mad, seeing a bear behind every bush.

Cecil made a note to hand the letter to Morton when he next saw him. The sense of something wrong in this whole affair grew stronger and stronger, but what that wrongness might be continued to elude him. He gathered up his papers and made his way to the Queen's rooms. He had conferred with her earlier that morning, but she had asked that he visit her again before dinner. Among other things Feria was still making a nuisance of himself over being refused lodgings in Whitehall and he was blaming Cecil for

Elizabeth's continuing refusal to consider her late half-sister's husband, King Philip, as a possible husband.

Now this was unfair, because Cecil was half-inclined to the match—since Philip seemed the best prospect in an unworthy collection of suitors which included most of the unmarried princes and monarchs of Europe. Early in her reign it might be, but Cecil was beginning to ask himself whether Elizabeth intended to marry anyone, now that Lord Robert was forbidden to her.

The fervour with which she attacked the business of ruling suggested to him that she would not lightly surrender her power to a husband. She was busy working her advisers, and him in particular, so hard that they were becoming exhausted while she, she showed no sign other than that she was blossoming under a burden which was destroying strong men!

Now there was this wretched business of Castleford which still hung over them. Morton's latest report seemed to show only that if Woodville was not the culprit, then it was difficult to decide who might be. The valet, with his aversion to blood, which had been secretly tested and found to be true, and Frampton, the other possible suspect, having produced evidence that he had spent the night playing dice with two friends, before getting royally drunk with them—or so they both testified—had been cleared.

Cecil sighed—he seemed to be doing it a great deal these days—gathered up his papers and went to wait on the Queen, where he spent half an hour debating with Her Grace over the question of how many of the late Queen's councillors they wished to retain in office. At the end of their discussion Cecil asked if he might speak to her in private, and once they were alone he raised the question of Castleford's murder again. For the first time he told her of his interview with Penelope Jermaine and of her evidence that she and Oliver Woodville had been alone together in the Flemish Room at the time Castleford was killed.

'And since Morton's investigations seem to prove that the other possible suspects could also not have committed the crime we are left in something of a quandary.'

His mistress's response to this was not at all what he expected.

'Alone for a long time in the Flemish Room, say you? What is the world coming to when my Maids of Honour seem to have no honour left! First Mistress Belsize misbehaves herself, which did not surprise me, and now Mistress Jermaine, which does!'

'Very true,' replied Cecil gravely, 'but if I may so advise you, it leaves us with the question of whether we believe that Mistress Jermaine is telling the truth. For if she is not, then Master Woodville's guilt must again be considered.'

The Queen lay back in her chair, exasperated. 'I do not think that Mistress Jermaine is a liar and she risks much by coming forward with her confession of misdemeanour. You are right to call this a quandary. If you wish me to advise you, then I suggest that you ought to delay any further action until after the Coronation—although your man must continue his work.

'In the meantime something might arise which would tell us why someone thought Lord Castleford worthy of death. I always thought him a pompous fool, over-inclined to see himself as a leader of the Catholic faction. Is it possible that someone decided that he might be a danger to them and so removed him, using Master Woodville's dagger to distract us?'

As usual his mistress had put her finger on a possibility which had not previously been considered. Cecil said, a trifle heavily, 'Perhaps, but my man said something about the murder which interested me. He said that it looked as though whoever killed him hated Castleford.'

'Which would mean that his death had nothing to do with either politics or religion.'

'Yes, but that does not help us, either.'

'To the devil with it then,' said Her Grace energetically. 'Let us leave it for the time being and hope that the mystery solves itself. We have enough to do in seeing that I am safely crowned without allowing such a piddling man's death to trouble us, even if it did occur in the palace precincts.'

Since this was Cecil's own wish, he bowed agreement and they went on to discuss how the business of government was to be organised once the Coronation was over.

'As with the Coronation,' Her Grace announced, 'we must not look in any way mean or miserable as a consequence of penny-pinching. The nations of Europe must not be allowed to look down on us, so I wish to hear no more talk of how to save money by reducing those of the court's expenses which are devoted to enhancing our regal state, either in public or private.'

Cecil moaned internally at this. He wanted to say, 'But will the Exchequer bear it?' He decided not to risk the Queen's displeasure by saying so. He also noted that her treatment of the Castleford affair—that of delaying a decision to wait on events a little—was something he would have to become used to. Only time would tell whether or not this trait of hers was a wise one.

Chapter Thirteen

If the powerful who ruled England were in a quandary, so, too, were those whom they ruled and who waited on their decisions. One good result of the Queen's policy of delay was that as the days passed and the Coronation drew near Oliver and Penelope found themselves no longer the centre of interest. They could attend the evening's revelries without fear of everyone's eyes being on them.

Oliver, however, began to have a curious feeling that he was being secretly watched: it was almost as though a shadow were following him. He frequently felt the hairs at the back of his neck rising at its presence, but when he turned round there was no one to be seen. He said nothing of this to Penelope, until the evening when the court was celebrating the feast of Epiphany, the last of the Twelve Days of Christmas, after an afternoon in which he had seemed to spend most of his time looking behind him—and seeing nothing.

After supper, the evening began with an exchange of presents. Oliver gave Penelope a small fan which he had brought back from Italy, and she gave him a handkerchief which she had embroidered with his initials. Among the many presents to the Queen were a pair of silk stockings—something quite new—which had all the court ladies envying her, since they were said to be so much more comfortable and exciting to wear than cloth ones.

Lord Robert had excelled himself that night. The evening's revelries began with a masque: a semi-theatrical diversion which mocked the clerics of the Catholic church. In it various birds and beasts were dressed as cardinals, abbots and bishops. The sight of bishops dressed as asses was particularly appreciated by the courtiers, who had eaten and drunk their fill at the lavish supper. After it, according to the shocked representative of the Duchy of Mantua, licence reigned supreme, with the whole court joining in on their last night of revelry before the business of running the country took precedence.

Penelope and Oliver were watching the courtiers playing an extremely boisterous and suggestive version of their favourite game of Blind Man's Buff when she remarked to him, 'You are quiet tonight, Oliver. Does something ail you?'

'No illness,' he told her, 'but I must confess to you that I am suffering from the delusion that I am being watched. I can almost feel someone's eyes on me, but when I look behind me there is no one there. It is like possessing an invisible shadow. I have not told you of it for fear I may brand myself a coward.'

Her response surprised him. 'If that makes you a coward, then I am also one, since I occasionally feel that there is an unseen presence near me. Fortunately it has not visited me today.'

Oliver gave a short laugh, not of amusement but of relief. 'Doubtless that is because the thing, whatever it is, has been following me all afternoon.'

He paused. 'I wish I had spoken to you of this before. To know that I am not alone heartens me. If I am going mad, then I am doing it in good company. Come, I feel myself a man again, let us join the game and forget these idle fancies.'

'Yes, indeed, but they are not idle fancies. I think that they are plaguing us because of our involvement in Castleford's murder. I have never had them before that—and I dare swear you have only suffered from them since then.'

Oliver was about to say, 'Yes,' but he suddenly remembered that he had experienced something similar in Rome just before, and just after, Harry Grantly's untimely death. The strange sensation had disappeared on the way home and he had decided that it arose from his distress over the loss of his friend.

Well, he certainly didn't feel any distress over Castleford's death so that could not be the explanation now, particularly since Penelope also shared in the same delusion—if delusion it were.

He looked at her anxious face and made a firm

resolution that he would not let it trouble him, and that he would do everything to prevent it from distressing her. He took her hand and pulled her into the game, where she was immediately caught by Roger Temple, who declared loudly that it was the Queen's Jester whom he had snared. In the laughter and the frolicking which followed they both, for a time, forgot the shadow which haunted them.

Penelope's evening, however, was not yet over. She was approached by the Queen's Steward and commanded to wait upon Her Grace immediately. Her heart sank. She had no doubt that the Queen had learned of her improper meeting with Oliver in the Flemish Room and was about to reprimand her for it.

Her Grace was laughing and talking with Lord Robert when she arrived before her. Were she not the Queen, Penelope would have described her as behaving like a flirt and she wondered what Master Cecil was making of it. For the first time she asked herself what had happened between them in private, since Lord Robert and the Queen were frequently alone together—as she and Oliver had been in the Flemish Room. She knew that Kat Ashley disapproved of these dubious secret meetings, and now the Queen was about to bring her to task over behaviour which was very little different from her own.

But then she was the Queen, and doubtless made her own rules, as her father King Henry had done when he had married all those different women—and beheaded them if they dared to behave in the same

way as he did—although no one believed that the
present Queen's mother had been guilty of the crimes
brought against her.

At last the Queen turned to look at Penelope—although it had been some minutes since the Steward
had announced her presence.

'Ah, Mistress Jermaine, I am sure that you must be
a little surprised that I have sent for you in the middle
of the revels: it is certainly not for you to play the
virginals for me. Master Cecil has told me of your
claim that you and Master Woodville were alone together in the Flemish Room during the time in which
Lord Castleford was murdered. It is not the behaviour
which I expect of my Maids, and I have no doubt that
when Mistress Ashley is informed of it—as she soon
will be—she is sure to think of a suitable punishment
for you. For the present, however, you will escape it,
since Master Cecil wishes to keep everything related
to Lord Castleford's murder a secret.

'Of all my Maids you are the one whom I would
have least expected to misbehave in this fashion. You
will continue to wait on me until Master Cecil tells
me that the matter of Lord Castleford's murder has
been solved. After that, we shall see. You may go
now.'

Penelope curtseyed, relieved that the Queen had not
subjected her to a fit of the renowned Tudor temper
which went so well with her red hair. Perhaps, after
all, Her Grace felt a little pity for her because of her

own obvious love for a man whom she could never marry.

She passed Master Cecil as she left. He put out a hand to detain her.

'I see that you have escaped the full force of Her Grace's wrath,' he said.

Penelope could not stop herself from replying, 'For the time being, sir.'

He laughed a little at that. 'Go to, Mistress. Your appearance may be demure, but you have a witty tongue in your head. Beware that it does not get you into trouble.'

Penelope curtseyed to him. 'I shall be sure to take good heed of your advice, sir.'

He laughed again. 'See that you do, Mistress, see that you do.'

She told Oliver of this after she rejoined him, watching the revels while they spoke, the Flemish Room being forbidden to them now. He listened carefully to her before saying, 'I am happy to learn that Her Grace has not treated you severely over our trysts. While you were with her I have remembered something which I ought to have thought of before. On both occasions on which I met Dr Dee he warned me that I had a secret enemy who was working against me and that I was in grave danger as a result of his machinations. I dismissed this as a piece of nonsense designed to make me believe that he was able to tell the fortunes of those around him.

'Now I am not so sure. I have found myself trapped

in a veritable spider's web of intrigue and perhaps Dr
Dee was not far wrong when he told me to be wary
at all times. He regretted that he could not tell me my
enemy's name since his spirits refused to reveal it to
him. Nevertheless, I feel that I am so embattled that
it might be wise to speak to him after he arrives again
tomorrow and ask him if his spirits have any further
information as to who that enemy might be.'

Penelope was not certain how much she believed
in Dr Dee's powers, but anything which would help
Oliver in his present plight ought to be pursued.

'I agree that it could be a wise move and one to
make as soon as possible. Who knows, by now he
might be able to help you. He must know of what
you are suspected and will not be surprised if you
consult him.'

'In the morning, then. And now let us join the
dance. The Galliard has just been announced and after
tonight we may not have a chance to enjoy it again.
Tomorrow the revels will be over and we shall all be
grave and serious until the Queen is crowned.'

'I once looked forward to that day,' sighed
Penelope, 'but no longer, for when it is over all your
troubles will start again.'

'True, but while we tread a measure together we
may try to forget them. Tomorrow morning may bring
us better news.'

Oliver was right about being watched. Two pairs
of eyes had been following him around. The owner
of one pair couldn't make up his mind when to arm

his unconscious messenger of vengeance by saying the magic word and then watch his enemy die. The other one didn't know why it was important that he should watch Oliver Woodville, but, all the same, he felt compelled to shadow him around the palace. The feeling made him uneasy: he could neither eat nor sleep properly. He had said a prayer to the Virgin the other night, but the feeling still persisted and would not go away until he did something, but what that something was, he did not know...

Early on 7 January Oliver was told that Dr Dee had particularly asked to see him. On his arrival in Dee's quarters the necromancer welcomed him warmly, saying that he was delighted to meet Master Woodville again. He had been given a large room at the back of the Palace. It was full of books and strange instruments. He was, he said, engaged in drawing up an astrological chart to determine Lord Robert's future.

'But I am more than happy to talk to you, Master Woodville. I hear that your enemy has moved against you, and I am not one of those who suspect you of the heinous crime of murder.'

'Thank you, sir. It is of that enemy that I wish to speak. I own that I was not entirely convinced when you told me of him, but recent events seem to have proved you correct. Two attempts were made to kill me and after that my dagger was used to murder Lord Castleford so that it would appear that I was his assassin. I have come to ask you if it is now in your power to name him, and if you cannot do that, to discover whether you are able to tell me anything, either good or bad, of my future.'

Dr Dee closed his eyes. 'You ask me some hard questions, young man. When I heard of the attempt on your life and that you were talked of as Lord Castleford's murderer, I called up my spirits and asked them whether they could tell me anything useful concerning your sad situation. Their reply was to assure me of your innocence and that an enemy was continuing to plot against you. They could not, alas, reveal his name because he had hidden it beneath a magic spell which all their arts were unable to breach.

'I am sorry to tell you this, but what I *can* reveal is that the spirits also said that you would survive these recent trials and live a long and prosperous life with the woman you love. So, take heart, all will yet be well.'

This was so vague that, as Oliver had thought before, Dee might simply be forecasting what was likely to happen, rather than what would happen. It reminded him of those magic words which jugglers and magicians at fairs used when performing their tricks. They might mean anything, or nothing. If he didn't survive to live a long and happy life then the knowledge of Dee's mistaken forecast would die with him.

He replied, as politely as he could, 'I thank you, sir, and am relieved to learn that you have offered me the promise of a happy future.'

'Give me your birth date and the hour on which you were born, if you know it,' Dee smiled at him, 'and I will draw up your astrological chart. It might be more accurate than my spirits are choosing to be. I shall begin work on it straightway.'

Oliver immediately did as he was bid. Dee then offered him hippocras to drink, and a plate of biscuits to go with it, and they talked together of Oliver's travels in Europe before he left with Dee's promise that his chart would be delivered to him shortly.

Preparations continued to go ahead for the Queen's move back to the Tower of London. Never mind that it was hateful to her, since it had always been the place in which previous monarchs had spent a night before their crowning she had no wish to begin her reign by flouting that tradition. It was enough that she was displeasing her Catholic subjects by refusing to follow many of their usual rites without appearing to ignore also the wishes of the citizens of London.

They, too, were making ready for the Coronation. Rightly or wrongly many felt that a bright new day was dawning and that Elizabeth's youth and beauty, when compared with the middle age and dour appearance of her half-sister, were a hopeful augury of better times ahead. The City of London was a Protestant stronghold and its inhabitants were truly delighted that they would be welcoming a sovereign of their own faith.

Thus encouraged, the Mayor and Corporation were spending large sums of money on erecting triumphal arches in the city streets as well as on organising elab-

orate and rich pageants and masques to greet the
Queen when she made her final ceremonial progress
through London.

The courtiers and officials who surrounded her had
begun to pack their belongings for their move to the
Tower, where they would stay for two nights before
moving, yet again, to the Palace of Westminster, this
time to spend Coronation eve there. All those who
were to be part of her progress, including her ladies,
had been given bright new clothes to match the splendour in which she would be dressed.

In the bustle which all this provoked, Oliver and
Penelope rarely met. Oliver's duties for Lord Robert,
who was in charge of everything connected with the
rituals surrounding Her Grace, kept him busy. He
barely had time to look at Dee's astrological chart,
which arrived on his last day at Whitehall. In it, he
had repeated his forecast that Oliver's future would
be a happy and prosperous one—much as he had earlier prophesied for the Queen.

Penelope, for her part, was engaged in trying on
her new crimson and gold dress and in waiting on
Her Grace, who grew more demanding of all those
around her the nearer the great day loomed. Master
Cecil was heard to swear repeatedly that it was not
right that a mere woman, with all her frailties, should
be in a position to dominate the wiser men around
her. It was quite common for her, after a hard day's
work and attendance at the evening revelries where
she frequently danced as many as six Galliards with

Lord Robert, to send her Chief Secretary a messenger after midnight bidding him wait on her in order to discuss yet another round of affairs.

Her remarkable energy only served to point up her difference from her immediate predecessors, including her father King Henry VIII himself, who had left the running of such matters to his chief minister and his fellow officials. One old man was heard to moan that by all accounts she was following in the footsteps of her tireless grandfather, King Henry VII.

Finally, all preparations having been successfully made, the Queen travelled by royal barge to the Tower, escorted by the Mayor and Corporation and representatives of the craft guilds in their decorated barges. She found a concert of music waiting for her in the royal apartments there.

'At last,' said Penelope to Oliver when they met, on their first evening at the Tower. 'I thought that I was never going to see you again.'

'Lord Robert has been a demanding master,' he explained. 'He is anxious that everything shall go smoothly and has driven us all hard. I looked for you once or twice while we were still at Whitehall and couldn't find you, but I believe that the Queen was being even more demanding than he was. If I had ever thought that being a courtier meant that I should spend a great deal of time walking round in pretty clothes doing nothing, then the last few weeks have proved otherwise.'

Penelope, looking more enchanting than ever,

laughed up at him, 'I don't think that life at court will always be as busy, nor, I hope, shall we be moving around so much—or spending our time being fitted out in new garments. I do have one question for you—are you still plagued by the sense of being watched?'

He smiled back at her. 'Not so much recently, possibly because I was kept so busy. Today, being more idle I have felt it a little—but not so strongly as before.'

'Dr Dee would doubtless say that it is someone from the spirit world who is spying on you.'

'Speaking of Dr Dee, I am no further forward with him. His spirits do not know the name of my enemy and when he sent me my astrological chart it simply said what he had already told me—that I shall have a long and happy life.'

'Nothing more than that?'

'No, indeed. Lord Robert and the Queen may believe in him, but I am not sure that I do.'

Penelope, mischief in her face, leaned forward and asked him conspiratorially, 'Do you think that he ever forecasts a short, unhappy and unprosperous future for anyone?'

Oliver's laugh at this was unforced and several persons nearby stared at them. Among them was the possessor of one of the pairs of eyes which had been watching him. Its owner decided that he had been remiss in not moving against him earlier, but the new Lord Castleford, who had taken him into his service, was being an even more inconsiderate master than the old one and needed to be dealt with, too. But not yet. That would not be until Oliver Woodville had been consigned to Hell or Valhalla: his would-be murderer did not mind which.

Tomorrow he would arm his tool by saying the magic word Azazel, which should see Woodville despatched and Jenkins assumed to have been Castleford's murderer. After that he could make ready for his next appointment with Fate. For tonight he would be one of the congregation in the Tower's chapel with the rest of the court and pretend that he was worshipping Christ and the Trinity—and not their chief adversary, Satan.

On the morning of her first full day at the Tower, the Queen conferred the honour of the Knighthood of the Bath on several of her chief ministers. Later she had decreed that her first day at the Tower should have its importance marked by Bishop Oglethorpe officiating at evensong. Most of her entourage would be present. The Bishop had decided that he would, while not openly reproaching the Queen, show his displeasure at her rejection of so many articles of the Catholic faith and her overt sympathy for Protestantism, in a sermon designed to accomplish this implicitly, rather than explicitly.

Oliver was one of the congregation, as was Bevis Frampton, who was attending as the new Lord Castleford's deputy, that nobleman having succumbed to a fit of the ague. Like many of the congregation he found the Bishop's sermon both long and tedious. The back row in the chapel had been reserved for a few of the many servants of those present. They had been chosen by lot. Among the fortunate ones was the valet Jenkins, who sat there, waiting for he knew not what, his dagger hidden in his pocket where he had recently, for some reason which he did not understand, felt compelled to keep it. He was feeling even more restless than usual.

The Bishop's sonorous voice echoed around the chapel as he reached the climax of his sermon.

'My children,' he said, more in sorrow than in anger, 'I beg of you to embrace our true faith and not be diverted from the path to God's heaven by the lures of Satan and his rebel angels. Attractive though his standard bearer, Azazel, might be, know that to follow him is to take the path that leads to the deepest pit of Hell.'

Two of his hearers were moved in quite different ways by his calling upon Azazel. Bevis was horrified: he knew that Jenkins was a member of the congregation and he could only wonder what might be the effect on him of hearing the magic word by accident. The word which he, and he alone, had thought to rouse him with—but not at an inopportune moment like this!

Jenkins, by contrast, was seized by a feeling of intense joy and fulfillment. The holy word had been said. Now he knew what it was that he had to do and that was to please the spirit which guided him by killing his enemy, Oliver Woodville, as soon as he saw him. After that he would confess to the authorities the sin which he had committed by killing his master so that he might be purged of it forever, no matter what the consequences for him might be.

His moment would come when the nobility and gentry sitting near the front processed out of the chapel at the end of the service. He secretly fetched out his dagger and slid it from its sheath. Now let young Woodville come near him and he would act before anyone could stop him.

The service duly reached its end. The Bishop bestowed his blessing on them all, Catholic and Protestant alike, after which the Queen and her chief ministers rose and marched out of the chapel, followed by the rest of the congregation in rank order. And there, walking immediately after Lord Robert Dudley, was Oliver Woodville side by side with Roger Temple who was on his right.

Jenkins rose, and, accompanied by the complaints of those he was discommoding, pushed his way along the row to be as near to the aisle as possible when his prey reached him.

Now!

He jumped forward, his dagger raised, ready to plunge it into Oliver's breast.

Oliver had attended the service with the suspicion that he had murdered Castleford still hanging over him. He prayed to God most fervently that he would save him from a shameful death which he did not deserve. Most of those who knew him thought him innocent, but that would be of no use to him in a court of law when his dagger—which had undoubtedly killed Castleford—was produced in evidence.

He had tried, during the last few days, to behave as though nothing was wrong, helped by Penelope who was not only his love, but his most fervent supporter.

'Who knows,' she had said to him, when she had met him that morning, 'what time may yet bring about? I cannot believe that they can try to sentence you on such flimsy evidence in the face of my own confession that you were with me on that fatal night.'

He wished that he could share her unshaken belief that he would come through this time of trial unscathed. He listened to the Bishop's sermon wondering wryly how little the man was saying had to do with life as it was lived outside the cloisters and the academies, where matters of religious theology were abstract things to be endlessly discussed. He could hear Roger Temple, who sat on his right, yawning as each leaden sentence rolled along.

Finally it was over. The great ones at the front of the chapel processed out and then it was his and Roger's turn to leave. Roger, who was on his right hand, was whispering something indiscreet about the Bishop's sermon and Oliver had turned his head to-

wards him the better to hear him, when suddenly the
world exploded around them.

'No,' Roger was shouting, causing heads behind
them to turn at this sacrilege in a holy place. At the
same time he was pushing Oliver backwards with
such force that Oliver found himself knocking the
man behind him down, but not before he found why
Roger was behaving with such surprising violence.

A man—could it possibly be Castleford's valet?—
was advancing on him with an upraised dagger while
Roger, having saved Oliver from it by shoving him
away, had caught the would-be assassin from the rear
as he pursued Oliver. Shocked and surprised though
Oliver was, he attacked the man from the front and
attempted to wrest the dagger from him before he
could injure either of them with it.

Jenkins was still screaming abuse at him, so that
there could be no doubt of who it was he wished to
kill. To Oliver it was like a scene from Dante's Hell.
One moment he had been walking peacefully along,
the next he was being attacked by a madman shouting
his name. The procession behind him had fallen into
immediate disarray. Bevis Frampton, in the middle of
it, was consumed by a fever of fear and rage as his
careful plan went awry.

The worst thing of all was that not only was that
swine, Woodville, fighting Jenkins off, with the help
of Temple and the members of the congregation near
him, but that Jenkins, having failed in his mission to
kill Woodville, had turned the dagger on himself for

some reason which neither Bevis, nor Jenkins, now completely in the grip of madness, could guess.

Trapped between Oliver and Roger, who had borne him to the ground, Jenkins's failure was compounded by the fact that he had only succeeded in wounding himself slightly and Oliver not at all.

Bevis found it difficult to prevent himself from crying aloud. Satan, his master, had deserted him and had allowed the Bishop to say the fatal word at the wrong time. He could only pray that the power of the command he had given to his tool had not failed also. If it had it was possible that Jenkins might blurt out his name to his captors and to Lord Robert, who, on hearing the hubbub behind him, had turned back on his tracks, had seen most of the action and was staring at the wretched valet, who lay on the floor of the aisle, helpless, trapped and bleeding freely. Despite that he was shouting curses at Oliver so that all could hear him.

'Dead,' he was howling, 'you should be dead—like Lord Castleford whom I killed with your dagger. Why did you not die when I pushed you downstairs and then I should not be here, betrayed by the spirits whom I had believed to be helping me?'

'The man is mad,' said Lord Robert impassively. 'Take him away, to be questioned and dealt with. It is a mercy that you were spared, Master Woodville— and that he has publicly confessed to the crime of which you might have been falsely accused.'

Oliver did not answer him. He was too busy watching Jenkins being hauled to his feet by the surrounding gentlemen before he was handed over to the Yeomen of the Guard who had entered the chapel prior to arresting him and taking him away.

'But I hardly know the man,' he said, 'and to find in this way that it was Castleford who ordered me to be killed...and that it was he who murdered Castleford...' Bewildered, he shook his head. 'I have you to thank, Roger, for acting so quickly and saving me from certain death. I was too busy trying not to tread on the heels of the man in front of me to see him begin to attack me.'

'Nonsense,' said Roger. 'I happened, by pure chance, to see him when you were paying attention to me and not to the rest of the congregation. And, by the way, who the devil was he?'

'Castleford's valet, Jenkins. I only met him once, and I do not understand why he should wish to murder me.'

Lord Robert, who had ordered the remaining congregation not to leave the chapel until Jenkins had been removed, said, 'You may be sure, Master Woodville, that he will be closely interrogated before he is tried and condemned. I understand that he also claimed that it was he who pushed you downstairs— which is another mystery solved. Now let us reform the procession and continue with our own business. I expect that Master Cecil will wish to question you and I give you leave to attend him before we sup with the Queen's Grace.'

* * *

'Castleford's valet tried to murder Oliver—and in the chapel, too! If it were not you telling me this, Mistress Ashley, I would think that you were jesting.'

Penelope had not attended the service, being required instead to help the wardrobe mistresses make ready the dresses of the Queen and her ladies for the procession into London and the Coronation which would follow.

'No jest, Mistress Jermaine. It seems that this fellow, who was Lord Castleford's valet, on his master's orders pushed Master Woodville downstairs. He then stole Master Woodville's dagger and murdered m'lord with it, before making another attempt to kill Master Woodville. One can only wonder why he committed these dreadful acts. One must suppose him mad.'

Penelope was not surprised to learn that Lord Castleford had ordered his valet to try to murder Oliver, since he had threatened both of them if they continued to see each other. What did surprise her was why the valet should wish to kill his master. She thought it wise not to discuss any of this with Kat Ashley. As usual, the less she said the better.

'What happened to the valet?' she asked instead.

'Oh, the Yeomen took him off to be questioned, summarily tried and sentenced. There is no doubt of his guilt—he confessed everything after he had failed to kill Master Woodville. It seems that he babbled a great deal about the spirits who had told him what to do.'

Penelope thought immediately of poor Alys Belsize who had said something similar. Perhaps the pair of them had been influenced by the presence at court of Dr Dee. Never mind that, the sooner she saw Oliver, the happier she would be, for now that the shadow of being suspected of killing Lord Castleford had been lifted from him they could enjoy life again.

'This beggars belief,' said Master Cecil. 'You say that this creature spoke, not only of his guilt in killing his master, but of the spirits who ordered him to execute Master Woodville as well?'

Lord Robert, Oliver and Roger Temple were all closeted with Master Cecil, who had demanded a full report of what had occurred in the chapel.

Lord Robert said, 'I arrived late on the scene but in time to hear Castleford's valet confess to having murdered his master. Masters Woodville and Temple and many of those around them will also bear witness to that.'

'So, all is explained which before was a mystery. I understand that he is already being severely questioned in the dungeons. We must be rid of him by tomorrow—such a miscreant must not be allowed to sully the rite of Coronation as he has already sullied the Queen's chapel. Her Grace wishes to speak to the three of you, once our meeting is over. She is waiting for you in the Presence Chamber. I shall join you later, after I have visited the dungeons to discover whether the questioning has revealed anything further.'

Master Cecil did not immediately leave on his unpleasant, if necessary, errand once he was alone, but sat for some minutes pondering on what he had just learned. He asked himself why it was that he still thought that there was something strange, something unexplained about the whole wretched business? All this babbling about spirits was disturbing to say the least.

He thought so even more when he stood in the underground room where so many had been tortured before in an effort to force truth, or at least a confession, out of murdering and conspiring villains. It was not that Jenkins, who was chained to the wall, was unwilling to talk, far from it. But what he was saying over and over again was what he had bawled at Oliver in the chapel: that after he had failed to kill Oliver Woodville when he had pushed him downstairs, he had been guided in all he did by the spirit Azazel.

Cecil spoke at last: so far he had been listening carefully to the madman's ravings in answer to the questions thrown at him, with the promise of the rack if he did not speak the truth.

'One moment,' he said. 'Has he mentioned the name Azazel before?'

'Frequently,' said the chief torturer, a big and burly man.

'Now that is interesting, for during his sermon

Bishop Oglethorpe spoke of Azazel—Satan's standard bearer. Have you questioned those around him as to his behaviour during the service?'

A clerk, who was busy keeping a record of what was being said, looked up. 'That has been done, sir. Before we brought the prisoner down to the dungeons we questioned his fellows in the back pews. They gave evidence that after the word Azazel was spoken he became extremely agitated, but he did nothing until the procession began to leave the chapel, whereupon he attacked Master Woodville.'

'Azazel,' shouted Jenkins. 'He is my master and none other. It is his bidding I do—and ever shall.'

Cecil rose and walked over to question Jenkins himself, using a mild voice. 'What else did Azazel bid you do?'

This simple question confused Jenkins, who said, 'Have I not told you, not once but many times? I did that which I was bid—and nothing more.'

'Has he spoken to you since you were brought here?'

'Nay, nor need he, for have I not been his obedient servant?'

'That is all that we can get from him,' said the chief guard. 'He will speak of nothing else. There is no doubt of his guilt—nor that he is mad with his talk of his spirit master.'

'Nor is there need to question him further,' Cecil said, 'nor torture him, neither. Mad or not, he must pay for his crimes. He has killed, and tried to kill, in the precincts of the court, and has so confessed.'

It was over, but Cecil still felt that there was something missing, something unexplained. A shadow hung over the court—but unless further evidence came along he would have to be content that at least the visible murderer had been dealt with. What was done was done; he had much to do, and no time to waste in brooding on mysteries.

Oliver left the meeting with Cecil in a state of happy relief. His innocence had been proved beyond a doubt and he need no longer fear a knock at his door, or the sight of guards coming to escort him to the dungeons to be tortured and questioned. Now he could approach Penelope's parents and ask them for her hand in marriage, secure in the knowledge that he had been proved a loyal member of Elizabeth's court.

At the same time he also knew that he had some hard decisions to make about his future—but they could wait until after the Coronation was over. Once they were alone together Roger shook him by the hand.

'I have come to know you too well,' he said, 'to believe the tales which flew about the court that since it was your dagger which was used to kill Castleford, then you must be guilty. But I greatly feared that you might suffer for the acts of another and what happened in the chapel proved you innocent and me right. I think I ought to tell you that once the Coronation is over and my marriage to Mary Jermaine is finally arranged, I shall be leaving the court. I have decided that this life is not for me.'

Oliver wondered how his future bride would receive this news, but said nothing to Roger, who had his own life to live without interference from others. In some strange way he felt that these few weeks he had spent at Elizabeth's court had changed him, but whether for good or ill he did not know.

He bade his friend good night and went to look for Penelope.

He found her with the Queen in the Presence Chamber: she was playing the virginals. Lord Robert and a small group of courtiers and ministers were seated near Her Grace, but Master Cecil was absent. Either what had happened in the chapel, of which she had undoubtedly been informed, or the atmosphere of the Tower itself was responsible, but there was an air of gravity in the room quite unlike the evening jollity which had reigned for the last few weeks.

The Queen looked up when he entered and beckoned to the waiting steward to bring him to where she sat, Lord Robert and another great gentleman beside her.

'I was greatly pleased, young man,' she told him, 'to hear that you not only survived an attack on your life, but that the attacker also confessed to the wicked deeds of which you were wrongly suspected. Once, however, I had heard Mistress Penelope Jermaine's account of your naughty behaviour in the Flemish

Room at the time of Lord Castleford's murder, I gave immediate orders that no action was to be taken against you until further investigations had been made. These are not now necessary. Once Mistress Penelope has finished playing for me I give you permission to go to her, provided always that you behave towards her, as Master Chaucer had it, like a very perfect gentle knight.'

Oliver bowed low. 'You are gracious, madam. I shall try to obey you in all things.'

'See that you do, sir, see that you do. Now go to your lady, for her song is at an end.'

Outside the Presence Chamber, hidden in one of the niches, the man who had watched Oliver ever since he had left the chapel was lamenting his tool's failure to carry out the fell task which he had been given. It seemed that the fates smiled kindly on Woodville as they had not done on Castleford and Harry Grantly. This was the third time on which, by chance, he had escaped death, and it might be that these same fates were telling him something. He would try to conjure up one of his spirits to ask him for advice, but they had been strangely silent of late and it might be that they thought him wrong to pursue his enemy so frantically.

He would think again of what to do before he decided on one last attempt to remove Oliver Woodville from this earth.

Chapter Fourteen

The day before her Coronation Elizabeth was carried in a richly ornamented litter through the streets of London on the way to the Palace of Westminster. Whatever else Lord Robert's other talents were—and there were those who doubted that he had many—he was a supreme master so far as arranging pageantry was concerned. He had given himself a major role by riding behind the Queen's litter while leading her palfrey.

Penelope was in the group of thirty-nine Ladies who followed him. They were all wearing crimson velvet robes with cloth of gold sleeves, the product of the hard work of the many seamstresses whose only part in the procession was to cheer it as it wandered through the streets of London. Behind them were more than a thousand mounted dignitaries. Oliver had his place there, thinking how fortunate he had been to survive to enjoy this day.

The Queen and her followers, riding at one point through a light snow shower, soon found that the City had outdone itself. At every turn of the road from Fenchurch Street onwards, the Mayor and Corporation had arranged for pageants, shows, heralds and even children to be ready to welcome their new Queen and to celebrate the Protestantism of the City itself. No expense had been spared in order to demonstrate to their new ruler the profound support which she enjoyed from all classes of society.

Most of the pageants centred around stories from the Old Testament and morality plays and all of them, as several foreign diplomats disapprovingly noted, were based on the principles of the Protestant faith. The Queen made no objection to this: far from it— she welcomed the frequent references to the one true religion which she was supposed to symbolise, and when the procession was stopped so that she might hear yet one more fulsome panegyric addressed to her she seemed always able to find the right words to thank those who were offering them.

Many of the watchers commented on how much she resembled her late father, the old king, something which pleased all those who remembered his reign as glorious by contrast with whose which had immediately followed him and who hoped that his younger daughter would be his true heir.

Finally the procession reached the City limits at Temple Bar, shortly before its journey ended at the Palace of Westminster, where the Queen was due to spend the night. It took some time for them all to enter; Elizabeth was very tired since she had spent the whole day smiling and thanking the cheering crowds, making several impromptu speeches along the lengthy route, but she never once betrayed how weary she felt.

In the hubbub which followed their arrival as members of the court tried to discover where their future quarters were, Penelope looked for Oliver. She had almost given up searching when she saw him and Roger come in from the stables where they had been caring for the welfare of the horses.

'Mistress Jermaine,' Roger said, forestalling Oliver. 'Your new gown becomes you well.'

Penelope offered him a saucy curtsey.

'I thank you, sir.'

'May I also praise your appearance, Penelope?' asked Oliver.

'Indeed you may. But the ladies are not the only splendidly apparelled members of the court on show,' was her riposte. 'All of the gentlemen, including your good selves, also look very fine.'

They both bowed back at her as gracefully as she had saluted them.

Roger, ever tactful, and mindful that Penelope and Oliver really needed to speak together now that the latter had been cleared of all wrong-doing and was safe from his mad enemy, who was due to be executed once the Coronation was safely over, said, 'I will leave you two turtle-doves together—I have no wish to be a fifth wheel to your carriage.'

Oliver grinned as Roger walked away. 'He is a good fellow and I can only hope that Mary understands that. He will look after her if she will let him.'

Penelope nodded agreement. 'I am not sure how happy she will be when she learns that he intends to retire from the court.'

'But she will not change his mind. What would you say to me, Penelope, if I told you that I might follow Roger's example, although I have not yet quite decided what my future will be?'

'It must be your wish,' said Penelope gravely, 'since if you decide to stay, yours will be the harder task. I will support you in whatever your choice may be.'

Oh, if only he could kiss her for those few kind words, here, where they stood in full view of everyone who came through the door to the mews. She had never looked more lovely than she did now in her brilliant crimson dress, her eyes sparkling at him. Desire roared through Oliver, choosing, as usual, the most inconvenient moment to attack him.

He tried to think of something commonplace to say to calm his unruly body down.

'At least we now have no need to worry that someone will be waiting around the next corner to assassinate me,' he said—but he still remained a slave to temptation.

'True,' said Penelope, smiling at Oliver, which undid him all over again. 'What *I* have to worry about is that Kat Ashley will notice that I am missing and will be getting ready to subject me to one of her sermons on duty and punctuality, so I will bid you farewell until the morrow.'

Oliver watched her measured walk along the gallery towards Kat and conscientiousness, his painful desire slowly subsiding. He was finding it hard to wait for the day when it would be his duty to please and to pleasure her, and not a sin to be avoided.

Everything, many of her subjects said afterwards, even the weather, was favouring Elizabeth Tudor when she awoke on Coronation day, Sunday, 15 January, to find a cold and frosty, but fine morning, waiting for her. Fortunately the Queen and her entourage had only a short journey to make to the Abbey. She was being conveyed there in a chariot, which was merely a litter pulled by two mules, and was wearing yet another splendid set of robes—her over-gown being made of cloth of gold. An ermine cape covered her shoulders and she wore her hair loose both as a symbol of her virginity and in memory of her mother. The so-called chariot was decorated in scarlet.

Lord Robert, on horseback and leading her palfrey, was again her chief attendant, but this time her Ladies walked behind her, their beautiful long gowns trailing in the gravel once the spectators outside the Abbey had torn up the blue carpet laid down for the Queen after she had walked on it. It was remarked that the crowds that watched the regal procession were as ecstatic as they had been the day before.

Afterwards Penelope remembered the Coronation service as a blur of light, music and noise, more a superb piece of theatre than a religious ceremony, particularly at the end when Bishop Oglethorpe asked the congregation if they accepted her as Queen and they loudly shouted 'Yes', with one voice and all the bells began to ring at once. If so, she afterwards conceded, it served its purpose, for when Elizabeth emerged from the Abbey wearing a light crown made for her mother, and not the over-weighty crown of state, and carrying the orb and sceptre, the crowd again went wild as she walked in procession, smiling at them, all the way back to Westminster Palace.

After the service came the banquet at Westminster Hall. It began at three of the clock in the afternoon and ended at one in the morning. The peers were present as well as the ministers and courtiers who served the Queen. Oliver was not seated near Penelope, but that was to be expected. He and Roger found themselves far away from the great powers in the land, at the end of one of the long tables each of which led to where the Queen sat—in yet another gown, this time of purple velvet—beneath a canopy of state, waited on by two of her nobles.

The meal was an elaborate one and the wine flowed like water. For once Roger, who was usually abste-

mious, indulged himself, but Oliver, remembering the
advice which the physicians in Italy had given him
after Henry's death, was more careful. He was again
plagued by the feeling that someone was watching
him, but looking around the huge chamber at all the
dignitaries assembled there, he felt that he must be
mistaken.

He was not wrong. Bevis had been chosen as one
of those who had been delegated to serve those fortunate enough to sit at table. This was considered
something of an honour, since even the Queen was
waited on and handed her food and drink by two of
England's most prominent noblemen, her great-uncle,
Lord William Howard, and the Earl of Sussex. In
Bevis's case this gave him every opportunity not only
to watch Oliver, but to have one more chance to harm
him.

He was carrying round a great pitcher of hippocras
to refill the drinkers' goblets. He avoided serving the
part of the table where Oliver sat until the feasting
had reached the pitch where most of the company
were flown with the wine which they had already
drunk, then he made it his business to walk to where
he could see that Oliver's goblet stood half-empty.

He took great care to fill it while Oliver was turned
towards Roger, so that he remained unseen, pouring
a great draught into the goblet as well as a smaller
one from a phial similar to the one he had given Alys,
except that its contents, brought from Italy, were even
more deadly. It was a potion supposed to be similar

to those the Borgia family had used to subtly murder
their victims.

He then walked rapidly on. Oliver, still trying to
keep a steady head while everyone about him was
busy making theirs as flighty as possible, made no
effort to drink what he had been served. Roger, by
contrast, now almost ready to sink to the floor,
clapped him on the shoulder, saying, 'By the Lord
God, Woodville, if you do not wish to drink up
hearty, then I will do the business for you.' On Oliver
laughing and replying, 'Pray do,' Roger seized the
poisoned goblet, intending to drain it.

He was saved only by the diner on his right, now
even more drunk than he was, deciding to clap *him*
on the back, just as Roger turned to steal Oliver's
drink. The blow struck Roger on the elbow instead,
with the result that the goblet and its contents were
knocked to the floor, the wine spilling in all direc-
tions.

At this happy sight one of the many greyhounds
who were lying before the wall behind them, all of
whom were busy snapping up the stray bones and
other dainties which the guests threw to them, leaped
to its feet and eagerly lapped up the spilt liquor.

'Happy to see that someone appreciates good wine
better than you do, Woodville, even if it is only one
of Her Grace's dogs,' was Roger's comment on that.
Whereupon the surrounding company began to laugh,
one of them going so far as to offer a toast to the
greyhound, commending its taste.

It was not, however, to the dog's liking. The greyhound, which had lain down again after its unexpected good fortune in inheriting Oliver's hippocras, rose on all fours and began to bark frantically before falling to the floor, writhing in agony while being violently sick.

'Good God!' cried one drunken reveller, 'I never knew good wine affect a dog like that before.'

The only person not amused by the sight of the stricken dog lying still and quiet after its dreadful spasm of illness was Oliver. He rose to his feet and, choosing a clean piece of floor, knelt down and gently examined it. As he had suspected, the poor creature was dead—dead from drinking the wine which had been meant for him.

What to do?

To inform the revellers of the dog's death after it had drunk from his goblet something which had killed it on the instant would mean drawing attention to himself again: attention which he did not want. He remembered feeling that he was being watched—and perhaps that feeling was a true one, even if he could not explain it. Fortunately no one was taking any notice of him or of the dog. Even Roger was too far gone to grasp that there was something odd about the dog's sudden death.

Where had the poison come from—and who had doctored his drink? It was certainly not Lord Castleford's valet, who was lying chained in one of the Tower's dungeons, waiting to be executed, but if

were not he, then who could it be? He took from the
purse attached to his belt his finest handkerchief,
which he had bought in Florence, and laid it carefully
under the poor creature's head. In a sense it had died
for him—and for Roger, who had been about to drink
his unwanted hippocras.

He returned to his seat. No one remarked on him—
or the dog. He said casually to Roger, 'Did you notice
who served me with my last drink?'

'Not I,' said Roger blearily. 'Too busy enjoying
myself.'

Oliver looked around him—at the diners and at the
crowd of servitors both gentle and simple—but he
could recognise no one whom he thought might wish
to kill him. He did not see Bevis because he had already left the Hall pleading illness—which was not
altogether a lie, since the sight of a dead greyhound
and not of a dead Oliver Woodville had not only sick-
ened him, but confirmed him in the belief that his
enemy was being protected by some power greater
than himself or his attendant spirit. Could it be that
the wretch Dee was looking after him? If so, then it
might well be unwise to continue to try to kill him.

So the shadow which lay over him was still there,
was Oliver's reaction to what had just happened. He
could not believe that the greyhound's death was an
accident, coming as it did after so many varied attempts to harm him. It was particularly galling that it
had happened so soon after he and Penelope had been
happily agreeing that, as a result of Jenkins's arrest

and his repeated confessions, all danger to him was over. Despite that, he was more resolved than ever that he would say and do nothing which would cast a shadow over the celebrations of the Queen's Coronation.

He refused to drink anything more, but tried to enjoy his dinner and join in the general merriment. Gradually the sense of horror at the dog's death, which might have been his own, dimmed a little. He was even able to present a happy face to the world, while privately deciding that he would say nothing to Penelope about this latest incident. She did not deserve to be worried. After all, the whole business might have been an accident, or perhaps the dog had eaten or drunk something else which had killed him.

But Oliver did not really believe this, however much he tried to convince himself that such an explanation could possibly be true.

Later, much later, when all the guests, led by Her Grace, had left the Hall to the servants and porters to clean and tidy, the dead dog was taken away with the other litter, leaving the chief steward to inform the Queen that one of her pets had succumbed to overeating, which was not surprising considering how much food the nobility and gentry had been throwing at them…

Virtually everyone in the Palace of Westminster, except the Queen and her chief minister, William Cecil, woke up half-way through the next morning with a thick head and very little memory of how they had managed to stagger up to bed.

Oliver was no exception. Despite the shock which he had suffered at dinner, he had, to his own astonishment, slept what was sometimes called the sleep of the just. His head was not quite so thick as everyone else's, because he had refused any further drink after the dog's death.

Shortly after he had dressed himself, a little page arrived with a letter for him from Penelope. It seemed that Mary, who had been staying with her parents, had written that now that the Coronation was safely over they wished both her and Oliver to visit them at their home in the Strand as soon as possible.

'I know not,' she wrote, 'what Mary has said to them, or why they should wish to see you. She did add that Roger had also been invited, but, again, gave no reason why. We must try to meet today as soon as our duties are over.'

This was, indeed, passing strange—unless Roger, whom he knew had visited Mary at the Jermaines' home after she had left the court, had said something to them about him and Penelope which had aroused their curiosity.

Now he had yet one more thing to worry him. If he visited Penelope's parents as they wished, then what would they say to him if he asked them for their daughter's hand in marriage, seeing that he had not been considered to be a good enough husband for

Mary? His life's complications seemed to be growing by the minute!

Oh, never mind that! What was it that Harry Grantly was given to saying to him when he had worried or busied himself overmuch with his plans and arrangements during their continental tour? *'Courage mon ami, le diable est mort!'* Which roughly translated meant 'Courage, my friend, the devil is dead!' with the added rider that consequently there is no need to fret.

Suddenly Oliver knew that the attempts on his life, even the suspicion in which he been briefly held, far from weakening him, had strengthened him. He was his own man and no one else's—not Lord Robert's nor William Cecil's—and he would allow no hidden creature to frighten him, nor trouble himself with what the Jermaines might say to him. He had not Roger Temple's prospect of a peerage, but he came of a good family, better even than the Jermaines, and he truly loved Penelope and would care for and protect her.

Better than that, he had already done so when Castleford had played his unpleasant trick on her, and although he could not tell her parents of it he knew what he had done and that he would do it again, if need be.

Oliver laughed at himself a little. Where had all this sudden maturity, this belief in himself, come from? No matter, he would act on it and give the dead devil a kick into the bargain. So he sent the page back with the verbal message that he would try to see his love as soon as possible.

Thus, when he met Penelope later that day, she was surprised by the joy with which he greeted her and pleased that, unlike most of the court, the previous night's excesses had left no mark on his face.

'Tomorrow,' he said. 'I have spoken to Lord Robert and he has given me leave to visit your parents tomorrow.'

'And the Queen's Grace is allowing me to have the whole day to myself tomorrow because she says that I have worked hard enough to deserve it.'

'And Roger will accompany us. Have you any notion as to why I have been invited? I can guess why he has.'

'None at all, but I can hope.'

'And I also.'

She looked so loving that Oliver was tempted to kiss her. Instead he said, 'Now, before I accompany you to the Strand, I must first tell you of the decision which I have come to, before I ask you an important question—for your answer may rest on my decision.'

He looked so serious and earnest when he said this that Penelope had an insane wish to kiss his anxious face and make it happy again. She contented herself with replying, 'Tell me of your decision, my dear heart. I am sure that you have not come to it without due and careful consideration.'

Oliver inclined his head. 'It is this. When I went abroad with Harry Grantly I had it in mind that when

I returned I would wish to join Princess Elizabeth's court when she inherited the crown. I wanted to serve my country and so when we visited the courts of France and Italy I studied their manners and customs most seriously in case they might help me when I achieved my ambition. Some of the things which I saw disturbed me a little, but I became increasingly convinced that I possessed the powers which would lead me to success. Even when I first arrived back home and became one of Lord Robert's men I soon discovered that my talents were such that I felt that little was beyond my reach.

'However, as time passed I also found that one of the talents necessary for success was an ability to lie, to deceive and to cheat my fellow men. This ability I also possessed but the more I used it the more I came to dislike myself. I suddenly grew to believe that if I were not careful I would come to resemble not only Lord Castleford but also many of the men who, for one reason or another, lost not only their honesty, but their lives, in pursuing such worldly ambitions.

'At first I thought that to retreat would be cowardly, brought about by the attempts to disgrace and kill me. Then I asked myself, could I be sure that I would not behave like that? I also asked myself whether my life would be more honest, more devoted to the service of God and the right if I were to return home, run the family estates for my father who was old before I was born, and try to ensure that my family, servants and tenants had a happy and fulfilled life.

'I thus intend to relinquish my post at court and the prospects of promotion which both Lord Robert openly and Master Cecil secretly have offered me, and retire to the country. Would you be happy with a simple gentleman on his lands rather than a courtier on his way to dubious glory?'

He was saying what Penelope had come to believe. She thought of unhappy Alys and of a life which, as Oliver was saying, depended on deceit, trickery and flattery: all of which attributes the saints and the Bible condemned.

She nodded her head gravely. 'I can see that you have been thinking deeply on this matter. You said that you have also a question to ask me. I should like to hear it.'

'Can you not guess what it is?'

Penelope put her head on one side and replied coyly, 'Of course, I can't. Oh, yes, I have it. You spoke recently of you singing, and me playing for Her Grace—if she would wish it—that old song about the spring which we practised together before you went to Europe.'

'That is truly a sweet thought, but no. What I have to say to you is this.' And then, although they were in the long gallery at the top of the stairs and might be seen by anyone, he went down on one knee, took her hand, and said, 'Miss Penelope Jermaine, as I love you, and I trust that you love me, then I ask you to allow me to approach your father in order to ask him for his consent to our marriage.'

Penelope, her eyes sparkling, clasped her hands together and said, 'Yes, Oliver, oh, yes: what else can I say? At one time I thought that you would never ask me—but I do understand why you delayed until you were out of danger. As for your decision to leave the court and go home, I support it with all my heart. I, too, am fearful of the kind of person I might become if I were to remain here much longer. I may also tell you that, like Ruth in the Bible I would cleave to you whatever you decided.'

If Oliver had not been so delighted by her frank answer—so typical of the woman he loved—he would have felt worried over the fact that by not telling her of the previous night's incident with the greyhound he might be deceiving her as to his safety, but as it was he could scarcely contain himself. Only the knowledge that at any moment someone might come along prevented him from taking her into his arms.

That could wait—but not for too long, he hoped.

All that now remained was for her father to agree to the marriage—and he could not take that agreement for granted.

Late the following day Bevis Frampton was told the rumour that Oliver Woodville was planning to retire from the court to settle on his father's estates. He already knew that Roger Temple was leaving now that the Coronation was over. In some sense this latest failure to kill Oliver by poisoning him had frightened him. How was it possible that his victim had managed to escape with his life on every occasion when, by rights, he should have lost it?

Was the collapse of this latest attempt a sign that fate was taking a hand against him? And if Woodville was retiring into the country, had he not in a sense defeated him in a different fashion by convincing him that court life was too dangerous and thus he must abandon his hopes for a public life there? If so, then he would wave him a silent goodbye and allow him to settle down as a country bumpkin, his revenge accomplished after a different fashion.

There would be other battles for him to win in the future—no doubt of that: even to influence the life of the Queen might not be beyond his powers.

The Jermaines' home on the Strand was an impressive one, with miniature turrets set at its four corners, standing as it did among those even grander houses which belonged to the great nobles of the Tudor courts. Their gardens ran down to the river, and Oliver, Roger and Penelope were rowed along it to the steps which led up to the Jermaines' premises: the Thames was London's principal highway—being easier to use than any road.

'Cold though it is to travel on the river,' Roger had said, when calling for a wherry, 'it is easier than trying to find one's way through the city's crowded streets.'

Oliver was in full agreement with that. If Roger was surprised that he had also been invited to dine with Penelope's parents he was tactful enough to say nothing. Penelope was wrapped in furs and accompanied by her maid; Gib, armed, and acting as a footman, accompanied them.

The roaring fire in the Great Hall to which they were led by the Jermaines' Steward, who was still delighting in the family's new importance, was an extremely welcome sight to the shivering travellers.

It was Penelope's father who rose to greet them from his vast armchair—another symbol of his new station in life.

'My lady will greet you later,' he told them. 'Penelope, my dear, Brewster will escort you and Roger to your mother's room while I talk on matters of importance with Master Woodville before we dine. I trust that you will excuse us, Master Temple.'

Roger indicated that he would. He liked Mistress Jermaine, who he thought to be a less self-important person than her arrogant husband: he was pleased to leave Oliver to him.

Oliver, however, was not sure what was coming. Master Jermaine motioned him to an armchair opposite to him.

'You will wonder, Master Woodville, why I have summoned you here. It is of my daughter, Penelope, that I wish to speak to you. I understand from my other daughter, Mary, that her late betrothed husband, Lord Castleford, wished to disown her, despite the fact that they were pledged *de futuro* and were shortly to sign the binding *verbis de praesenti* contract. It appears that he had decided that he preferred to marry Penelope instead. His violent death, however, has left both my daughters free to marry whomsoever I should please.

'I shall today give my consent to Mary's marriage to Master Roger Temple, a most worthy young man, since I understand that he is the eldest son of a father who is the heir to an Earldom. Now, as to Penelope, I also understand from Master Temple that you were kind to her when Lord Castleford pursued her after he threatened to throw off Mary even though Penelope did not desire to marry him. I would therefore, wish to know what *your* intentions are towards Penelope. Pray do not be afraid to speak your mind.'

He stopped. Oliver stared at him. It was quite plain that John Jermaine, who had not wished Mary to marry him, was now urgently asking him to make an offer for Penelope! He could only wonder what had caused this dramatic change of heart.

'I came here today,' he said, 'to ask you for Mistress Penelope's hand in marriage. Do I understand that you would be only too willing to agree to such a union?'

'Most heartily. You are a worthy young man of good, if not great, family, and she, being quiet and learned, is not likely to attract the male flibbertigibbets of the court—or of such lying fortune-hunters as the late Lord Castleford. I have learned since his death that he had repeatedly deceived me about his wealth and the size of his estates. I count his untimely end as a piece of great good fortune.'

The world had turned upside down indeed! He had come here to plead with John Jermaine to be good enough to allow him to marry Penelope and instead her father was eager to agree to their marriage. So shocked was Oliver that he did not immediately offer the man an answer.

Finally he said, his manner grave. 'Before you give me your consent, I ought perhaps to tell you that as soon as the matter may be arranged I shall be leaving the court to return home to help my father manage his estates—as you know, he is growing old. I have no intention of continuing to be one of the Queen's courtiers. Penelope is only too willing to retire to the country with me.'

John Jermaine gave a great sigh. 'If that is what you both wish, then I will respect your decision. I have been greatly disappointed with what I have learned of the conduct of the court during the late Queen's reign and I doubt me that the new Queen's will be any different.'

Oliver bowed his head. 'To speak plainly, sir, I wish to tend my own garden and not that of the monarch. There are many others who will wish to do that, and my blessing goes with them.'

'Then, Master Woodville, I will freely give my consent to your marriage to my daughter, and that being so, I shall give the order for my wife, Master

Temple and Penelope to join us. After that we may make arrangements for all the necessary legal formalities to go ahead as soon as possible. Both of you are above the common age of marriage and the sooner you are able to bless your father and myself with grandchildren, the better.'

It was done, and all his and Penelope's fears about the nature of her father's answer when Oliver made his offer for her hand had been groundless. Later, after they had eaten and drunk their fill and settled on the arrangements which needed to be made for both the legal and ceremonial aspects of their two marriages, which would take place as soon as possible, the four lovers were permitted to walk alone in the garden running down to the Thames.

'I can't really believe that this is happening and that we have not suddenly found ourselves in an old romance or a new play,' Penelope told Oliver, her breath visible in the freezing air. 'Not only has my father softened towards you since he has learned that in London he is but a minnow, whereas at home he is the pike who rules the river, but Mary and I have become reconciled. I think that Castleford's double-dealing with us both may have taught her a valuable lesson. She even told me that Roger is her true knight and that, like me, she will go where he wishes to, forsaking her dreams of being a great lady at the court.'

'And you don't mind surrendering that dream?' Oliver asked her.

'Not I,' she said with a vigorous toss of her head, 'for that was never my dream, but my father's. I nearly became lost in it until I saw what happened to Alys. Oh, I know that she has married Jack, but all the same her love for him so nearly ended in tragedy. Besides, I couldn't avoid seeing how sad the Queen's life is. Even if his wife dies soon, as everyone says she will, they will never let the Queen marry Lord Robert—and I am not sure that she even wishes to.

'I can't help thinking how much luckier we are— that we have each found our own true love and can settle down together. As for Mary, she will be much happier with Roger than she would have been with Lord Castleford.'

'And you, will you be happier with me than you might have been with Lord Castleford?' he asked her naughtily.

'Wretch,' she said, stroking his face with her gloved hand. 'I have loved you ever since I first saw you when I was only a little girl and you but a tall thin boy, and now my dream has come true and we are to be married. Master and Mistress Woodville, living in the country, their children around them, far from the dirty city.'

'No regrets, then?' he asked, catching her gloved hand.

'None,' she replied. 'Only that if it were spring we should be able to celebrate our luck in a much more time-honoured way instead of merely walking sedately in the winter's cold.'

Oliver leaned forward and kissed her cheek, saying, 'It may be winter, but it is also the spring of the Queen's reign and of our love. Soon, soon, when my parents have come to London, and the lawyers have done their work, I shall show you what true love means, whatever the time of the year or the weather.'

'And I will show you a token of mine,' Penelope told him, and took from the pouch at her waist his ring which Mary had thrown away on his first visit to them when he had returned to England.

'I give you this,' she said, 'which Mary did not want and which I have treasured ever since she rejected you. It is now a true pledge of our love and it is my wish that you will receive it in the same spirit as that with which I give it to you.'

Oliver took the ring from her and kissed it before slipping it on to his finger. 'Eros has blessed it again,' he said, 'and that which was rejected has become his greatest treasure. You know, I have come to believe that I always loved you, even when I was hankering after Mary, but I was deceived by vain show before I could recognise true worth. I promise to love it— and you—always.'

This promise he kept, and many others, for their union was a blessed one, and like the Queen's reign began in joy and ended in what for them was success. The Queen, not so severe a woman as she later became, allowed them to leave the court and retire into private life, much though she had come to treasure them both.

Oliver later thought that she had hoped in rewarding them that the gods might be kind and allow her to crown her life with Lord Robert's love—but that was not to be. His and Penelope's success lay in doing their duty to those around them, as well as in the creation and rearing of a happy family. The shadow which had hung over Oliver while he was a member of the Queen's court had disappeared forever.

Dr Dee's forecast of a prosperous future for him had thus come true, and whether that was the result of his necromancy, or merely the workings of chance, mattered little as they lived out their days in peace.

Turn the page for a preview of
LADY IN WAITING
from
Anne Herries
The summer of Elizabeth's reign…

*With hopes of marriage dashed by
scandal, and constant threats to her
crown, Queen Elizabeth takes a young,
spirited woman into her close court circle.*

*Available April 2004
from Mills & Boon®*

Chapter One

September 1560

'Come, Mistress Catherine, a visit to the fair will do you good on this bright day. And besides, I do not like to see you downcast, sweet Cousin. My good Aunt Elizabeth would have driven you out into the sunshine before this, I dare swear.'

Catherine Moor laid down her embroidery with a sigh. She would as lief have sat quietly over her work, though others had already left for the delights of the fair that had come to visit, but she knew only too well the determination of her cousin Willis Stamford. Both Willis and her aunt, Lady Helen Stamford, were concerned for her, believing that it was time she put aside her grief for her beloved mother. Lady Elizabeth Moor had died of a putrid inflammation of the lungs in the spring of the year 1560, and it was now September of that same year.

Catherine no longer spent hours weeping alone in her bedchamber, but the ache of loss was constantly present and she had no real wish to visit a fair, even though she had always loved them when her parents had taken her. However, Willis would give her no peace until she acquiesced, which she might as well do with a good grace since she knew him to be a kind-hearted lad, some five years her senior. Most lads of his age would not have concerned themselves with a girl of barely eight years.

'Will you wait a moment while I fetch my cloak and purse, Cousin?'

'Martha has your cloak ready in the hall,' Willis replied, smiling at her. 'And you will have no need of your purse, as it is my pleasure to treat you to whatever you desire. You shall have sweetmeats, ribbons and trinkets, as many as you shall please.'

'Then I can only thank you, Cousin.'

Catherine stood up, brushing the stray threads of embroidery silk from her grey gown. Her dress was very simple, the full skirts divided over a petticoat of a paler grey, and the laced stomacher braided with black ribbon. More black ribbons attached the hanging sleeves to a plain fitted bodice and were her only ornament apart from a tiny silver cross and chain that her mother had given her just before she died.

Martha, her nurse and comforter since Lady Moor's death, was waiting to fuss over her in the hall, clucking like a mother hen with a chick as she tied the strings of Catherine's cloak and warned her not to stand in a chill wind.

'You take good care of her, Master Willis, and don't let her overtire herself.'

'Trust me, good mistress,' he replied and planted a naughty kiss on Martha's plump cheek. 'I shall let no harm befall my cousin, I do promise you.'

'Get on with you, you wicked boy!' cried Martha, blushing at his teasing. 'Or I'll take my broom to your backside.'

The threat was an idle one, as both Catherine and Willis were well aware. Martha's heart was as soft as butter straight from the churn, and Willis knew exactly how to twist her round his little finger.

'I hope it will not tire you to venture as far as the village,' Willis said after they had been walking for some minutes. He glanced anxiously at Catherine's pale face. She had been ill with the same fever that had carried off her mother, and though long recovered, he knew his mother considered her still delicate. 'Perhaps we should take a short-cut through the grounds of Cumnor Place?'

'Do you think we ought?' Catherine turned her eyes on him. They were wide and of a greenish-blue hue that made Willis think of a clear mountain pool he had drunk from on a visit to the Welsh hills as a young boy…deep and mysterious and deliciously cool. 'Will the lady of the house not mind us using her grounds as a short-cut?'

'Poor Lady Dudley never leaves her bed they say.

She has a malady of the breast and is like to die soon enough…' Willis stopped abruptly, wishing he had cut his tongue out before saying those words to his cousin. He hastened to repair his slip. 'Though I dare say that is merely gossip and the doctors will make her well again.'

'You need not protect me, Willis.' Catherine's serious eyes turned to him and he thought how lovely she was; the wind had whipped a few hairs from beneath the neat Dutch cap she wore so that they clustered about her face in dark red curls. 'I know that people sometimes die when they are ill, no matter how hard the physicians try to save them, as my dear Mama did. If we take this short-cut you know of we must be very quiet, for we do not want to disturb the poor lady.'

'As to that, I daresay she would be glad of some company, for it is certain that her husband is often at court and seldom visits her…but it is this way, Catherine.' Willis stopped and held out his hand to her. 'See the gap here in the hedge? If we squeeze through it will save us half an hour of walking.'

Catherine looked at the gap doubtfully. She could see that it was well used and realised that local people must often take this route rather than walking around the perimeter of the grounds. Willis was beckoning to her and she followed him through, looking about her guiltily as they began to walk across an open sweep of grass. The house was some distance away, and she was relieved to know that they could not possibly disturb the sick woman if she were resting on her bed.

Ahead of them was a small wood, and once inside it they would lose sight of the house altogether and would soon rejoin the common ground grazed by pigs and cows belonging to the village folk. Catherine glanced back at the house and paused for a moment, her eyes narrowing as her attention was caught.

What was that? She shaded her eyes, puzzled by what seemed to be happening close to the house. Something odd had occurred, causing an icy chill to fall over her. She could not see clearly enough to be sure, but it was like a creeping black mist that appeared to hover just above the ground. Where had it come from so suddenly? It had not been thre a moment ago.

'Willis!' She called out to her cousin, pointing back towards the shadow, which had become more upright, looking almost like a man's form now but less defined, not quite substantial enough to be a human. A shiver of fear went through her. She was not a girl given to superstition, though she knew the common folk believed in all kinds of evil spirits and demons that stalked the night, but this was broad daylight! 'What is that…back there…near the house? Do look, Willis.

She tugged at his arm to make him look back.

'What? I see nothing.'

'There…' But she had taken her eyes from it and when she looked again it had gone. 'It was by the house. I cannot describe it…a strange shadow. It was sinister, evil. I felt its evil, Willis.'

'A trick of the light, no more. I can see nothing, cousin.' His eyes studied her with concern as she shivered. 'Come, Catherine, you have let your imagination lead you astray. There is nothing there to disturb you. We must hurry or the pedlars will have sold all their best wares before we arrive.'

She knew he was right, and yet for a moment her feet seemed almost glued to the ground and she felt as if she were unable to move. A sense of some evil having taken place here seemed to hang in the air, making her throat tight so that for a moment she could scarcely breathe. Catherine felt cold all over, her skin covered in goose-pimples. The feeling of terror was so strong in her that she was afraid she might faint. She had seen something that had frightened her but she did not know what it could be.

'Come along, Catherine!'

There was a note of impatience in Willis's voice. Catherine found that her feet were no longer leaden and she hurried after he cousin. Since whatever it was had gone, there was no point in trying to explain to Willis. Besides, all she wanted now was to leave this place.

She would make sure that they returned home by another route.

April 1571

'Do not look so at me, Catherine,' pleaded Sir William Moor as he saw the mutiny in his daughter's fine eyes. She was a beautiful girl of almost nineteen years, her long red hair flying about her face as she came in from some hard riding that morning. 'Your aunt is determined on this trip to London, and, God forgive me, I have neglected the question of your marriage. It is time a husband was found for you, my dear child.'

'Why must it be so?' Catherine asked, fire sparking in the bottomless depths of those green eyes. Her life had been so peaceful and serene these past years, and now it seemed that all must change. 'Why may I not stay here to take care of you for always, Father? Why must I marry and leave all that is dear to me?'

'It is true that my estate is not entailed…' Sir William hesitated as he sensed the mutiny in his much loved child. He had put this same argument to his sister the previous evening and been roundly scolded for his trouble. 'But it would be selfish of me to keep you here, Catherine. You must be presented at court—and a husband must be secured, if one can be found to please you.' He looked at her doubtfully, knowing her stubbornness of old.

'You will not force me to marriage I cannot like?' She seized on his hesitation like one of the little terrier dogs the bailiff used for chasing rabbits from their holes. 'Promise me only that, dearest Father, and I shall go with a willing heart.'

'When have I ever forced you to anything you did

not like?' He gave her a chiding look, for they both knew that he had spoiled her these last years, never remarrying after his beloved wife's death as most widowers did to gain an heir. Catherine was child enough for Sir William and he would miss her when she married. 'I swear I should not mind if you married, my dearest Cat, but your aunt is determined you shall have the chance…and I believe my Elizabeth would have wanted this for you.'

'Then of course I shall go,' Catherine said, for any mention of her mother's wishes was sure to soothe her rebellion. Their mutual respect for a woman still loved and missed was a bond between father and daughter. 'But I wish you were coming with us, Father.'

'I shall join you soon enough,' he promised, eyes warm with affection. His Catherine was a high-spirited girl with a temper upon her when she chose, but he knew the sweetness and goodness of her true nature. 'Go up and tidy yourself now, Daughter. Your aunt awaits you in the best parlour.'

Catherine nodded, walking slowly up the wide staircase of the manor house that was her home. It was a sturdy building erected in the early days of King Henry VII's reign by her great-grandfather: half-timbered, with overhanging windows above good red bricks, it had a large open hall with stairs leading to a gallery above. Some of the walls were hung with bright tapestry, which lent colour and warmth to the rooms. Recently, Sir William had had the small parlour and the principal bedchambers panelled with good English oak in the latest fashion, and the new wood glowed with a rich golden colour.

Catherine's own bedchamber was furnished with an elaborately carved bed, which had two posts and a tester overhead; below the tester was suspended a canopy of silk tied with twisted ropes. Heavy brocade curtains could be drawn about the bed at night if the room was cold, though she seldom used them, preferring not to be enclosed.

At the foot of the bed there was a planked chest, and there was a counter beneath one of the small windows. This was a plain chest on joined legs that had once been used by the stewards for counting and storing money; but having found it lying neglected in a store, Catherine had had it removed to her own chamber, because the extra height made it useful for her personal items. She had spread an embroidered cloth over its scarred surface, and her beaten-silver hand mirror, combs and perfume flasks lay on top together with gloves, a string of amber beads and some feathers for a hat. Inside the cupboard were stored gloves, hats and various articles of feminine attire.

A number of triangular stools stood about the room, one by a harp, another in front of a tapestry frame, her much prized table desk set on a board and trestle with yet another stool near by; these, her virginals, several items of silver set upon the board and rich hangings proclaimed this the chamber of a privileged and a favoured woman.

Taking a few moments to wash her hands in cold water from a silver ewer stored in a curtained alcove, Catherine finished her ablutions and then glanced in her mirror to tidy her wayward hair. Her careful work had restored the damage of a mischievous wind, and she was now neat enough to meet her aunt. Lady Stanford was a fastidious woman who always dressed richly, as well she might, having survived three wealthy husbands.

She was standing before the fireplace in the best parlour when Catherine entered, holding her hands to the flames of a fire that had been lit for her benefit. It was now April of the year 1571 and fires were seldom lit until the evening once the worst of the winter was over, because Sir William and his daughter, being busy about the estate, had no time to sit here during the day.

'I hope I find you well, Aunt?'

Lady Stanford turned as she spoke. Eyes that had once been described as sparkling were a little faded now, as was the complexion she embellished with paint, and the sparse grey hair she hid beneath a wig as red as Catherine's own hair. Painted cheeks and lips were the fashion for ladies of the court who needed a little artifice to aid their looks, but seemed strange to Catherine, who was used to fresh-cheeked countrywomen.

'Well enough, Catherine,' Lady Stamford said and

smiled thinly. It was more than four years since she had seen her neice, for they lived some many leagues distant and travelling was hard enough in summer, almost impossible in the depths of winter. She was pleased to find that Catherine had matured into a beauty. Taller than some men of the age, she was perhaps too slender to please those who found more roundness their ideal, but child-bearing would no doubt change that soon enough. 'You look even prettier than when I last saw you. I had feared that at almost nineteen your looks would have begun to fade, but I see it is not so. I think we shall have no problem in establishing you at court, and then who knows? If Her Majesty is pleased with your conduct she may arrange a prestigious match for you.'

'You are kind to trouble yourself on my account, Aunt.'

Catherine thought it wise not to impose her own thoughts and wishes too soon. She had her father's promise and did not wish to quarrel with Lady Stamford for nothing. Her aunt had shown her great kindness over the years, especially when she had gone to stay at her home in Berkshire after her mother's untimely death.

'I have often wished for a daughter, but most of my babies did not survive their first year. Willis has given me my heart's desire in part, for Margaret is a good wife to him, and they have a son already. A beautiful boy and strong, praise God.'

'You must be thankful for it,' Catherine agreed,

only too happy to change the subject. 'I trust the child will continue healthy and that they will have more babies.'

In an age when babies were fortunate to survive their infancy, the need to produce strong sons was often paramount, second only to the importance of marrying for wealth and position.

'I pray it may be so—but to other matters, Catherine. Your gown is sufficient for country wear but will not do in town. Before you can be presented at court you must be properly dressed. It is my intention to leave for London on the morrow. We shall have time to visit the silk merchants and my own dressmaker—a Frenchwoman of some skill—before we are summoned to attend the Queen.'

Catherine hid her sigh. Since both her father and her aunt were determined on this she must accept with a good heart. Yet she was aware of regret and an unease she could not name. Given her choice she would have remained at home, but perhaps no gentleman would be brought to offer for her and then she could return to her old pursuits in peace.

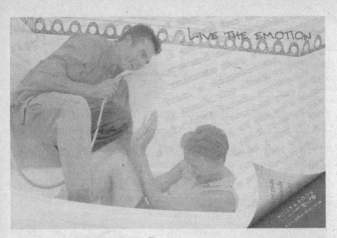

LIVE THE EMOTION

Modern Romance™
...seduction and
passion guaranteed

Tender Romance™
...love affairs that
last a lifetime

Medical Romance™
...medical drama
on the pulse

Historical Romance™
...rich, vivid and
passionate

Sensual Romance™
...sassy, sexy and
seductive

Blaze Romance™
...the temperature's
rising

27 new titles every month.

Live the emotion

A *Mother's Day* Gift

A collection of brand-new romances just for you!

Margaret Way

Anne Ashley

Lucy Monroe

On sale 5th March 2004

Available at most branches of WHSmith, Tesco, Martins, Borders,
Eason, Sainsbury's and all good paperback bookshops.

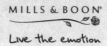

MILLS & BOON®

Live the emotion

PENNINGTON

BOOK TEN

Available from 2nd April 2004

*Available at most branches of WHSmith, Tesco, Martins, Borders,
Eason, Sainsbury's and most good paperback bookshops.*

PENN/RTL/10